BEDEVILED

BEDEVILED
(A FATHER JAKE AUSTIN MYSTERY)

by John A. Vanek

coffeetownpress
KENMORE, WA

coffeetownpress

A Coffeetown Press book published by Epicenter Press

Epicenter Press
6524 NE 181st St.
Suite 2
Kenmore, WA 98028.
www.Coffeetownpress.com
www.Epicenterpress.com
www.Camelpress.com

For more information go to:
www.coffeetownpress.com
www.Camelpress.com
www.Epicenterpress.com

Author website: www.JohnVanekAuthor.com

This is a work of fiction. Names, characters, places, brands, media, and incidents are the product of the author's imagination or are used fictitiously.

ISBN: 9781942078586 (trade paper)
ISBN: 9781942078593 (ebook)

Printed in the United States of America

For the many fine authors who have guided me on my writing journey, and for friends, family, and the readers who have supported me throughout.

ACKNOWLEDGMENTS

It takes a village to write a book—or in my case, a small city. I am extremely grateful to my wife, Geni, for her advice and patience, and to Jessica & Randy Dublikar, Jen & Matt Vanek, Father Thomas Winkel, Sterling Watson, Laura Lippman, Les Standiford, Michael Koryta, and Dennis Lehane for their help and encouragement. Special thanks to Dean Jollay, Luis Castillo, Gale Massey, Abe Spevack, Susan Adger, Barbara Schrefer, Sue Peck, Ann O'Farrell, Lee Summerall, Jeanne Hirth, and Richard Erlanger for their brutally honest critiques over the years. I am grateful for input and support from Patti & Ron Poporad, Linda & Al Vanek, JoAnn & Jim Gavacs, Kathy & Emil Poporad, Mary Winter, Alex Trouteaud, Nancy Janus, David Wood, the Pinellas Writers, and the Oberlin Heritage Center. I wish to thank Jennifer McCord and Phil Garrett at Coffeetown Press for guiding me through the morass of the publishing world. I also want to express my gratitude to all of the readers who have supported the first three novels in the series (*DEROS, Miracles,* and *Absolution*) by recommending them to friends and posting kind reviews online.

The characters, settings, and all of the events in this mystery are fictional and the product of the author's imagination. The short poem about human trafficking in the novel is my original work (copyright © 2020 by John A. Vanek). If you enjoy the Father Jake Austin Mystery Series, please tell your friends. Word of mouth is the lifeblood of independent presses and their authors.

CHAPTER ONE

Tuesday, March 25, 2003, 3:00 p.m.

Sheriff Tremont "Tree" Macon eased his cruiser onto Route 58 and began a slow and silent journey north toward town. There was no need for sirens or flashers. The time for action was past.

Neither of us spoke. There were no questions to answer, nothing to say. What could you say? Life—as a great thinker once said—is a riddle, wrapped in a mystery, inside an enigma. Only today, it was also shrouded in a body bag.

My day had been routine until I received a telephone call from a woman in Pennsylvania who told me that her sister, Mildred Rojas, was not returning her telephone calls. Because it was a long drive from Pittsburgh to Mildred's home, she had asked me to make sure her sister was okay.

Although she was in her eighties and lived fifteen miles south of Sacred Heart Catholic Church in Oberlin, Ohio where I was acting pastor, Mildred was an active member of my congregation and a regular participant at potluck dinners and bingo. The last time I had seen her was at Mass on Ash Wednesday, nearly three weeks earlier, and her sister's phone call had set off a jangle of alarm bells in my head.

One of my parishioners lived on Mildred's street, so I'd phoned and requested that he knock on her door. He called back an hour later to say that there had been no answer, but the lights were on upstairs and the doors were locked. The alarm bells grew louder.

I wanted to do a welfare check on her, but I didn't think I could, or should, enter her house. With concern for a person's well-being, the police can legally enter anyone's house. The law is less clear about priests wandering through people's homes uninvited, so I had asked my friend, the county sheriff, to accompany me.

When we arrived, Tree used his six foot, six inch frame and two hundred and fifty pounds of determination to muscle open a window and boost me inside. The living room curtains were drawn and it was pitch black except for a faint blush of light at the top of the stairs. I called Mildred's name and announced myself, got no reply, then stumbled my way through the darkness, tripping over a hassock before finally reaching the front door to let Tree into the house. I flipped on the room lights, and we searched the downstairs, which was unoccupied and undisturbed.

The air in the house hung heavy and we followed a pungent, sour smell up the stairs. Mildred lay in bed dressed in gray flannel pajamas, her eyes open. She had no pulse or respirations and was cold to the touch. The flies swarming the room and her body made it clear that she had been dead for a while. I recalled the many times this kind and gentle woman had delivered food, laughter, and joy to our church community. The thought of her dying alone filled my eyes with tears.

My friend noticed and walked away as I dabbed them dry, then Tree notified the local police and county coroner. He explained our presence in Mildred's house, and told them he saw no evidence of foul play and suspected that she had died of natural causes. From my time as an Army medic and my years working in hospitals, however, I was certain I had never seen a death that looked *natural*.

When the local authorities arrived, Tree and I left. Our journey took us past corn fields stippled with the brown-stalk remnants of last season's harvest until we turned onto the highway toward home. Although Oberlin is a far smaller city than its eastern neighbor Cleveland, it feels like a metropolis compared to some of the rural areas to the south and west of town. The fact that Mildred had been willing to drive all the way to Sacred Heart Church on Sundays to attend Mass and listen to my sermons made me miss her all the more.

Tree was all business on the solemn drive home, his head swiveling back and forth as he scanned his county for signs of trouble. He was one of those folks who *lived* the job, never flipping the off switch.

I finally broke the silence. "Thanks for coming with me, Tree. I was worried about her and wasn't sure what I might find."

"No sweat, buddy. I didn't want you busted on a Code 12."

"A what?"

"Breaking and entering. Knowing you, locked doors wouldn't have kept you out. You do have a history of … let's call it *defying convention*."

"Don't tell my bishop. He gets a facial tic every time I walk into his office. By the way, I called your house last weekend to invite you and Sonya to dinner, and she said you were at some big, important meeting."

"Yeah, you can get meeting'ed to death in my job." He ran one hand over his shiny, shaved scalp the way he used to when he had hair. "I was a speaker at the National Black Police Association conference in Elyria. Sonya wants me to run for reelection, so I gotta keep my constituents and supporters happy. She's my boss—well Sonya, the District Attorney, the Governor, and pretty much everyone else in the county." A smile danced on his lips, then fell away, his face transforming to black granite. "Hang on Jake. I got work to do."

The sheriff punched the accelerator, hurling me back against the passenger seat. Telephone poles flew by my window and a mile of asphalt slid behind us in seconds as the cruiser gained ground on a red truck in the distance.

"What's going on, Tree?"

"Not sure."

The battered F-150 pickup ahead of us was weaving erratically. We closed the gap and the sheriff reached for the siren and lights, but before he could switch them on the old Ford abruptly slowed, veered off the road, bounced across a shallow ditch, and slammed into the trunk of a giant pine.

Tree skidded the cruiser onto the berm, brought it to a screeching stop, and we ran to the pickup. Although steam was seeping from the radiator, the damage to the truck's front end appeared minimal. The airbag hadn't deployed, but the teenager in the seatbelt was unconscious.

Tree put a hand on the boy's neck, turned to me, and said, "I can barely feel a pulse. Take over, Jake. You're better at this than me. Do what you can, while I radio this in."

My medical training kicked in, and I checked the teen's vital signs. Not only was his pulse weak, but his heart was racing and his respirations were rapid and shallow. No need for CPR yet, but that could change quickly. He had a knot on his forehead with early bruising and a cut over his right eye from contact with the steering wheel. Although his pupils were of equal size, they were dilated and sluggish.

My first thought was that he had been stoned and driving under the influence. I was running through a mental list of other things that might cause these signs and symptoms when I caught the faint scent of alcohol on his breath. But neither booze nor grass accounted for the combination of a fast, thready pulse and dilated pupils. Which left a short list of more mind-bending drugs and uglier possible outcomes.

"This is bad, Tree," I shouted. We were far out in the country where the road cut through a thick stand of pines, not far from the middle of nowhere. I spotted a soybean field a hundred yards down the road, pointed to it, and hollered, "How fast can you get a helicopter here?"

"I tried. None available."

"How far off is EMS?"

"ETA ten minutes. Fifteen more to Oberlin hospital."

"I don't think he's got that kind of time. The sooner we get him there the better. Let's grab him and go."

The sheriff hesitated a moment, then sprinted over, unlatched the teen's seatbelt, and began to pick him up.

"Wait, Tree. I want to immobilize his neck before we move him, in case whiplash fractured his spine." I reached around Tree and placed my hands and forearms like splints along both sides of the young man's head and neck. "Okay, let's get him out. Easy does it."

Tree slowly lifted the teenager from the car as if he were weightless, and we carefully moved him into the backseat of the cruiser. I hopped in, knelt on the floor next to him, and checked his vital signs again, which were unchanged.

With his lights flashing and siren wailing, Tree gunned the engine and radioed the emergency room with a description of the boy's condition. Halfway there, the teen stopped breathing and I began mouth-to-mouth.

We wheeled into the Oberlin Community Hospital ER entrance, where a doctor and two nurses met us. They eased the teen onto a gurney and took over, much to my relief. We had done all we could, and now his life was in their hands—and by the looks of him, in the hands of the Almighty.

Tree and I watched in silence. As they rolled the youngster into the Emergency Room, the wind made a mournful noise, like God sighing. Dark storm clouds blanketed the sun, and a lone turkey vulture circled a nearby field. I slumped against the cruiser, feeling every one of my forty-eight years.

"Been a bitch of a day, Jake. I could use a beer or two. You?"

I nodded. "As a Catholic, I probably shouldn't quote Martin Luther, but he was spot-on when he said, 'Whoever drinks beer is quick to sleep; whoever sleeps long does not sin; whoever does not sin enters Heaven.' I know the gospel truth when I hear it."

Tree forced a tired grin and opened the cruiser door. "Hop in. I'm buying."

"Give me a second." I called Colleen Brady, the nanny I had hired to care for my nephew when I wasn't at home, and asked if she could stay an hour more. When she agreed, I slapped Tree on the back and said, "Let's get that beer, buddy. Time to drink our way to Heaven."

CHAPTER TWO

Wednesday, March 26, 7:45 a.m.

The next morning, I dropped off my nephew at preschool, returned to Sacred Heart Church, and offered morning Mass. When I entered the sacristy after the service and began removing my vestments, I realized I'd missed a phone call. The voicemail was from Bishop Lucci, postponing my upcoming performance review. Since my arrival in his diocese nine months earlier, His Excellency had been less than pleased with my work.

Due to a shortage of priests, and despite his misgivings about my current living situation, Lucci had recently appointed me acting pastor at Sacred Heart Church. He disapproved of my role as my young nephew's guardian. He felt that raising him would be too distracting from my religious duties and wanted RJ placed for adoption with a two-parent Catholic family. That was not going to happen. The boy was all the family I had left, and when my sister was dying, I'd promised her that I would care for him. I had no intention of breaking that promise, whatever the cost.

The bishop and I had a love-hate relationship. He tolerated my role as RJ's custodian because I had helped save his life in July. More importantly, St. Joseph's Hospital needed physicians to care for the indigent in the county. My parish was small, so I was able to treat patients there part-time. I was a member of the Camillian Order and had taken a fourth vow to minister to the sick, in addition to vows of poverty, chastity, and obedience. I had come late in life to the priesthood, after a stint as an Army medic and a decade as a physician, so the Camillian's commitment to treating both the body and the soul was a perfect fit for me, and for them.

As I removed my long white alb, my cellphone played "I Shot the

Sheriff," the ringtone I had selected for Tree Macon—not the guitar-powered, Eric Clapton version, but the more soulful one by Bob Marley with the drums and melodic bass driving the one-drop reggae beat. Tree and I had been best friends since junior high, and we could not have been closer if we had been blood relatives. A few months earlier, when my life had been in danger, he'd almost taken a bullet for me. My ringtone was a reminder of how I had nearly gotten us both killed.

"Top of the morning, Sheriff. What's up?"

"Got a little follow up on that teenager you helped me with yesterday. His name's Anthony Pagano."

"How's he doing?"

"Lousy. The ER in town stabilized Tony, then transported him to the intensive care unit at St. Joseph's Hospital. The boy's still in a coma and under the care of a neurologist there."

"Good. From what I saw at the scene, I'm betting on a combination of drug overdose and head trauma. I doubt he simply passed out from too much booze."

"Yeah, me too. After what you told me, I requested a full toxicology evaluation. Results aren't back yet. When I got to the cop shop, I ran his name through the system but got bupkis. No arrests, incidents, or sealed juvie records. Zip, zero, nada. The reason I'm calling is the family is with him now and his mother asked to speak with you. She wants to thank you in person for what you did. A nurse told her that your CPR saved Tony's life."

"No problem. I need to visit a couple hospitalized parishioners there anyway. As soon as I change out of my vestments, I'll head over. Tell her I'm on my way."

"Roger that. And I wanted to thank you too, Jake. If I'd been there alone, the boy would've probably been a goner."

"No sweat. Just repaying you for your help with poor Mildred Rojas. Breaking and entering would have looked bad on my resume, and Bishop Lucci's already close to benching me as it is. By the way, Mildred's sister in Pittsburgh had a fruit basket delivered to the rectory. Guess I owe you an apple."

"Yeah, yeah. You're a real peach, Jake, but I'll stick with my red-meat cop diet. Later buddy." Click.

I slipped on a clerical shirt with a Roman collar and stepped outside into slanting rays of sunlight under a Wedgewood sky, the morning as still and beautiful as an oil painting. After a long, hard winter, spring had arrived like a benediction. I took a leisurely drive along a backroad past newly-plowed fields, basking in the glorious warmth. With the window rolled down, the car filled with the invigorating aroma of tilled soil and rebirth.

At St. Joseph's Hospital, I took an elevator up to the intensive care unit and was greeted by the familiar acrid smell of disinfectant that inhabits hospitals like the ghosts of patients past. It wasn't powerful enough, however, to mask the scent of vomit that the parchment-pale man in bed one was depositing into an emesis basin.

I found Tony Pagano in bed number four, motionless and plugged into two IVs. An oxygen mask misted his face, partially obscuring a sprinkling of freckles on his cheeks. There was a sutured laceration over his right eye, and a spill of honey-colored hair draped the edge of a nasty blue-green bruise on his forehead. Tony looked as though he had gone a few rounds in the ring and lost the fight by a knockout. The good news was that he wasn't hooked up to a ventilator and his EKG monitor showed a normal pattern and heart rate.

A middle-aged couple stood at the foot of his bed in the midst of a heated discussion. The man wagged a finger at the woman. He was big and beefy, wearing a plaid lumberjack shirt and overalls. She was dressed in jeans and a flowered peasant blouse. Although half his size, she was giving as good as she was getting.

They didn't notice my approach, so I stopped and listened. He held up a hand and his voice dropped to a low growl.

"He shouldn't be here, Edna. We oughtta take him home, care for him ourselves. What will Reverend Flood say? The whole congregation'll be watching me, watching us."

"You think being a deacon somehow safeguards our son? Nonsense! And I don't give a damn what *anyone* thinks! Flood was here most of the night praying. What good did it do? Tony's still unconscious."

"You gotta give prayer time to heal. You can't rush the Lord!"

"The Lord will hear our prayers perfectly fine from the hospital, Virgil. I will *not* put my only child's life at risk for your vanity, your ... *reputation!*" she roared like a mother bear protecting her cub. "I'd do anything to save him." Her voice dropped to a whisper, almost a hiss. "Including burn for eternity in Hell, if I had to!"

"What's wrong with you? You've lost your faith, woman. I'm downright ashamed of you!"

He stepped away from her and noticed me. I approached and introduced myself.

"A Catholic priest? What do you want? We don't need you here. We shouldn't even be in a Catholic hospital. We're Christians!"

I had no idea what to say to that. This was the wrong time to point out that we Catholics were the *first* Christians. I turned the other cheek and just smiled at him.

Edna jumped in. "For goodness sakes, Virgil, Catholics are Christians!"

"With all them idols and graven images? They're not *real* Christians in my book."

I finally found my voice. "Sorry for the interruption. Sheriff Macon said you wanted to see me. He and I drove Tony to the hospital yesterday."

Anger drained from Edna Pagano's face. She stepped forward, took my hand in both of hers, and squeezed it gently.

"Thank you so much! I'm more grateful to you than you'll ever know." She paused and studied my clerical attire. "They said you performed CPR on my son, kept him alive till he got to the hospital." It was more a question than a statement.

"No thanks is necessary. I was just doing my job." I tapped my hospital staff ID badge. "I'm also a physician here."

Virgil Pagano looked me up and down and scowled. "You been thanked. Don't need no more help. You can leave now."

Mrs. Pagano flushed, fixed her husband with an icy stare, then turned to me. "Thank you again, Father. You'll be in my prayers."

Flustered and a bit mystified by what I had encountered, I stepped into the hallway outside of ICU and nearly bumped into Dr. Marcus Taylor. He was the Head of Neurology and Chief of the Medical Staff at the hospital. I counted him as a friend.

He narrowed his coal-black eyes. "Jake, what are you doing here?"

"Sheriff Macon and I found Tony Pagano by the roadside and brought him in. Truck vs. tree. Unconscious, smelling of booze. He stopped breathing on the way to the hospital. How is he?"

Taylor ran a hand through snow-white hair, the same color as his bushy eyebrows. "Headed in the right direction, but until he wakes up and I run more tests, I won't say he's out of the woods. His x-rays were negative, no fractures, and his CT scan showed no hemorrhage or contusion from the crash." Taylor's gaze drifted to the window, and he seemed lost in thought.

"Marcus, are you all right?"

He pulled a stethoscope from the pocket of his white coat and refocused on me. "Yes, but frustrated … and confused. This is personal for me. I *know* Tony Pagano, and I don't understand how this could happen. He's a good kid and doesn't have time to get into trouble. I hired him to help out on my farm. Feed the horses, muck out the stalls. He's worked for me for a couple of years. When he's not at school or helping out at my place, he's working on his parents' farm down the road."

It was common knowledge that Taylor was a wealthy man. When the weather was questionable, he drove his sleek new Mercedes to work. On sunny days, his Lamborghini was parked in the hospital garage. I said, "You, a farmer?"

A grin creased his lips. "*Gentleman* farmer. My daughters talked me into riding lessons and then into buying horses. My girls are grown and on their own, but the horses are still with me and my grandkids come over to ride now."

His grin evaporated and the wrinkles returned to his forehead. "What's so frustrating is that Tony's bloodwork just came in." He draped his stethoscope around his neck. "His tests showed that he was slightly over the limit for alcohol but had sky-high levels of *amphetamine*. Can you believe that?"

"Could it have been prescribed for ADHD or some other legitimate reason?"

"No, Jake, I checked. His blood levels are way above normal therapeutic doses. This makes no sense." Taylor was always the consummate medical professional and had years of experience, yet he was visibly shaken. "Tony's the most down-to-earth, dependable kid I've ever met. Works hard, top of his class in school, and volunteers at his church. I *thought* I knew him as well as my own children. Now I'm not so sure."

"Do we ever *really* know anyone, Marcus? We all wear masks in public—you and me included. Especially teenagers." I had more than a passing acquaintance with substance abuse. Although I had once been an altar boy, my checkered youth included a foray into booze and drugs. "I agree though, the boy doesn't have the look of a tweaker. Good hygiene and teeth, no pimples or open sores, clean clothes."

Amphetamines in his system accounted for Tony's dilated pupils and rapid heart rate at the crash site, but I wanted to give him the benefit of doubt. "Maybe he was experimenting and accidently OD'd. Kids sometimes lose the path, slip and fall. It happens. Thank God they usually don't plunge into the abyss."

"Hope you're right. Tony's outgoing, not the least bit withdrawn, irritable, or anxious like most meth-heads. He's on the *chess team*, for Christ-sake!" Taylor blushed. "Sorry about my language, Father. I mean, Tony plays clarinet in the marching band, and he's never stolen anything from me. He doesn't fit the pattern of a user. I hate to think I've been completely wrong about him for all these years." Taylor patted me on the shoulder, headed for the ICU, then turned and added, "Wish I had your faith, Father."

CHAPTER THREE

Wednesday, March 26, 12:15 p.m.

I had missed breakfast and decided to eat before visiting my hospitalized parishioners. Against all common sense and good judgement, I called Emily Beale and asked her to join me for lunch.

Emily and I had dated in high school. After I returned to town, we rekindled our friendship. Much to our surprise, there were still sparks between us. His Excellency, Bishop Lucci, knew about my conflicted feelings for my former high school sweetheart. He had instructed me to burn that bridge to my past, but I couldn't force myself to strike the match. God help me, I was addicted to her company. My feelings for her still ran deep and our long history together drew me to her, which made keeping my vow of chastity challenging at times.

I was leaning against the wall at the entrance to the hospital cafeteria, thinking about poor Tony and the toll that drugs were taking in this country, when I heard the patter of Emily's cane coming down the hall.

Emily and her father both suffered from hereditary adult-onset blindness. Together, they ran the hospital snack shop operated by the Society for the Blind. They also lived in the hospital dormitory, serving as counselors to the medical interns and residents residing there.

Although Emily was sightless, I had seen her super-senses in action, so I was not surprised when she tapped her way directly to me and said, "Fee-fi-fo-fum, I smell the cologne … of a *clergyman!*"

My once-upon-a-love ex-girlfriend spouting fairytales. She gave me *that smile*, the one that had always made me see rainbows and butterflies—and still did.

"Very perceptive … and poetic, Em."

Her paisley printed dress in crimson and black accentuated her figure. She wore very little makeup and was every bit as beautiful and mesmerizing as she had been in high school. I gazed at her a moment too long as Don Quixote whispered in my ear to stop tilting at windmills.

"I'm surprised you're here today, Jake. Isn't this your day off?"

"It is, but I promised I'd cover Urgent Care for Dr. Poporad this afternoon. Her daughter has a softball game. I told her I'd arrive by two o'clock and fill in for her until she gets back."

We joined a line of interns and residents trying to grab a quick bite before returning to the clinics and wards. Institutional food is always a roll of the dice, so I played it safe and chose a hamburger and fries. Emily was feeling optimistic and selected the fish entrée.

I carried our trays to a vacant two-top table near a window. We sat and she filled me in on the poetry therapy workshop that she led two days per week. Besides being a compassionate person, Emily was an accomplished poet. Allowing patients and their families to express their fears in writing sometimes opened doors and broke down defenses when standard therapy and medication failed. Much to my surprise, the Psychiatry Department had encouraged her. They had also integrated art and music therapy into their arsenal of treatments.

"How are things with your dad, Em?"

"Getting better." She removed her sunglasses, revealing sorrow in her blue eyes. "Slowly."

Emily and her father had been close—until he confessed that he'd intercepted the love letters I had written to her while I was a young recruit overseas in the Army. Emily had assumed that our high school love affair had merely been a fling for me and I'd forgotten all about her. When she didn't respond to my letters, including one in which I had asked her to marry me, I felt as if she had deserted me.

The problem was that his action had betrayed both of us and changed forever the course of our lives. She had a disastrous marriage followed by divorce; I turned inward, found my faith, and became a priest. Now a small fire flickered between us, and we were like two moths circling it, unable to fly away. The closer to the blaze we got, the hotter it burned.

"Give the guy a break, Em. Your dad was only trying to protect you." I had forgiven him; Emily was still working on it. "Heck, I was *feral* in those days. If I had a daughter, I wouldn't want her dating a guy who behaved the way I did, drinking and drugging, especially one who was hip-deep in a bloody war half-a-world away."

"I understand intellectually, but…." Emily shrugged. "Dad and I have declared a truce. We'll reach detente … in time." She forced a sad smile. "So, how's the little guy?"

Emily referred to the two most important people in my life as the big guy and the little guy—Tree Macon and my nephew, Randall James.

"His mother's illness and death shut him down, but over the last few months the real RJ's beginning to emerge. He was pretty shaky about preschool at first. To be expected, I guess. Heck, all of a sudden the poor kid's living with an uncle he barely knows, then I send him off to school. But he seems to be adjusting. Truth be told, he's the best thing that could have happened to me. RJ's become the center of my world, and I can't wait to hear about his day when he gets home from school."

The week prior, I had received an unsolicited letter that began, "Thank you for your interest in joining the Episcopal priesthood," followed by procedural information, and the address and telephone number for the Episcopal Bishop of Ohio. Of all the protestant denominations, theirs was closest to the Catholic liturgy and sacraments—and Episcopalian priests were allowed to marry. *The "M" word.* I had not requested the information, however, and it could only have come from either Emily or Tree Macon.

"Did you send me any snail mail of a religious nature recently, Em?"

I watched her expression as she answered the question.

"No. What in the world are you talking about?"

Not the slightest hint of deceit.

I told her about the letter and she chuckled. "So *that's* what Tree thinks you and I should do. Ha! I love the big guy but sometimes…." Emily finished the last of her meal and took a sip of tea. "What do you know about the Church of Eternal Release, Jake?"

"Not much. Fundamentalist. A rural church south of town. Why?"

"The Lorain Journal had an article about it. Word is, the preacher is a real showman, extremely charismatic. Reportedly, he arrived in the county a few years ago and within months, hallelujahs were echoing from the walls of his church. His zeal has been spreading like a brushfire, and I quote, 'on the winds of righteousness.' Now he has a huge congregation."

"Wish I could say the same. He sounds like a force of nature."

Emily tilted her head and her short auburn hair caressed the side of her face. Our knees touched under the table and I should have pulled away, but didn't.

She slipped her sunglasses on and asked, "How late are you working?"

"Till five."

"Are you doing anything special afterward?"

"I was thinking of taking RJ to the park. Why?"

"I'd like to go to the seven o'clock church service there tonight and hear what all the fuss is about. Would you be willing to drive me? It would give you a chance to meet a fellow clergyman."

"Really? Tonight?"

She nodded. This would not have been high on my to-do list, but I'd always had a hard time saying *no* to Emily. The woman had my number and knew it.

"Let me see if Colleen can babysit for RJ." She was someone I could always count on, and without her help I could never have juggled being a physician, priest, and a parent. I called her and when Colleen agreed to help out for the second night in a row, I hung up and said, "I'll change clothes after work and pick you up at six thirty."

CHAPTER FOUR

Wednesday, March 26, 4:30 p.m.

After lunch, I visited two hospitalized parishioners, changed into scrubs in the doctors' lounge, and threw on a white coat. Such was my life, transforming from mild-mannered clergy to hard-charging physician and back again.

In Urgent Care, I worked my way through a logjam of patients with the usual complaints. Colds, sprains, headaches, and seasonal allergies. Everything went smoothly until four thirty, when the receptionist rolled an agitated, elderly man to the nursing station in a wheelchair.

"Sorry Dr. Austin. I know this is unusual, but Mr. Webb told me he developed blurred vision in the waiting room." She leaned in close and whispered, "He thinks he's having a stroke."

I introduced myself, took the man into exam room three, and helped him from the wheelchair onto the examination table. He was disheveled and smelled of cigarettes and booze.

"What's going on, Mr. Webb?"

"I came here 'cause the damn rheumatism in my hands is killing me. It's been painin' me for years, and I'm fed-up with it."

He moaned as I examined his swollen, arthritic knuckles.

"But it's my vision, Doc, that's got me scared. I was sittin' out there waiting my turn, you know, and suddenly I can't see right." He pointed to his eyes. "Things got all blurry."

Worried about a possible retinal detachment, I grabbed an ophthalmoscope and asked him to take off his glasses. He set them on the exam table, and I assessed both of his eyes. His retinas and optic nerves looked normal. I began a neurological examination and was thinking about ordering a CT scan or MRI to rule out a bleed, stroke, or tumor when he put his glasses back on.

Somehow, I managed to stifle a laugh. "Let me get this straight, Mr. Webb. You had no problem with your vision until you got here?"

"That's right."

"Interesting. I'll be with you in a minute, sir." I walked out to the waiting room and asked our receptionist where my patient had been sitting. She pointed to the far corner. I marched over, got down on my hands and knees, and found my patient's lens next to his chair.

When I reentered the exam room, Mr. Webb was slipping a small flask into his pocket. He wiped his lips on his sleeve, belched, and gazed at me. Not wanting to embarrass him, I asked for his eyeglasses and turned around so he couldn't see what I was doing. Popping the missing lens into the frame, I wiped away so many greasy fingerprints that it felt as if I was tampering with a crime scene.

"Good news, Mr. Webb." I handed him his glasses. "You're not having a stroke."

He put them on and glanced around, completely dumbfounded. "Well I'll be damned! Everything's real clear again, Doc. Thanks so much." He burped again. "It's a darn miracle, that's what it is."

I only wished that all miracles were that easy to perform.

"The lenses are loose, sir, and that caused the blurriness. No big deal. But have your glasses fixed, so you don't have any more problems."

I wrote him a prescription for his arthritis and gave him a bottle of samples to get him started.

Dr. Poporad returned from her daughter's ballgame, peeked into the room, and thanked me for covering for her. I was out of the clinic door well before Mr. Webb, happy to be spending an evening with Emily.

CHAPTER FIVE

Wednesday, March 26, 6:30 p.m.

Emily was waiting outside for me in the cool night air beneath a streetlamp. She was bathed in an island of light, her gentle blue eyes directed up at an equally placid azure sky. She looked lovely in a jade green skirt and matching jacket over a white silk blouse. She wore only a touch of makeup, and in my opinion, didn't need any at all. She folded her collapsible cane and slid it into her purse. I opened the passenger door, guided her in, and we headed south on Route 58. The sun was low in the west, painting the clouds in shades of pink and marmalade. As we drove, they rolled east like parade floats.

We had both exhausted our supply of recent updates over lunch and had little to say, but we'd always been comfortable in each other's company in the quiet moments. I tuned the radio to a soft-rock station and "Spirit in the Sky" filled the car, which seemed an appropriate soundtrack for a drive to a church service. When I saw a sign for the Church of Eternal Release, I turned west onto a two-lane highway, passing a few isolated farms. Another sign directed me left onto a dirt road, and we rumbled across shallow potholes into a large gravel parking lot. I pulled the car under a massive oak tree stippled with green buds, one of the few remaining spots in the crowded lot.

I helped Emily from the car. She took my arm and we strolled to the entrance through a twilight perfumed with the scent of pines and newly-plowed earth.

The Church of Eternal Release was a simple whitewashed clapboard structure in the Greek revival style with a steeple rising above its inset entry door, giving it the look of a pastoral postcard in the waning light.

The remnants of a cornfield, as yet unplowed, nestled it on the right and a small pond flanked it on the left. A stand of skeletal trees awaiting spring's arrival fenced the back of the church. As we approached, the postcard luster gave way to the reality of years in harsh Ohio weather that had pitted and peeled the building's skin.

The door was wide open, and a frail, elderly gentleman with an aluminum walker greeted us warmly and offered us each a church bulletin. We made our way down the center aisle and found two available seats. The nave was nearly filled with a predominantly blue collar crowd of mixed ethnic origin, with a few stragglers still wandering in. The altar area was simple in design, practically stark compared to Catholic churches. The one oddity was what appeared to be a miniature traffic light above the altar, which glowed red. I described the room for Emily, including the lovely stained-glass windows and sandstone floors.

Most of the congregation was casually attired, and I felt conspicuous in my button-down shirt, tie, and sport coat. In contrast, the folks seated in the first two rows marked RESERVED wore what used to be called Sunday-go-to-meeting clothes. Elegant dresses, jewelry, stylish hats, and tailored suits.

Somewhere in the church a gong sounded, and I nearly leapt out of my seat. As the ringing faded, a choir wearing burgundy robes trimmed in white entered the sanctuary from a side door. They laid down an old-time spiritual that I recognized from Civil Rights marches, and their three-part harmonies made me want to jump up and shout hallelujah.

Then the gong rang out a second time, the pipe organ launched into an entrance anthem, and a tall, broad-shouldered man with dark, slicked-back hair strode out to the altar. He had a regal bearing and appeared to be in his mid-forties.

Dressed in radiant vestments, the Reverend Jeremiah Flood led his congregation through a few hymns and a surprisingly undistinguished service, making me wonder how he managed to fill the pews on a Wednesday night—and yes, leaving me more than a little jealous.

When Flood ascended to the pulpit for his sermon, however, everything became clear.

CHAPTER SIX

Wednesday, March 26, 7:30 p.m.

Reverend Flood stepped to the microphone and hurled fire and brimstone at the sinners huddled below him like Zeus throwing lightning bolts. Amens filled the church, and hands waved in the air. *Charismatic* was the word that came to mind, and my own homilies seemed insipid and uninspired.

Without warning, he went silent, raised a fist into the air, and slammed it down on the heavy wooden lectern. "I have had enough! I'm fed up with Death." He continued in a whisper. "Its gaunt face, its smell, its presence on this earth." Flood's voice slowly began to rise. "My beloved friends and neighbors, Death is the Devil's henchman—and I'm *sick to death* of them both!"

The people in the first two rows of pews stood in unison, and the rest of the congregation followed suit. In minutes, the entire crowd was swaying to his words.

"Years ago they said death was natural, just the way it was, the way things had to be. Suffering was to be expected—the *natural* state of the world." He paused. "They also told us the world was flat, that smallpox and the plague were unavoidable, and that even *slavery* was part of the natural order!" Flood swept his eyes across his mesmerized parishioners. "We. Know. Better!"

He moved closer to the microphone and cranked up the volume, his voice ringing from the rafters.

"Death is strong, but *God* is stronger! I am stronger. You are stronger." He stopped and dropped his volume by half. "So in this church ... we close the door to Death!"

Emily, I, and many in the congregation literally jumped as the elderly man who had greeted us slammed the entrance door shut right on cue, then hobbled to a back pew with the aid of his walker.

Flood let his parishioners settle down for a moment before resuming the service. "In this house of worship, we close the door to Death ... and open the door to life everlasting! How do I know?" He pointed at the miniature traffic signal above the altar. The green light was now flashing. "As you see, we are in the presence of the Lord," he said, as if the connection between the light and the Almighty was obvious and logical. "God is here in this very room with us!"

With a few long strides, Flood descended the pulpit and leapt down into the Nave like a paratrooper, then walked among his flock.

"*Only God* can heal your soul. Your heart. Your mortal body!"

More shouts of praise, hallelujah, and amen. All those who could stand were now on their feet, many swooning.

Flood stepped up to a sallow-looking gentleman wearing a white shirt tucked into his blue jeans. He placed both hands on the man's shoulders and whispered in his ear. They leaned their foreheads together for a minute. A hush fell over the room and Flood handed him the microphone.

"Praise the Lord, Reverend, for He is with us! *He* will cure my failing heart!"

A young woman stepped up to Flood, and he followed the same ritual, placing his hands on her shoulders and his forehead against hers.

"Praise God, I feel the Spirit!" she cried. "Praise His presence among us. By His love, I will be saved. I will conquer my cancer!"

He said something to her, and she teetered and collapsed into his arms. Two young men helped lay her down on a pew. After a few seconds, she started to stir.

A woman in front of us turned, stared at Emily's sunglasses, and took her hand. "You poor thing. You're blind? Let the pastor lay his hands upon you and pray. Pray like you've never prayed! It's a powerful thing, for he is filled with the Spirit."

I glanced up at the blinking green light above the altar and thought, *filled with something.*

Emily thanked the woman, removed her sunglasses, winked at me, and mouthed one word. "Wow."

On and on, Flood ministered to his congregation. People cried, applauded, hugged. As the excitement grew, Emily stood and out of solidarity, I joined her. When the fervor peaked, Flood returned to the pulpit and waited for his flock to settle down. He gave them a not-so-subtle reminder of their obligation to tithe, veiled in a vague threat of divine retribution for those who failed to open their hearts and their wallets. I suspected that the man guarding the entrance door was not about to open it until every possible penny had been collected.

The offertory began with a flourish of collection plates. Purses, money, and donation envelopes materialized as if by magic. When the collection came to me, I reached for a twenty, reconsidered, and threw in two dollars, glad that Emily couldn't see the paltry sum. Heck, I was a priest who had taken a vow of poverty, and I was currently borrowing from St. Peter to pay St. Paul in order to raise my nephew.

After the Offertory, Reverend Flood approached the microphone, and said, "In this house of worship, everyone is invited to partake of Communion, no matter what denomination or faith."

Baskets containing small squares of bread were passed throughout the church. Emily took one. I pretended to and passed the basket to the elderly lady on my left. She paused and gave me a long hard stare before taking a piece and passing it on, then she cleared her throat as if to say, "I saw what you did!" Her disapproval reminded me of the nun who had terrified me in grade school, Sister Mary Nancy. We had called her Sister Very Nasty, a nickname she had earned.

There might have been no need to justify my behavior had I worn my clerical collar. I certainly did not intend to offend anyone. But the Catholic Church's teachings were clear on the matter. Only those clergy whose line of ordination was unbroken back to the apostles could consecrate bread and wine into the Holy Eucharist, the body and blood of Jesus Christ. That meant Roman Catholic and Orthodox Catholic priests. This was a decree I was not allowed to ignore.

Flood raised a loaf of bread, broke it in half, and took a small piece between his thumb and index finger. With his other hand, he pointed at his flock and said, "The body of Christ is *not* in this bread. It is in all of us here in this room."

I knew that most Protestants didn't believe in transubstantiation, but the conviction that the Communion bread actually *became* the body of our

Lord was so deeply ingrained in my Catholic brain that my head jerked back as if I had been slapped.

Flood surveyed his flock and continued. "Hear me, brothers and sisters. I am, you are … we as a *congregation* are the body of Christ on earth. Do this in His memory." He placed the bread in his mouth and everyone around me did the same. Then he raised a silver chalice and said, "Remember our Lord and drink the wine, just as Jesus did at the Last Supper."

Trays with tiny, plastic Communion cups containing red wine were passed throughout the congregation. Emily picked up a cup, glanced at me, and drank. My elderly neighbor gave me another angry look. Images of Sister Very Nasty and her ruler raced through my mind and God help me, I took a cup and passed her the tray. I studied the wine in my hand and pondered my next move. *Now what, genius?* At a loss, I casually set my cup in a hole in the hymnal holder provided for empty cups. The old woman glared at me, reached over, took it and drank. I wasn't sure, but I thought I heard her whisper "heathen" under her breath.

After Communion, Flood read a gospel passage and then, brandishing his Bible like a sword of justice, he interpreted the reading in such a unique and convincing manner that he left the impression that *his Bible* contained God's-own truth, whereas all others were merely filled with suggestions, proverbs, and questions.

Afterward, he took the opportunity to remind his followers that although a sin might be in the past, its stain was with us forever. He segued into prayers for the sick, naming those in need one by one including Tony Pagano, the teenage boy in a coma at St. Joseph's Hospital.

Following the Doxology, the organist and choir launched into "What a Friend We Have in Jesus" with all the energy and emotion befitting an old-time Southern gospel song. I only knew the first verse by heart and picked up a hymnal. The woman next to me kept glancing over to make certain that I was participating to her satisfaction.

Flood raised his arms heavenward. "Open the door to life everlasting." Right on cue, the elderly man threw the entrance door open, and the cool night breeze glided through the church like the Holy Spirit. "Go now and shout His praise to all you meet!"

The Benediction concluded the service, and the congregation departed to a rousing rendition of "Stand Up, Stand Up For Jesus," sending us all out into the world to spread the good news.

Jeremiah Flood was at the door to receive us as we left the church.

I shook his hand. "An inspiring service, Reverend. I've heard great things about your ministry. I'm Jake Austin, the pastor at Sacred Heart Church in Oberlin."

His smile wavered for only an instant. "Thank you for coming. You're welcome here anytime, Father," he said, moving on to greet the man behind me in line.

Emily took my arm and I led her out into a crisp, clean evening. A last vestige of crimson and violet streaked the western sky, which hung low and heavy with stars. A gentle gust of wind rustled the budding tree branches, adding a light snare drum accompaniment to the last few strains floating from the church.

"What did you think, Em?"

"I said it before and I'll say it again." She grinned. "Wow!"

Wow indeed.

"I haven't been to many Protestant services, Em, but as a Catholic, the order of things seemed a bit odd to me. Other than that, Flood touched all the bases and definitely hit a home run."

"That's an understatement. The man is a phenomenon, definitely a force of nature. His style reminds me of the charismatic preacher in *Elmer Gantry*, that classic movie I saw before I lost my vision."

I'd had the same reaction, and when the light hit him just right, he even looked like a young Burt Lancaster. After the traffic signal gimmick that supposedly signified the presence of God in the room, I had half-expected Flood to do a baseball slide down the center aisle as Lancaster had done in the movie.

"To be honest, Jake, it was exciting. I haven't been moved like that in church for a long, long time."

That, of course, included all the times she had attended Masses that I'd offered. But as she went on bubbling about Flood's hypnotic style and charisma, I had to smile. I hadn't seen Emily this revved up in ages. I tried to set aside my petty jealousies, but her enthusiasm highlighted the stark contrast between Flood's approach and mine. The Reverend Jeremiah Flood had left me feeling like a third-string, benchwarmer on Team God.

I was guiding Emily around a pothole when a soft voice behind me said, "Father?"

Edna and Virgil Pagano approached us. "What a pleasant surprise to see you here," Edna added. "I'm so glad you came."

Virgil fixed me with a cold, dead-eyed glare and nodded.

"My pleasure. It was an interesting and enjoyable service. How's Tony?"

"We been praying and he woke up this afternoon," Virgil replied. "He's a bit groggy but he'll be okay, with the Lord's help. Doc Taylor has to run more tests, but I have faith that God will heal Tony, same way He cured the lame and the blind."

At the word *blind*, Emily squeezed my arm.

Virgil started to walk away. Edna took hold of his arm and stopped him. "Thank you again for all you did, Father. You're welcome to visit our son anytime you're in the hospital."

"I'll stop by tomorrow if he's still there."

"He won't be," Virgil added and led Edna away.

When we got in the car, Emily asked, "What was that about?"

"Long story." I gave her the CliffsNotes version of my encounter with Tony Pagano, and later with his parents at the hospital. I left out the part about the drugs in Tony's bloodstream.

"Thanks for bringing me tonight, Jake. I'm really jazzed."

No doubt about that! Emily was as restless and fidgety as RJ was after two cans of soda pop. She was seldom this talkative and never used words like "jazzed."

What concerned me was that I knew her excitement was about more than just Flood's service. Although she put on a brave face for the world, the onset of blindness in her twenties had been a crushing blow. Conventional medicine had nothing left to offer her, and she had recently placed her hope for a miraculous cure on a bleeding statue—and she'd had her hopes dashed. Now Flood and his laying on of hands? I didn't want to watch her go through another heartbreaking disappointment.

"I have an idea, Jake."

"What?"

"Let's stop at The Feve for a drink. What do you say?"

I couldn't say anything and nearly swerved off the road. The Feve was a local watering hole. Emily rarely drank, was not a partier, and would never have suggested anything like this in the past. I fought off the urge to call Colleen and ask her to babysit my nephew a while longer. There was nothing I would have loved more than to spend time with Emily for a couple hours over cocktails, but scandalous, unfounded rumors about the priest and the blind lady were already spreading like a virus throughout the hospital and the county. We both knew our relationship was under the microscope and had vowed to be more cautious about adding grist to the rumor mill. Now, a drink together at a pub in town? Clearly she *was* jazzed.

"I wish I could, but I have to put RJ to bed."

"Party-pooper! How about some tunes."

She reached over, found the radio controls, turned on a music station, and sang along, chair-dancing in the passenger seat the entire way back to St. Joseph's, all wiggles from the waist up.

As we pulled into the hospital parking lot, Tanya Tucker's alto filled the car with the 1970's classic country song, "Delta Dawn." I glanced at Emily and stiffened. The story of someone in their forties still clinging to the memory of a lost love struck way too close to home for me. Why couldn't I let go of my feelings for her? Maybe *I was* as "crazy" as Delta Dawn.

I escorted Emily to the residence hall where she lived rent-free in exchange for serving as an advisor to the interns and residents who stayed in the hospital dormitories.

We said goodnight, and I was walking through the hospital lobby on the way to my car when I spotted Tree Macon. He did not look happy.

CHAPTER SEVEN

Wednesday, March 26, 9:00 p.m.

Tree finished a phone call and pocketed his cell. He was unaware of my approach and startled when I called his name.

"Hey, Sheriff, too much caffeine?" I snickered. "What're you doing here this late at night?"

He did a double take. "I could ask you the same thing. Aren't all kindergarteners, little old ladies, and priests in bed by eight o'clock?"

"That's not far from the truth." Tree was all business and wearing his game face. Given what Dr. Taylor had told me about amphetamines in Tony's system, I was confident I knew why Tree was here. "What's up, big guy?"

"It's what's *not* up. Tony Pagano. When we pulled him from the truck, he was stoned. I came to ask him where he got the speed, but he's still too loopy to give straight answers."

"Come on man, tell me you didn't interrogate the boy without his parents present! I just saw them at church."

"It was a pleasant chat, not an interrogation."

I had seen Tree play fast and loose with the rules once before in a case, and I hoped to God he was being straight with me now.

"Doesn't make sense, Jake. He was higher than a kite when we brought him in yesterday, but he should have come back to earth by now. I don't know, maybe he also got a concussion when his pickup hit that tree, but my bet is that he's playing me." He released a massive sigh, befitting his two hundred and fifty pound frame. "I'm tired of punk kids taking dope and thinking it's all harmless fun. I'm the one who has to deal with the collateral damage. DUIs, brawls, drive-bys, overdoses."

I remembered what Dr. Taylor had said. "I don't think Tony is a druggie or a punk. You saw him; he doesn't have the look of a tweeker. From what I've heard, he's a solid citizen. A good student holding down a part-time job and an altar boy, or whatever ministers call their assistants."

"Yeah? So what's your point?" Tree gave me the *stink-eye* he had perfected over time. "*You* were an altar boy too and as I recall, you were circling the drain back in high school. Heck, if Uncle Sam hadn't dragged you into the military, and if God hadn't reached down and saved your ass, I suspect you'd be wearing prison orange or be dead by now."

Hard to argue with that. All of this was true. Jesus had *literally* been my savior, and my time as an Army medic led me to a career in medicine.

"What's wrong with you tonight, Tree? It appears you could use a mood-enhancer yourself. I prescribe a bottle of Guinness when you get home. All I'm suggesting is that you take it easy on Tony until you know the full story. I realize you're only doing your job, but …."

"Fine. Maybe you're right. I've had enough for one day anyway. Think I'll go pop the top on a cold one. See you around." He saluted and headed for the cruiser parked illegally in front of the hospital entrance.

Before going home, I stopped briefly in the record room to sign a chart I'd forgotten about. As I put my pen away, Dr. Taylor walked in.

"You too, Jake? I swear, when I die they won't need dirt to bury me. They can just shovel the hole full of insurance forms and administrative memos."

"Sad but true." I spent as much time practicing my penmanship as I did practicing medicine. "I have a question. Why is Tony Pagano still out of it thirty hours after we brought him in? Why so long?"

"Although his amphetamine levels were off the charts initially, you're right, it's atypical. Took me a while to figure that out. Apparently, Tony has seasonal allergies. As he began to come around, he was sneezing and complaining, and his mother gave him some of his usual over-the-counter meds. It added to his already high levels of stimulant. I wanted to give her hell but couldn't bring myself to chastise a woman who'd nearly lost her son, so I slipped on my best bedside manner and asked her to refrain until Tony was well enough to go home."

He gave me a weary smile, and we walked to the parking garage together. It had been an exhausting day, and a bottle of Guinness sounded like exactly what I needed to cure what ailed me.

CHAPTER EIGHT

Thursday, March 27, 7:00 a.m.

The next morning, Colleen arrived to get RJ ready for preschool. She had grown up in the Aran Islands off the west coast of Ireland and was decked out in her favorite green Aran sweater. She wasn't simply my nephew's nanny. Given my hectic dual roles at the church and hospital, Colleen was the constant in RJ's life, and he'd become the child she'd never had. In truth, she had grown to be family, and RJ and I both depended on her. She was the engine that kept our strange, blended family on the tracks and moving smoothly through life.

"Top of the mornin', Father," she said, her bright eyes sparkling below her short white helmet of hair. "Shall I make a spot of breakfast for you then?"

"No thanks. I'm offering a memorial Mass in the hospital chapel in honor of Sister Agnes before my shift in Urgent Care and can't be late. She passed away on Monday."

"Aye, 'twas a sad day. A sainted woman that one was, though I hear she drank a bit, bless her heart."

Vintage Colleen. She was also the Queen of Gossip. She giveth the compliment with the right hand and taketh it away with the left.

I woke RJ. He gazed at me like a punch-drunk fighter, then grabbed his stuffed Pooh Bear, closed his eyes again, and rolled away. I felt the same way some mornings. I chuckled because he was having a bad hair day and his red locks looked like a raging forest fire. With great effort, I finally succeeded in rustling him out of bed, dressed him in a Cookie Monster t-shirt and jeans, and plopped him and his beloved Pooh Bear at the kitchen table as Colleen finished making pancakes. I desperately wanted to spend the morning with my little man, but duty called. I gave him a hug, kissed him goodbye, and made a quick exit before Colleen could volunteer any more rumors and innuendos.

When I arrived at the hospital chapel, a large crowd of worshipers was pouring in. Sister Agnes had been one of three nuns whom I'd come to think of as my "Three Owls" because they each wore large, round glasses and were always perched in the front pew at morning Mass. She'd cared for some of my patients on the medical floors and we had become friends. Her passing greatly saddened me.

During the service, I glanced over to where Agnes usually sat. My *two* remaining Owls forced smiles and nodded. They had intentionally left Agnes's seat vacant, which looked to me like a hole in the heart of the universe.

Agnes's years of hard work, compassion, and innumerable kindnesses had filled the small chapel with many hospital staff of various religious denominations. Midway through Communion, Dr. Bhat stepped forward to receive the Eucharist. Bhat was a Hindu, but had participated once before at a funeral Mass. Afterward, I had explained that the Eucharist was intended for Catholic worshipers only. He'd replied that as a Hindu he worshiped many gods, and he included Jesus among them.

Bhat stood before me, waiting patiently to receive the body of our Lord. I started to say something, scanned the long line of communicants behind him, and gave him the host. Who was I to judge?

After Mass, the chapel emptied and a young nun approached me. A few errant blond curls peeked out from under her white wimple veil. She said she was a friend of Sister Agnes, thanked me for the service, and asked if we could speak privately.

"Sister Agnes told me that you might be willing to get involved, Father. That in the past you'd done some courageous things. She told me you were … different."

I cocked my head. "Different?"

"Sorry, that didn't come out right. *Different* in that you'd been in the Army and had become a physician before you joined the priesthood."

"All true. So what can I do for you Sister …? Sorry, I don't know your name."

She reached out, took my hand, and gave it a firm shake.

"Angelica." She smiled and her entire face lit up.

"How can I help?"

"My younger sister, Miriam, is missing. We were raised west of here in the village of Kipton. She's only seventeen and a very troubled kid."

Angelica's eyes grew moist and she glanced away. "I have no idea how her life unraveled. She was quiet as a kid, a mouse of a girl." She showed me three photographs, one of her sister beaming at the camera in her Brownie uniform, another of a cute young lady blowing out fifteen candles on her birthday cake, and the last of an adolescent with fluorescent-green hair and a defiant expression. "All she ever did was go to school and fool around with her PlayStation—until her late teens, when all hell broke loose."

Angelica shook her head. "Miriam went from a straight arrow to a loose cannon overnight. Suddenly she was hanging around with a bad crowd, dabbling with drugs, making bad decisions. It's ironic, I guess. Her name means 'rebellion' in Hebrew—and hers began at age fifteen."

She drew a deep breath and continued. "Miriam's missing and the authorities don't seem to care. They assume she's probably a runaway, shacked up in some motel, and doesn't want to be found. But that's not like her. We were *close* … even after her rebellion. She kept in touch for a while after she dropped out of school and disappeared. Said she was okay and working as a waitress, but wouldn't tell me where. I haven't heard from her in over a month. She wouldn't do that to me, stop calling. Not on her own. Something bad has happened."

I flashed back to my welfare visit for Mildred Rojas—to her lifeless body, the scent of death, and the swarm of flies in the bedroom buzzing her corpse. I willed the image away.

"What can I do for you, Sister? This sounds like a police matter."

"That's exactly why I came to you. Maybe you can get their attention. Sister Agnes said that Sheriff Macon is your friend."

I wasn't sure what was coming and just nodded.

"Will you talk to him for me, Father? Get him involved? Our last name is Riley." She gazed away from me, lost in her nightmare. "Our dad drank a lot. He passed away a year ago, but after our mom died and I went off to the convent, he may have … abused her. I wasn't there for her when she needed me, but I want to be there for her now." She looked up at me, her eyes pleading. "Please! I have nowhere else to turn."

She'd caught me completely off-guard and my head was spinning. "I'll speak with the sheriff and do what I can to help. No promises."

"Thanks, Father, I'd appreciate that. Take these photos of her, if they'll help." Her eyes drifted down. "I know what happens to runaways, especially girls, and I'm scared." She hesitated. "I'm not paranoid, Father. I belong to a local group that's committed to ending human trafficking in our community. I believe that *this* is my purpose in life, what God put me on earth to do. Will you help us?"

I had boxed as a young man and had a nose that angled slightly to the left to prove it, and her request hit me like a right hook. *Human trafficking?* I'd watched a special about the flourishing slave trade in Asia and the Middle East—but here in the heartland? I had been so wrapped up in my day to day challenges that this issue hadn't even shown up on my radar.

"Sorry, Sister, I'm not up to speed on all this. How can I help?"

"We've been e-blasting social media but we want to do more. I know it's asking a lot, but could you distribute these?"

She handed me a stack of 4x3 inch stickers that read ARE YOU SAFE? NEED HELP? CALL 1-888-373-7888 or TEXT "BeFree" (233733). The website for the Human Trafficking Resource Center was printed near the bottom.

"You've lost me, Sister."

"A group of us are sticker-bombing all the public restrooms in the county. Not just hospitals, but bars, liquor stores, strip clubs. Anywhere kids in trouble might be taken and have some privacy." She held up her stack of stickers. "I'm putting mine on the inside of stall doors in all the ladies' rooms at the hospital. Please do the same in the men's rooms."

I thought about requesting permission from the hospital administration, then considered the usual red tape and bureaucratic BS. What was the worst that could happen if security caught me? The hospital needed my services, and the Pope certainly wouldn't excommunicate me. Heck, maybe God would give me brownie points toward Heaven for getting involved.

"Okay. I'll speak with the sheriff about your sister and plaster the men's restrooms with these stickers."

"You may also come across victims at the hospital or at the church, Father, and not realize it. The warning signs may be subtle. This might help."

She handed me a printed list of bullet-points entitled, "Red Flags of Human Trafficking". It included visible bruises, multiple cell phones or hotel keys, avoiding eye contact, inappropriately seductive clothing, fake IDs. I had much to learn.

"Count me in, Sister."

"One other thing. Our members are all volunteers and our funding is running low. A lot of victims are Latina women who are Catholic with nowhere to turn for help. Could you ask the bishop for financial assistance from the diocese? I tried but … he wasn't receptive. He and I have banged heads in the past."

"I'll speak with him, but I doubt it'll do much good. He and I have a love-hate relationship."

"Give it your best shot. And thanks for your help," she added and left the chapel.

Human trafficking in the Midwest? E-blasting social media and sticker-bombing restrooms? Heck, I still had an old Rolodex on my office desktop. In my head I was twenty years old, but in fact I was a middle-aged dinosaur.

After a hard, painful slap of reality from Sister Angelica, I walked over to Urgent Care. What I needed was something to lighten my mood. What lay ahead, of course, were sick people and frustrated patients who had been waiting a long time to be seen. Fortunately, I had a competent second year resident to assist me, and we promptly got the situation under control.

Emily had told me that she had a doctor's appointment and couldn't meet me for lunch, so instead of heading for the cafeteria, I called Tree Macon at noon and asked him to look into Miriam Riley's disappearance.

The big guy was in a lousy mood and growled at me. "I'll do what I can but don't get your hopes up, Jake. Most runaway teens get picked up by a predator within a week, disappear, and are trafficked. And I'm not only talking prostitution, but also forced labor on farms, in nail salons, or as domestic help."

"I've read about the problem overseas, but here in America? In rural Ohio?"

"The slave trade is no longer just about race; it's about enslaving the weak and powerless of all skin colors. Women from Asia and South America are particularly vulnerable. Some are trying to pay off huge family debts. They work for pennies and may be trapped because they're here illegally, or they've had their passports confiscated by their employer." He paused. "Look, buddy, I gotta meeting and have to go."

"Thanks, Tree. Do what you can for Angelica's sister and keep me posted."

After I hung up, I called the Diocese of Cleveland and asked to speak with Bishop Lucci as Angelica had requested.

"His Excellency has left for the day. He'll be in a grueling meeting all afternoon … fundraising."

I thanked her, hung up, and smiled. On a lovely, warm spring day in Ohio, I suspected that his *meeting* would indeed be grueling—especially the dogleg on the sixteenth fairway and the water hazards near the eighteenth green, prior to cocktails at the club.

I took the opportunity to affix Human Trafficking Resource Center stickers to stall doors in the men's rooms. The task took longer than I'd anticipated and I was only halfway done by the end of my lunch break. Instead of grabbing a quick bite to eat, I hurried to ICU to check on Tony. The neurologist was examining him when I arrived, so I returned to work.

By the end of my shift, I was fading physically and my empty stomach was expressing its displeasure when I received a phone call from Dr. Poporad. She told me that she would be late to relieve me in Urgent Care. I called Colleen, explained the situation, and again asked her to hold the fort with my nephew. She was none too pleased.

"Have no worries, Your Lordship. We peasants were born and bred to serve the whims of the nobility." She mumbled something in Gaelic and hung up.

As the clock slowly ticked on, I stepped into examination room three and found an elderly gentlemen complaining of a fever and sore throat. There were no tongue depressors available so I grabbed a new box from the supply cabinet, but when I reentered the room I saw him close a desk drawer and slip something into his pocket. It was the proverbial, back-breaking straw at the end of an exhausting day. I stormed up to him. "What do you think you're doing, sir?" I reached out, palm up. "Give it to me."

He blushed, reached into his pocket, and placed a sterile one c.c. syringe and needle in my hand, the kind used to inject insulin or for TB testing. "Sorry, Doc."

"Sorry? I should call security." He looked remorseful. I grabbed a tongue depressor and said, "Open up." The man did in fact have a raging pharyngitis and swollen tonsils. I took a swab for culture and wrote him a prescription for antibiotics, then asked, "What in the world was that about? Are you shooting drugs? Do I need to run a tox screen on you?"

I'm not sure what I expected him to say or do, but what he did was cackle uncontrollably—on and on until he started to cough.

"Boy, have you got the wrong guy, Doc. *Budweiser* is my drug of choice. I'm a fisherman and it's been a cold, hard winter. I'm going to the lake this weekend and I use these," he said pointing to the syringe, "to inject air into worms to make them float off the bottom. Fish eat that up. Literally."

My turn to chuckle. I had been waiting all day for a laugh, and the old man had finally delivered. I handed him the prescription, the needle and syringe, and wished him calm waters and a stringer full of walleye.

I left the room as Dr. Poporad arrived to relieve me. On the way to my car, Emily called. "Jake, where are you? You promised to pick me up for RJ's birthday party."

Crap! I had completely forgotten.

"Sorry, I'll be there in five minutes, Em."

CHAPTER NINE

Thursday, March 27, 5:50 p.m.

Emily was waiting for me at the curb holding a gift-wrapped present for RJ. As I guided her into the passenger seat, I realized that not only had I not bought a present for him, I didn't even have a birthday cake. *Double crap!* The hospital was a few minutes from a bakery that specialized in custom cakes. I broke the speed limit and wheeled into their parking lot just as a woman hung a sign on the door that read CLOSED.

I asked Emily to wait in the car, ran to the entrance and knocked, but the clerk shrugged and pointed to the sign. I begged her with my hands steepled in prayer position, then removed the clergy card from my wallet and held it up to the window. Not as effective as a police shield, but she relented and opened the door. I explained my predicament.

"Sorry, Father, but we have no birthday cakes left today and the baker's gone home."

I stood there forlorn, gazing at the tile floor, before turning to leave.

"Wait a second, this might work. I have a small chocolate cake for a young girl that no one picked up." She removed a cake from the cooler with vanilla icing reading "HAPPY BIRTHDAY RONDA" in large pink letters above the numeral 8.

"I could try to remove the name for you, Father."

Proof enough for me of the existence of God!

"My nephew's name is RJ. Can you remove just the letters N, D, and A, and alter the letter O so it looks like a J?" She looked at me as if I had just stepped out of a spaceship from Pluto. "Please, I'm desperate!"

When she had finished, I said, "Great. Now change the eight into a five."

Although the writing resembled that of a grade-schooler's when she finished, I hoped it was good enough to fool RJ. And for the first time ever, I was grateful that Emily was blind, so she wouldn't realize what a total jackass I was. I knew, however, that Colleen would not fail to point out my shortcomings.

I thanked the woman, paid for the cake, handed her the last ten dollars in my wallet as a tip, and hopped into my car.

"Problems, Jake?"

"No, just running late." I needed to redirect the conversation. "How'd your doctor's appointment go today?"

After a long pause, Emily managed, "Fine. No problem." Her hesitation and her expression suggested otherwise.

"Nothing serious, I hope."

"I'm okay."

I don't like being lied to, but I let it go for the time being and wheeled into the driveway at the rectory. Colleen met us in the hallway, tapping an impatient foot.

"Grand of you to finally come, Father. I did as you asked." She opened the hall closet and handed us helium balloons exclaiming "Happy Birthday" in large block letters.

"The lad's in the living room. I haven't mentioned his birthday, and he has no idea it's today. He ate a fine supper and is more than ready for dessert." She took the cake box from me and added. "I'll sneak this into the kitchen, add some candles, and get the present I bought for him. Be back in a jiffy."

RJ sat on the floor in the jeans and the Cookie Monster t-shirt I had dressed him in that morning, which seemed appropriate given his voracious appetite for sweets. He was finishing the roof on a Lincoln Log house when he looked up and noticed the three of us holding our balloons. His mouth dropped open and his silver-blue eyes grew large beneath his mop of red curls. He was speechless, a rarity.

"Surprise! Happy Birthday, RJ."

A huge grin lit his face. As we sang Happy Birthday, he jumped to his feet and bounced around the room like a human pogo stick. I crouched down, and he ran to me and leaped into my arms. If it was possible for my life to get any better at that moment, I couldn't imagine how.

"Wow, this is soooo cool!" He gave me a hug. "I love you, Daddy!"

And there it was, *Daddy*, the word I'd grown to love—and the word I could never quite live up to. My nephew had begun calling me that after my sister passed away from leukemia. With my erratic hours at the hospital and my inexperience with children, I was definitely a poor substitute for her. RJ's biological father had abandoned him, and I'd become his legal guardian because we had no other family, and because I didn't want my nephew warehoused in the foster care system—but I was still finding my way through a role I'd never even imagined I would have.

I had tried a few times to have RJ call me Uncle Jake, but when he gazed up at me one day with those sad eyes and said, "But *all the kids* at school have a mommy or daddy," I relented. There was no doubt that we filled a void in each other's life. The Vatican had permitted priests to adopt on rare occasions, and I'd decided to pursue adoption proceedings. It would be an uphill battle, but I was committed to doing whatever it would take to make it happen.

RJ gave me another squeeze, then noticed the presents that Emily and Colleen were holding. "Are those … for me?"

"You bet they are, birthday boy!"

The five-year-old center of my universe morphed into Genghis Kahn, immediately pillaging wrapping paper and looting gift boxes.

Colleen's present was largest and RJ attacked it first, removing a Tickle Me Elmo doll. My nephew didn't have many cuddly toys and was a fan of Sesame Street, so he was thoroughly delighted. He wrapped his arms around Elmo and danced across the living room as the doll giggled at him.

But Emily's gift was the highlight of the party. She knew I had purchased a DVD of the movie *Toy Story* for RJ and had taken him to see the most recent sequel at a local movie theater. When he removed a Buzz Lightyear action figure from the box, he shrieked with delight and resumed his human pogo impression.

Then it was my turn. Time to pull a rabbit from my hat. RJ had been begging me for a bicycle since the snow melted, so I promised to take him this weekend to pick one out. RJ rewarded me with another hug, but visions of scraped knees and tears danced in my mind.

Colleen had placed five candles on the birthday cake, and hurricane RJ wasted no time blowing them out. She appraised the cake, raised an eyebrow, and said, "A fine job of planning on your part, I see, Father. I offered to bake one but no," she added shaking her head, "that wasn't special enough for your Highness."

I could only shrug.

I watched my nephew consume his body weight in cake and ice cream. I didn't take a slice, however, since I'd given up my favorite food groups for Lent—sweets and junk food. As I watched the three of them descend on the cake like a swarm of locusts, I would have traded my medical degree for one small bite.

Afterward, Colleen drove Emily to the residence hall at the hospital on her way home. With RJ on a sugar high, I had a devil of a time getting him bathed and into his GI Joe pajamas. I had to read him several bedtime stories before he finally conked out.

I booted up my computer in the study, checked my email, then settled into my recliner in the living room to watch The Father Clement Story on television. I had never seen the movie, but I knew about his life and was indebted to him. In 1981, he obtained permission from Rome to adopt and raise four African American children. His example caught President Clinton's attention and led to the founding of the national "One Church-One Child" program, which encouraged people of faith to adopt at-risk kids.

I was thoroughly engrossed in the story as Lou Gossett, Jr. portrayed Father Clement's confrontation with Cardinal Cody over the issue of abandoned and orphaned children. Tree Macon's phone call returned me to reality.

"Got a minute, Jake? I could use your help."

"Sure." I muted the TV. "What's up?"

"Tony Pagano finally came back to planet earth today and was discharged from the hospital. I ran a background on him and like you said, the boy's squeaky clean. Good student, hard worker, regular church-goer. Hell, my grandmother looks a lot dirtier than this kid. I gotta assume this was his first experiment with drugs. I have no interest in busting him, and hopefully, the experience scared him straight."

"Okay, so?"

"A little community service is all I'd ask for from the D.A. in exchange for giving up the name of his drug dealer. I'm sick and tired of the carnage these lowlifes cause, especially to young folks. But when I asked him where he got the uppers, Tony stonewalled me and his father went nuclear. I thought his old man was gonna throw a punch. I know you've got rapport with the mother. Would you talk to them, so I don't have to lean on the boy with the threat of jail time?"

"Of course. I'll stop by their place tomorrow." Time for some quid pro quo. "Did you find out anything about Angelica's sister's disappearance?"

"Working on it." A weary sigh. "Patience, buddy. I got a few other things on my plate."

CHAPTER TEN

Friday, March 28, 7:15 a.m.

Usually RJ was up with the sun, but that Friday he slept in. When I woke him, he began to cry.

"What's the matter, RJ?"

"I had a dream … about Mommy." He wiped away tears on his sleeve and sniffled. "She was *right here* with me … and you woke me up. It's not fair!"

Not fair indeed. Life surely wasn't. Many times since my sister's death, I had turned to tell her something or let her in on a joke and was once again painfully reminded of the bottomless void that her death had produced.

In the past, I had tried to paint a child's picture book portrayal of heaven, angels with harps on clouds, his mother sitting in radiant sunshine at the Lord's right hand smiling down on us. It hadn't worked. I had no words to comfort RJ's kind of pain, so I hugged him until he finally gathered himself, then changed the subject to his best friend at school and got him dressed.

I was late for Mass and Colleen offered to drive him to preschool. Because of an afternoon teacher's meeting, RJ only had a half day. I asked her to pick him up and stay with him in the afternoon, so that I could speak with Tony Pagano and his family. She agreed. Without a doubt, Colleen had become more than my Girl-Friday at the rectory. She was the glue that held my hectic life and blended family together. Without missing a beat, Colleen set a steaming bowl of cinnamon oatmeal in front of my nephew, handed me a cup of coffee, and I hurried from the rectory to the church sacristy.

The Lenten season was a time to honor and remember the forty days that Jesus had spent in the desert praying and fasting. For me, Lent was a time of self-reflection and an opportunity to evaluate my personal shortcomings, which never seemed to be in short supply.

I donned my purple vestments and walked to the altar. RJ's ongoing suffering over the loss of his mother had unsettled me, but I set aside my flagging spirit and troubled thoughts. This was *my time* with the Lord and as necessary for me as food and water. I inhaled the faint aroma of incense and flowers, and let the ageless rhythms of the Mass wash over me, marveling at how my convoluted journey through life had somehow led me to this amazing inner peace.

After Mass I walked to the rectory, changed into a polo shirt and Dockers, and attacked the mountain of church-related paperwork burying the desk in my study. I muddled through the quarterly financials and budget, paid a bill for a plumbing repair at the church, and returned a few phone calls from parishioners, then began preparations for the upcoming Holy Week and Easter service, which is the spiritual equivalent of the Super Bowl for a priest. Time slipped away and I was putting the finishing touches on my sermon when I heard Colleen return with RJ.

She made tuna salad and tomato soup, and we settled in at the table and listened to my nephew's detailed account of his day at school—the world according to RJ—including his favorite part, recess. When he tired of entertaining us and went to play with his Lincoln Logs, I hopped into my car and drove to the Pagano farm south of town.

Edna Pagano met me at the door, invited me in, and offered a cup of freshly brewed coffee. She said her husband was in the barn caring for a sick calf. Given my initial hostile encounter with Virgil, I doubted he would be forthcoming with me anyway. Tony's school bus had not yet arrived, so I got down to business.

"Mrs. Pagano, do you have any idea where Tony could have gotten amphetamines?" She shook her head. "The police can't look the other way much longer. I don't want them coming after your son, so please help me get to the bottom of this. Are there any family friends or relatives who use drugs? Anyone who might have influenced him?"

"No one. Honest, Father. My husband's family members have all passed, and I'm an only child. Most of our friends are from the church and barely drink alcohol, let alone do drugs. None of this makes sense. I *know* my son. Tony's a good boy. Could the blood test have been wrong?"

"No, they ran it twice when Tony was in the hospital. What about his pals from school? Could one of them be involved? Peer pressure can be powerful."

She gave me the names and addresses of her son's two best friends, Tyler and Ryan, but was confident that neither was involved with drugs. From my years at the church and in the hospital, I have become a good judge of character and she seemed genuinely bewildered.

Tony opened the front door, heard the word "drugs," and became as motionless as one of RJ's toy soldiers. Edna guided him to the couch, and I asked my questions as gently as I could. He continued to deny purchasing or using any illicit substances, but each time he answered he glanced warily at his mother.

Edna had nothing useful to add, and I wanted to speak with Tony alone. I studied him and said, "Take a walk with me, son." I glanced at Edna for permission and raised an eyebrow. She nodded her approval, and Tony and I went outside.

The air was laced with an odd blend of scents: mowed grass and fragrant flowers mixed with the pungent aroma of fertilizer. Halfway to the barn I stopped, placed a hand on Tony's shoulder and said, "Son, this is not going to go away. You have to talk to someone. Better me than the police. I'll do what I can to help, but please stop lying to me."

"I'm not lying! I never bought any drugs, honest."

"Then explain why you were so high you ran your truck off the road and stopped breathing."

"I … I don't *know*." He was quiet for a long time, and I let the silence weigh on him until he spoke again. "I get that my whole story sounds crazy. I do! But it's the *truth*. The only thing I can think of is …." He stopped and stared at the ground.

"Is what, son?"

"What I did before that." He ran a hand through his honey-colored hair. "Please don't tell my parents!"

"I may have to tell the sheriff, but I'll try to avoid telling your folks if possible. So, what were you doing before the accident?"

"I'd just finished sweeping out the church nave. I help out there when

I have time. Nobody was around and ….." He looked up, his eyes moist. "I pray hard and work hard, and I wanted … to be like the chosen ones." His mouth opened, closed, then more words spilled out. "I took a little of the altar wine reserved for The Blessed."

"I don't understand. Who are The Blessed?"

"Members of the congregation who are righteous in the eyes of God. Reverend Flood says they have a special place in the front pews at church, in Heaven, and in the Lord's heart. No matter how much I do to help out there, they say I can't be one until I'm twenty five. That's all I wanted. Heck, I do more for the church than all of them combined!"

Tony's words held the ring of truth. Trying to make sense of what I'd heard, I remembered my visit to the Church of Eternal Release with Emily and the well-dressed folks in the first two pews. An icy chill slid down my spine.

Flood had shown The Blessed an inordinate amount of attention during the service. And while the ushers passed out Communion to the rest of the congregation, he had personally dispensed the sacraments to them.

"Wait, Tony. What did you drink? Didn't most Protestant churches switch from wine to grape juice after the Reformation?"

"Reverend Flood teaches us that the Bible is the word of God. It says wine in scriptures, so we use wine."

Dr. Taylor's description of Tony's bloodwork came roaring back to me: Slightly over the limit for alcohol, but sky-high levels of amphetamine.

"How much wine did you drink, son?"

"Not much. Maybe one glass. That's all." He opened a gate in the split-rail fence and we walked silently toward the barn, then he stopped. "I've had wine in the past, and I sure as heck didn't drink enough to get drunk, or I wouldn't have gotten in the truck to drive home."

"Do your buddies, Tyler and Ryan, do drugs? Come on, be honest with me."

"Heck no!"

"Anyone at church or at school?"

"There's some kids at school who smoke grass, but I don't know anyone who does anything stronger."

I thought for a moment. "Did the wine taste okay?"

"It tasted … like *wine*. I haven't had enough to know the difference."

"What else did you do before leaving the church that day?" I was grasping at straws, struggling to ask the right questions. "Use any cleaning products? Eat any food? Drink water or something other than wine?"

"No, nothing. I had cows to milk, so I got in the truck and drove home—well, tried to. I don't know what happened. All of a sudden I felt dizzy, totally out of it. That's all I can tell you, sir." He kicked a clod of dirt down the path. "I gotta go help my dad in the barn now." He took a few steps and added, "Please don't tell my folks. This would kill them."

I had no idea how Edna would react. Having met Tony's father, I suspected he would go off like a roman candle. I had no desire to tell him anything until I had more facts. And from Tony's reaction, I was confident he wouldn't repeat his mistake or do anything else reckless in the near future.

I pulled out my cellphone and began to dial Tree Macon's number but stopped. The gears in my head were grinding but not quite meshing.

I used the drive back to the rectory to reevaluate the facts and ponder the discrepancies.

CHAPTER ELEVEN

Friday, March 28, 4:30 p.m.

Colleen had left me a note that she had taken RJ to the park and would be back in time for supper, so I ran a Google search on Reverend Jeremiah Flood. He had been an assistant pastor in Wyoming, and then the pastor at a fundamentalist church in Arizona prior to establishing the Church of Eternal Release four years earlier. Upon his arrival in town, he had become active in a local homeless shelter and the county food bank. There were photos of him ladling out soup at the shelter and stocking shelves with canned food. A newspaper article about his ministry at the prison in Grafton noted the uptick in inmate participation at worship services since his arrival.

Given the many online accolades about him and his burgeoning congregation, I was beginning to feel like a slacker. Reverend Flood was definitely the cleanup hitter on Team God and I was riding the pines—and if I didn't step up my game, I would be sent to the ecclesiastical minor leagues.

I found nothing untoward or suspicious, but the details were sparse. Given that the Sheriff's Department had much better ways to check backgrounds, I phoned Tree, got his voicemail, and asked him to call. Just as I opened the most recent issue of the New England Journal of Medicine, my mobile came to life.

"Got your message, Jake. To quote the bunny, 'What's up doc?' "

I told Tree about my conversation with Tony. Because I was not in a formal relationship with Tony or his family as a priest, I owed them no confidentiality as far as the Catholic Church was concerned.

"So the wine might have been drugged? That's a really weird tale. I thought I'd heard every excuse in the book. Never heard that one before. Druggies usually clam up, or deny things, or try to finger someone else. Tony's story makes him sound more like an innocent victim. You believe him?"

"I think he was straight with me. His story's too strange not to be true. He's more afraid of his parents than the police. And it fits with his squeaky clean image." I paused. "There's one thing I don't get. I'm told that amphetamines have an odor and taste bitter. Tony didn't notice anything when he drank the wine. Then again, he probably wouldn't know the difference between a thousand dollar bottle of Château Lafite Rothschild and a corked bottle of two dollar rotgut."

"Drug dealers sometimes add flavoring and fragrances, kind of like their trademark. The taste of powdered speed is pretty mild, and its bitterness could easily be masked by a sweet wine." Tree stopped talking. "Hold on. I gotta take a call on the other line."

When he returned, Tree said, "I don't know. It doesn't add up. That amount of wine in a boy his size might put him over the limit for alcohol, but there would have to be a shitload of speed in the glass to send his blood levels off the charts. When you attended the church service there, were the parishioners pinging off the walls?"

"There was definitely a fundamentalist zeal, though I wouldn't call it pinging. But no church offers full glasses of wine. You'd know that if you ever attended services, you heathen. They pass around trays containing thimble-sized Communion cups. If the wine was laced with amphetamines, an ounce might give everyone a nice buzz, but nothing more."

"Did *you* get a nice buzz?"

"I didn't partake, on religious grounds."

"That's a shame. You would have made a terrific guinea pig."

"I'm against animal testing, especially if I'm the animal. I'm with PETA on this one. Next you'll be locking up animals in cages. Oh I forgot, that *is* what you do for a living."

"Yeah, yeah. Very funny. Problem is, it'll be tough to get a warrant to test the wine on the basis of what you told me. Hearsay is the legal equivalent of rumor and gossip. This helps a lot though, Jake. When I spoke with Tony, he didn't tell me squat. I'd better send a deputy over to their place to get a written statement from him about the wine and his activities at the church. Maybe Tony will add a few more details to his story and we'll get lucky."

"Is there any way you can avoid involving Tony's parents? He begged me to keep them out of it. He's filled with shame and genuinely spooked. His dad's a church leader, and he has a short-temper."

"Unlikely, but we'll try. Guess I'll stop by the church under some pretext and size up the good reverend."

"His name's Jeremiah Flood. I Googled him but couldn't find much about him before he came to town."

"I'll run him through the system, see if he's got any warrants, wants, or priors. Thanks for your help, buddy."

I remembered how jazzed Emily was after our first visit to the Church of Eternal Release and said, "Wait a second, I almost forgot. Emily *did* drink the Communion wine and her behavior on the car ride home was out of character. She was restless, extremely talkative, and she was chair-dancing in the passenger's seat. She even wanted to stop at a bar afterward for drinks. At the time, I didn't think much of it and wrote it off to her enthusiasm about Flood's service—but now, I'm not so sure."

"Emily? That *is* odd. Doesn't sound like her. Pity I didn't know that forty-eight hours ago. I might have asked her for a blood sample. Not much use now."

I slipped into Sherlock Holmes mode, considered in detail what I'd seen at Flood's church, and grinned. Since becoming involved in a couple of Tree's investigations, much to my surprise I'd found that I *enjoyed* the deduction needed to solve a puzzling case, the same way that I enjoyed helping a patient by making a difficult diagnosis.

"There's more, Tree. While the ushers passed out wine to the congregation, Flood personally served the folks at the front of the church, a special group that Tony called The Blessed." I gave him the details, then hesitated. "But if Flood was dispensing drug-laced wine to them, then why did *Emily* act so strange on the way home?"

"That paints a different picture. Maybe the drugged wine was intended for the congregation, and Flood was sparing The Blessed, or he was serving them a *special* cocktail."

"Flood's style was mesmerizing and his service stirred the congregation into a frenzy. I suppose Emily might have simply been swept up in the excitement and her reaction had nothing to do with drugs. Who knows?"

"Well, I'm not going to solve this sitting on my backside, chatting on the phone. Time to invest some shoe leather. Thanks for your help. Call if you hear anything else."

Click, and he was gone.

As I wandered into the kitchen to get a cup of coffee, Colleen returned with RJ.

"If you've no need of me, Father, I'd prefer to leave a mite early today. At our last Legion of Mary meeting, I volunteered to visit a shut-in gal in South Amherst. Poor soul, thin as a rail she is. I wish to prepare a nice casserole for her, so that she might have more than her usual Meals-on-Wheels fare for a change."

"Of course. I appreciate all the extra time you've been putting in with RJ." Given all she did for my nephew and me, the church, and the community, I wanted to give her a hug. Knowing how she would react, however, I had added a substantial bonus to her weekly wages as a sign of my gratitude. I handed her the check. "Don't forget, I'm working at the hospital till three tomorrow."

Colleen looked at the amount, smiled, and said, "I'll be here early with bells on, Father." She kissed RJ on the top of his head and departed.

After my near-debacle with RJ's birthday, I wanted to make our time together special and decided to forego a mundane dinner of leftover meatloaf. I had my nephew make a pit-stop in the bathroom, and we headed to Walmart to examine their bicycles. The selection was small, so we drove to a local bike shop. RJ got excited when he saw a metallic blue Huffy in his size. I was less excited when I saw the price of the bike and helmet, but bit the bullet and wrote the check, adding another major dent to my bank account. As my father used to say, *I wasn't broke, but I was badly bent.*

We finished our boys-night-out with spaghetti & meatballs in town at Lorenzo's and a hectic bike-riding lesson in the empty church parking lot until dusk. Although his bike was equipped with training wheels, my little Kamikaze managed several death-defying crashes. Medical school had trained me to deal with the stress of performing CPR and Heimlich maneuvers, and the seminary had taught me to guide people through harrowing life events, but neither had prepared me for watching my boy hurtle toward the asphalt.

Despite a scraped knee, RJ was undaunted. By the time we went inside,

I was exhausted from running along beside him. The electrical current in my nerves was arcing and sparking, and I was in desperate need of an adult beverage.

After getting my pint-sized tornado asleep in bed, I realized that I'd forgotten my cellphone in the study when we went out. I had only one voicemail, from Bishop Lucci.

"I must speak with you, Father. Tomorrow morning. Come to my office before Noon."

The bishop did not sound happy. He knew I was scheduled to work at the hospital until three o'clock and that summoning me to his headquarters was a major inconvenience. Most likely, this was another Lucci power play. His Excellency could be petty and officious. He enjoyed flexing his bureaucratic muscle to remind his underlings of their place in the pecking order. Nevertheless, Lucci was my boss and as volatile as nitroglycerine, so I had to handle him with care.

It was too late to return his call. I decided to deal with him in the morning, but I had no idea which of my many alleged shortcomings he intended to address. I slept poorly that night.

CHAPTER TWELVE

Saturday, March 29, 11:30 a.m.

I had been trying unsuccessfully all morning to find someone who could relieve me in the Urgent Care Clinic so that I could drive to the bishop's office. I was awaiting a call from my last possible candidate when my cell played "Onward Christian Soldiers," the ringtone I'd chosen for Bishop Lucci, my Commander-in-Chief. I apologized to my patient, excused myself, and stepped into an empty exam room.

"You hadn't forgotten about our meeting had you, Father?"

"No, Your Excellency. I'm having trouble getting coverage at the hospital. I was just about to phone you."

A derisive grunt. "Yes, well, I must leave early for an urgent meeting, but I still needed to speak with you."

Outside the window, bright sunlight had banished the morning mist, and a gauze of white clouds streaked a cerulean sky. I suspected that an early tee time made polishing his golf clubs quite urgent.

"Before I left for the day, Father, I wanted to express my continued concern over the financial weakness of your parish. I went to bat with your Superior General to get your hospital income reinstated so you could care for your nephew. In return, I require that the fiscal solvency of your parish become your utmost priority. Sacred Heart's red ink is bleeding my diocese dry. It has to stop and *soon*. I would hate to have to shutter its doors."

His rant sounded like a threat and contained his usual quota of half-truths. Lucci had helped convince my Camillian Order to allow me to keep *part* of my hospital salary, but that was primarily intended to decrease the expense to his diocese. As for shuttering church doors, I had my doubts. Sacred Heart had a thriving congregation, and I had reduced the red ink in the ledger by half since my arrival nine months earlier. His Excellency was, however, a bean-counter, and he'd had absolutely no qualms about closing parishes to save money in the past. It sounded as if he wanted me to take Reverend Flood's approach, spewing fire and brimstone from the pulpit until every member of the congregation tithed their ten percent to the church. That was not going to happen. Many of my parishioners were blue-collar workers barely making ends meet.

"I inherited a deep financial hole, Bishop, but we're clawing our way out of it. If you look at the recent quarterly statements, you'll see that I'm making progress."

"Progress? I am looking, Jacob … and waiting, and waiting."

Time to change the subject. Recalling my encounter with Sister Angelica, I said, "Your Excellency, it's come to my attention that a local grassroots organization is engaged in a righteous battle against human trafficking. That's one crusade I think the Church *should be* involved with. A lot of victims are Catholic Latinas with nowhere to turn for help. The group is in need of funding, and I was wondering if the Diocese could provide some seed money until they get on their feet."

"Wonder no more. Absolutely not. That is out of the question, and it's a job for the Community Foundation, not the Church. If you ever get Sacred Heart's finances back in the black, maybe the parish could do a fundraiser." Another derisive snort, followed by a pause. "Let me guess. You've met Sister Angelica."

Best to play dumb with Lucci. "Oh, you know her?"

"Know her? She spends more time in my office than I do! She's always trying to raise money for one cockamamie scheme or another, but only succeeds in raising my blood pressure. I've had it with that meddlesome, self-important woman. She's been a thorn in my side since the day she was assigned here. Was she wearing her habit when you met her?"

"Yes, she was."

"Well that's unusual. Last time I saw her, she was wearing torn blue jeans and a Browns football jersey, like she was on her way to a bowling alley or a garage sale rather than a church. She's another one of those radical, *activist* nuns trying to transform the Church into some sort of socialist utopia. They're worlds apart from the pious sisters who taught me in grade school. Angelica even belongs to the L.C.W.R. They think soup kitchens and women's shelters are more important than spreading the gospel. Next thing they'll be pushing for gay rights, contraception, and God help me, female priests!"

As a firm believer in income equality, an opponent of starving people and battered women, and a proponent of women priests, I opted not to voice my solidarity and instead asked, "What's L.C.W.R.?"

"Leadership Conference of Women Religious," Lucci replied, spitting out each word. "Their ranks are growing. I've heard that the Congregation for the Doctrine of the Faith may investigate them, so hopefully that will put an end to their seditious influence." The bishop sighed, leaving me to ponder ecclesiastical infighting and church politics. "Anyway, Father, what I also need in return for my help with your nephew's lodging and care is for you to be my eyes and ears. Keep me informed about what Sister Angelica is up to."

Here we go again! Lucci had recently tried to enlist me in a plot to undermine a local priest and his parish. Apparently he thought I was the pastor at Our Lady of Perpetual Surveillance. The last thing I wanted was to be a diocesan spy for His Deviousness. What I *could do*, however, was be a double agent.

"Rest assured, Bishop, I will keep my eyes and ears open." And my mouth shut.

"Glad to hear it, Jacob. Well, I must be going. Keep me posted on Sister Angelica's … activities. I look forward to seeing improvement in your next fiscal quarter. Good day."

I finished evaluating my last patient of the morning, sticker-bombed the remaining stalls in the men's restrooms with Human Trafficking Resource Center hotline phone numbers as I had promised Angelica, and grabbed a chicken salad sandwich for lunch. I was on my way back to Urgent Care when my phone struck up "I Shot the Sheriff."

"Hi, Tree. How're things in the wonderful world of law enforcement? Hopefully, better than in the world of diocesan politics. Last time we spoke, you were going to talk with the Paganos about amphetamines and altar wine. How'd it go with Tony?"

"Wrong question, buddy. The question is *where* did Tony go? He's missing."

CHAPTER THIRTEEN

Saturday, March 29, 12:30 p.m.

I was speechless for a moment. "What do you mean Tony's missing? How? What's going on, Tree?"

"Wish I knew. My deputy got to Tony's house before his bus arrived yesterday afternoon, but he wasn't onboard. CCTV at the school showed him getting into a red compact car, a Honda Civic. The license plate was too covered with mud to read the number. The driver's side window was down though, and we got a quick glimpse of the guy behind the wheel. Light brown skin, shaved head, and a rat's-nest of a beard. My computer geeks are running his mug through our facial recognition program, but my hopes aren't high. Not a good camera angle. His left arm was resting out the window and there's a Puerto Rican flag inked on his forearm. He has a second tattoo on his biceps that's harder to make out. Picture's grainy, but my lab techs are trying to enhance the image. Maybe one of his tattoos will be distinctive enough to get an ID." I heard someone shout Tree's name. "Hang on, Jake."

When he returned to the phone, Tree said, "Sorry, buddy. Sometimes my rookies need a map to find their own butts." He drew a deep breath. "Anyway, I showed Tony's parents a photo of the guy in the Honda taken from the CCTV feed, but they denied knowing him. Normally, we don't get involved until someone's been missing more than twenty four hours. But Tony's behavior is so out of character for him that his parents panicked and begged me for help. They claim their son is an *atypical* teenager—obedient and considerate—unlike you and I were as kids. Sounds like Tony is the white sheep of the family, maybe of the entire generation. Guess there has to be *one* left in existence, but the species is damn-near extinct now-a-days. His folks said he would never get in anyone's car without calling home first. And yet … he did."

"Maybe he was bribed or threatened or tricked, Tree."

"Who knows? I'm worried about his safety given the drug connection, so I put out a BOLO on him."

"Did Tony appear to be under duress before he got in the car?"

"Nah, he looked kinda confused."

"Crap, I don't like the sound of this, Tree."

"You're gonna like it less when I tell you that a cruiser on patrol spotted an abandoned red compact near Carlisle Reservation, that Metro Park in LaGrange. The car was stolen and somebody wiped the fingerprints from the steering wheel and driver's door. Unfortunately, there's no CCTV out there. I got helicopters and uniforms combing the area, but it's two thousand acres, overgrown, and heavily-wooded. We're organizing volunteers to help in a grid search at two o'clock. You available?"

"I'm working, but I'll try to break free."

"Great. Any volunteers you can recruit, Jake, would be appreciated."

"Will do. Did you have a chance to interview Flood?"

"The Good Reverend is out of town at a spiritual retreat and unavailable. I didn't want to press the issue and spook him, so I'll intercept him after his church service tomorrow. Starts at 11:00 a.m. You interested? I'd appreciate your insights. Besides, I can't get a court order to test the altar wine because I don't have enough evidence yet, so I could use a human guinea pig … to see if the wine's spiked with anything. Might involve a little blood donation on your part."

"Very funny. Forget law enforcement, Tree. You're in the wrong profession. You should get a gig doing standup comedy. And when it comes to blood drawing, I've always thought it was better to be the draw-er than the draw-ee."

Tree and I have had a symbiotic relationship since junior high. The word "No" wasn't in either of our vocabularies.

"Okay, Tree, if Colleen can hold the fort with RJ after morning Mass tomorrow, I'll join you at Flood's service."

"Thanks, buddy. I owe you."

I telephoned Sacred Heart Church and asked the nuns to call our parishioners and commandeer volunteers to help search Carlisle

Reservation, then called Sister Angelica and requested that she rally her troops at the convent and hospital.

I contacted my colleague, Dr. Poporad, explained the situation, and requested that she relieve me early in Urgent Care. When she arrived at 1:30, I jumped into my car and hurried to LaGrange.

The sheriff gave everyone instructions and assignments. I was stationed along the western edge of a branch of the Black River. In the parking lot near me, the abandoned red Civic was being swarmed by CSI techs wearing gloves, gowns, and booties. I waited with the other volunteers until several cadaver dogs and their trainers led us through the tall grass, proceeding slowly and cautiously, calling Tony's name.

Knowing that the park included wetlands, I'd slipped into surgical scrubs at the hospital, but I had no change of shoes and my wingtips were soaked and mud-covered within minutes. My assigned route took me along the river bank. Spring rains had been heavy, and the water was running high, fast, and wide. I stopped several times to examine submerged logs, hoping I wouldn't find Tony's body lodged in the branches. Using a long stick to clear undergrowth, I worked my way through waist-high grassland and thick brush, past intertwined fox grape vines, and into a mature forest of beech trees and sugar maples.

I soon entered a stand of tall pine trees, where I lost sight of the volunteer to my left. The canopy above cast deep shadows everywhere, and walking on the brown, matted pine needles muted the sound of footsteps, mine and anyone else's who might be nearby. It occurred to me that whoever had abducted Tony might still be out here.

Having been a combat soldier in my youth had not steeled my nerves. In fact, my most enduring souvenir from the war was a hyper-alert vigilance verging on paranoia. Self-preservation is a powerful instinct. To this day, in public places I sit with my back to a wall facing the door, my eyes scanning for danger. So I froze when I heard a rustling from a nearby bush—and nearly jumped out of my shoes when a rabbit scampered out and dashed directly in front of me.

My heart rate and respirations began to slow and I continued, reassured that I could hear the nearest searcher somewhere to my left shouting Tony's name. One hundred yards ahead, next to a briar patch, the beige pine needle floor became dark red. As I rounded the thicket, lines of crimson lead to a heap of something deep in the shadows. I gasped, and cool spring air lodged in my lungs. Having worked with Tree Macon before, I approached cautiously, avoiding what appeared to be a blood trail, trying not to disturb any evidence.

I didn't want to call for the police until I could be sure the finding was important, but without a flashlight the forest cast an eerie gloom and it was difficult to see clearly. I willed myself to move closer, approaching the bloody mass cautiously, fearing the worst.

The remains looked too small to be Tony's, but the carcass had been savaged and was so mangled that I couldn't make out a face. On the other hand, it wouldn't take long in these secluded woods for scavengers to dismember and devour any recent kill. I was about to holler for help when I identified what had been the head—and the sunken pits that had once been eyes. A fawn. There were coyotes in the area, and I had no doubt that this was their handiwork.

I slogged my way out of the woods into swampy wetlands, happy to see the sun and my nearest searcher again. Low dark clouds, however, had formed in the west, and a thunderstorm was putting on a light show somewhere over Toledo and heading our way. Time was running out. When the authorities finally called off the search, I spotted Tree Macon and asked if anything had been found. He shook his head and offered me a lift to my car. Neither of us had anything to say on the drive to the parking lot.

When I returned to the rectory, RJ was gobbling macaroni and cheese as fast as Colleen could fill his plate. I poured a cup of coffee, sat next to him, and he launched into an enthusiastic, in-depth review of a new television cartoon featuring puppies that could drive cars and fly helicopters, my TV viewing options ever expanding.

As much as I wanted to hear about RJ's day, I needed a warm shower to drive the chill from my bones and the darkness from my heart. When I returned, I slipped a Toy Story DVD into the player for him. He hopped onto the couch and snuggled up with his two best friends, Winnie the Pooh and the Buzz Lightyear action figure Emily had given him for his birthday. Seeing my nephew safely cocooned in the living room made me worry even more about Tony's welfare.

I went into the kitchen, wolfed down left-over lasagna for supper, and was about to join RJ when Emily called.

"Hey, Jake. I told my friend, Todd, about the Reverend Flood's church and how much I enjoyed his service. He offered to take me again tomorrow. I realize you're not a fan, but you're welcome to join us if you'd like."

"I'm not sure that's wise. Tree's been working on a case that may involve the church, and I think it might be safer if you waited a few weeks until he sorts things out."

"Safer? What're you talking about? Are you involved?"

How much to tell her? Enough to keep her out of potential danger, but not enough to compromise Tree's investigation or worse, tweak Emily's curiosity further. She was a strong-willed woman and once she set her mind to something, there was no stopping her.

Or was I simply being petty and defensive because she was choosing to attend Flood's service instead of mine?

She must have sensed my hesitancy. "Is this something I can help with? You and I made a good team on the bleeding statue investigation. If this is cloak and dagger stuff, Sherlock, and the game is afoot, I want to be involved. What's going on?"

"I don't know. That's the point." I had asked for Emily's help with the bleeding statue since her involvement had not placed her in jeopardy. A teenager associated with the church was missing, and if Flood was somehow involved with the drug trade, all bets were off. I didn't want her anywhere near that place. "I'm serious. Please don't go, not tomorrow."

"Jake, you're being ridiculous. That church has been holding services twice a week without incident for years. And I *enjoyed* it there."

No question about that. Emily had been so hyper on the drive home that I'd wondered whether her Communion wine had been laced with the Holy Spirit or with uppers.

"Stay home if you like. I'm going with Todd."

"Come on, Em, listen to me. That's not—"

"I stopped listening when you started talking nonsense. I've heard enough. Bye." Click.

One more disappointing setback in an already frustrating day. Depressed and completely spent from trudging through mud and undergrowth at the Carlisle Metro Park, I snuggled up with RJ on the couch and watched Woody try to save his friend from the evil kid next door. Having encountered more than enough evil in my lifetime, I prayed that some hero would miraculously appear, rescue Tony, and provide us all with a happy ending.

CHAPTER FOURTEEN

Sunday, March 30, 11:00 a.m.

After offering morning Mass at Sacred Heart for the safe return of Tony to his parents, I changed into a shirt and slacks, and drove to the Church of Eternal Release. Instead of the elderly gentleman who had greeted me on my previous visit, a burly young man with the physique of a weightlifter shook my hand and offered a church bulletin. Because Reverend Flood's welcome had been less than warm at our initial meeting, I chose a pew near the back of the nave and blended in with the crowd.

Emily and Todd arrived, and he guided her down the center aisle. They took seats several rows ahead of me. When I first returned to town, I'd assumed that he was her lover. And much to my dismay, that thought had resurrected jealousy I was certain I'd buried years earlier. Later I had learned that Todd was gay, a close friend, and an important part of Emily's support system, and I was grateful she had him in her life.

Tree Macon was not there, which was no surprise. When you're a black man the size of a refrigerator and your photo is often in the newspaper, it's nearly impossible to blend in anywhere. I suspected that he intended to intercept Flood after the service.

By the time Reverend Flood strode to the altar decked out in crimson and gold vestments befitting a Greek god, even standing-room-only space was scarce. Although the morning was cool, body heat had already raised the temperature of the room to uncomfortable levels.

The service started as it had during my last visit. The box resembling a miniature traffic signal above the altar winked its green eye as Flood led his congregation through several hymns. Then he stepped up to the pulpit for his sermon like Zeus ascending Mount Olympus. A sudden hush fell over the gathering. He began, as he had the first time I'd seen him, in a slow, nearly inaudible whisper.

"Brethren, do not be complacent. Being righteous is not enough. Do not underestimate your enemy, for he is powerful. He is cunning, devious, and shrewd. He can appear anywhere, in any form ... or as anyone. Do not be deceived."

Flood stopped and swept his eyes over the congregation, his voice gradually increasing in volume.

"Make no mistake, my friends. Satan is among us, today as always—even in this house of worship! I feel his presence, smell his evil scent." Flood raised a hand and pointed at members of his flock. "He may be seated next to you! Or you! Or you!"

The intake of breath from the people around me was audible and a restlessness rippled through the church. The woman to my right gazed at me and slid farther away.

"Have no doubt. We are at war!" His voice had risen nearly to a shout. "The choice is yours. Eternal life, or death and eternal suffering. Will you stand up for what you believe, or will you cower in the corner?" The people in the first two rows of pews, the select group that Tony had called *The Blessed,* stood in unison. Soon others began to rise. "Will you stand with the righteous ... or will you forsake them and join the Devil's evil minions? Those are your only two choices."

Flood removed the microphone, stepped down from the pulpit, and strolled up and down the aisles. He lowered his voice again to a whisper, and the congregation leaned toward him to hear every syllable.

"Today I want to remind you of Satan's many forms, his many disguises, his many faces. I say unto you ... where you least expect him, he is there. The lesson is clear. Even *Jesus* was betrayed by a friend." He paused before his volume again ticked up. "It's written throughout our history. The Nazis were quick to claim that God Almighty was on their side. Islamic extremists kill innocents in the name of Allah. But those are *obvious* perversions of the Word."

Flood stopped next to me and glanced in my direction, then continued. "Was Prohibition righteous? The *intent* may have been, but there were those who sought to use government policy to ban wine from churches, to withhold the sacred, redeeming blood of Jesus from the faithful—the same way they'd banned peyote for years from the Native Americans, and tried to ban Christian spiritualist from Brazil from using Hoasca. Was banning hallucinogens responsible, reasonable? Maybe, but I refuse to judge how others seek the Almighty."

He raised a fist into the air and upped his volume. "The quest for oneness with God is a personal and sacred right that should never be abridged by unbridled authority. Be vigilant that all our God-given constitutional rights are *never* shoved down that same slippery slope into the abyss by government overreach!"

A few amens and hallelujahs echoed in the rafters. Flood walked slowly down the center aisle.

"I'm sure all of you are aware of recent attempts in this country to suppress freedom of religion. Our great republic, founded on timeless Christian principles, is under assault. There comes a time when the righteous must stand up. Forewarned, my brethren, is forearmed. And you have been warned!"

The congregation was revved up and humming with excitement. Flood strode back toward the pulpit, nodding to parishioners and shaking hands. The man was a rock star! I suspected that if he leaned backward and fell into the nave, his followers would be there to catch him as if he had fallen into a mosh pit.

He snapped the microphone back into its stand, peered out over his congregation, and resumed the service. This time during Communion, however, I considered what Tony Pagano had told me and decided to volunteer to be a guinea pig. Instead of abstaining as I had on my last visit, I consumed the bread and drank one of the small plastic cups of wine that were passed, waiting to see if I felt any effects.

After an enthusiastic pitch for donations to the church's school building fund, Flood lead prayers for infirmed and hospitalized members of the congregation, then paused.

"Today, dear friends, is a dark, dark day. I ask you to devote your prayers in the coming days to the Pagano family. One of our own, someone you all know and love, has gone missing." Loud gasps sounded throughout the church. "Young Tony mysteriously disappeared from public school on Friday." He spat out the words "public" as if he'd bitten into something rancid.

Virgil Pagano, seated with his wife immediately behind The Blessed, bowed his head and moaned. Edna released a keening wail that must have pierced every heart in the church. Flood descended from the pulpit again, walked to her, and placed a hand on her shoulder. She stood and hugged him, wobbled unsteadily, and he guided her gently back onto the pew.

"Please take this opportunity to pray for Tony's safe return," Flood said, launching into the Lord's Prayer. The congregation responded in kind, *Thy will be done* and *deliver us from evil* hanging in the somber silence that followed.

The organist began the exit hymn, something complex and beautiful I had never heard. I looked over and recognized the young man at the keyboard. He was a student at the Oberlin Conservatory of Music and one of my parishioners who occasionally filled in when our regular organist was unavailable.

Wanting to speak with him, I stepped into the aisle and swam toward the front of the church against the raging current of people heading to the exits. Emily and Todd remained seated, no doubt waiting for the throng to clear. Despite her sunglasses and red-and-white cane, stepping into the center aisle too soon would have risked bodily harm. Hungry churchgoers can be an aggressive lot on their way to lunch. Patience is a virtue, but for a blind woman in a crowd, it's a survival skill.

When I finally arrived at the organ, I greeted the young musician warmly. "This is a pleasant surprise, Piotr. What're you doing here?"

"Ha! I think I might ask you the same thing, Father," he replied with a faint Polish accent.

"I hope you're not abandoning us at Sacred Heart. I'd miss your musical flair and smiling face at Mass."

"Oh no, nothing like that. I am here, how do you say it, to pick up 'brownie points.' One of my professors is a member here and she requested that I participate ... so I participate. And to be honest, it is an absolute joy as an organ major to play an instrument this exceptional, especially for so large an audience."

Because Emily's behavior had been unusually animated after our first visit to the church, and because Tony had crashed his truck while high on amphetamines, I had convinced myself that the wine had been spiked. But I sensed absolutely nothing unusual after drinking the wine. Then again, I weighed nearly twice as much as Emily, and any drug would have had less of an effect on me. And who knows? If Flood did spike the wine, maybe he did so sporadically or on specific occasions. The seductive power of *intermittent* reinforcement is strongly linked to gambling and other addictions.

I looked at Piotr, the other unwitting subject in the room, and asked, "Do you participate in the sacrament of Communion here?"

"No, Father, I did not think that would be proper. Was I wrong? I was taught in Sunday school that only a Catholic priest can perform … what is it called, transub…?"

"Transubstantiation. Correct. We believe the bread and wine miraculously *become* the body and blood of Christ. For most Protestants, Communion is considered an act of remembrance, a tribute in honor of our Lord." In light of what the bread and wine might be laced with, I added, "And I think you made the right decision."

In truth, I was disappointed. I felt absolutely nothing unusual after Communion and had hoped another guinea pig might help confirm my hypothesis. Time to slip into my role as Dr. Watson and assist Sheriff Sherlock.

"Have you noticed anything unusual during your time at this church, Piotr?"

"Other than the large crowds and vibrant service? No. What do you mean?"

I wondered how to ask my question without stirring up too much dust that might make it back to Piotr's professor and eventually to Flood. "Just curious. I'm in awe of what Reverend Flood has accomplished here in such a short time. Do you know him well?"

"No, not well, but he has been most gracious in complementing my music."

"And how do the congregants feel about him?"

"The few I have spoken with absolutely … adore him. Ha, I almost said *worship* him."

"That's how it comes across."

With the crowd nearly gone, Emily stood, brandished her cane, and walked slowly out of the church with Todd as Tree Macon arrived and approached Reverend Flood at the entrance. Time to get to the nitty-gritty.

"It's so sad about that missing teenager, Piotr. Do you know him?"

"I do not."

He gathered up his sheet music and stepped away from the ornate pipe organ. Before he departed, I added, "There's a nice mixture of ages and ethnicity at Flood's service. Wish I could say the same at my parish."

He considered this. "Good diversity yes, but predominantly white."

"I saw some Spanish-speaking folks seated near me. By chance, have you noticed a Hispanic man with a shaved head, a beard, and tattooed arms?" Piotr leveled a quizzical gaze at me and I added, "He's an acquaintance of mine. He lives somewhere around here, but we've lost touch." A venial lie, but a lesser sin I was willing to exchange for Tony's safety.

"Funny you should mention that. I did see someone like that in the parking lot after the service last Sunday leaning against a car, smoking a cigarette. I think he had several tattoos."

"What kind of car?"

"A bright yellow sports car of some kind, Father."

"Is he a member?"

"I doubt it. I remember only because there was something ... *off* about him. He did not appear dressed for church. I am not sure why exactly, but he made me uncomfortable. He really a friend of yours? On a dark night, I would have crossed to the other side of the street to avoid him." He pushed the bench closer to the organ. "Sorry, Father, but I must be going."

CHAPTER FIFTEEN

Sunday, March 30, 12:45 p.m.

As I walked down the aisle toward the exit, Tree Macon saw me. He guided Reverend Flood away from the entrance doors to a quiet alcove hoping he wouldn't notice my presence, although I suspect Flood already had when he was preaching from the aisle near me.

Outside, the sky had taken on a menacing appearance as lightning wove unlikely paths from cloud to cloud not far to our west. The storm that had threatened our search for Tony in the park had slipped to our north and missed us, but a strong wind gust and the scent of rain carried a reminder of Mother Nature's schizophrenic edge.

I spotted Emily in the parking lot and caught up with her. She turned when I called her name.

"I'm surprised you're here, Jake, given the *grave danger* you warned me about. But let your heart not be troubled. I have survived another perilous worship service in a house of God without the need for armed bodyguards."

Ironic. Emily often accused *me* of being a smartass.

I shook hands with Todd. "Come on, Em, this is no joke. I meant what I said last night. I'm here at the sheriff's request."

She was about to take another dig at my paranoia when Tree caught up with us and introduced himself to Todd. Another wind gust rattled the tree branches and shivered us all. Todd wrapped his sport coat around Emily's shoulders and jogged off to fetch his car for her. When he was out of earshot, I asked Tree, "How'd it go with the good reverend?"

"Exactly as you'd expect. Great concern for Tony's welfare but not a clue what happened. A firm pledge of cooperation. Yada, yada."

"Did he appear edgy?"

"No, but neither do copperheads—till they rear back and bury their fangs in you." He glanced at Emily and continued. "It's too soon to lay my cards on the table, so I didn't show him the photo of the guy in the red Civic or mention …." Tree tilted his head toward Emily and shrugged.

Although blind, she didn't miss a thing. "What? Come on you two, what's going on? I thought we were *friends*, Tree."

I nodded and Tree said, "Okay, but this is in strict confidence, Emily. Let me ask you a question first. Did you notice anything after you took Communion? You feeling all right?"

"You too? I feel fine, Tree. What the heck is going on?"

He lowered his voice and told her everything: Tony driving off the road with high levels of amphetamine in his system, his denial that he ever bought drugs, his confession about sneaking Flood's altar wine, and his disappearance from school in a stolen red Civic two days earlier. I added that the organist may have seen the driver of the car in the church parking lot the week before, and told her our theory about drug-laced wine at Communion.

She furrowed her brow. "Whoa, really? Roofied at church? That sounds like a stretch."

"Not Rohypnol, the date-rape drug. Probably speed." Tree pulled a small spiral notebook from his pocket and scribbled down Piotr's name and information. "It's only a theory, but so far all the pieces fit together."

"Honestly, Tree, I don't feel drugged. Not even a hint of a buzz."

"Did you feel anything different on your last visit? Jake wondered if you were high after the service, said you seemed a bit … hyper."

She turned toward me. "I was not! I just enjoyed the sermon and a night away from my contracted world at the hospital." She refocused on Tree. "If you think it might help, you're welcome to take a blood sample from me and test it."

"Mine too," I added. "Though I feel fine."

"Thanks for the offers but bad idea. The lawyer for the department said our close personal relationships might be misconstrued as conspiracy or entrapment, and some wily shyster could use that to imply that the evidence is tainted. But not to worry. I had a neutral party inside who is willing to volunteer a blood sample. We'll know soon if the 'highs' that folks have been experiencing here are indeed *spiritual*." Tree stopped at his car and opened the driver's door. "And I hafta say, the content of Flood's sermon worries the hell out of me. Sounded as if he may have gotten wind of our investigation and was trying to rally his supporters."

"Some of his comments were way over the top," Emily replied. "Nazis and militant extremists? Stand up for what you believe. We're at war. What the heck was that all about, Tree?"

The big man wiped a meaty hand over his face. "Code words. I'm paid to be suspicious and that sounded a lot like a call-to-arms to me. *Government overreach?* Unbridled authority threatening the Constitution? That has the ring of anti-government rhetoric." Tree gestured toward the parking lot. "This is farm country, and half the pickup trucks here have gun racks in their rear windows. Forewarned is *forearmed* makes me wonder if Flood is gathering an army of resisters. I don't like the sound of that. The last thing I want in my county is another Jonestown Massacre or Waco bloodbath."

Emily gasped. I hadn't even considered the possibility and was speechless. When Todd drove up, we said our goodbyes. I helped her into the passenger's seat and they drove off.

"Any progress on Tony?"

"The BOLO hasn't helped, but we've issued an Amber Alert and plastered the area with Tony's photo and description. I also notified the FBI's National Crime Information Center. Their mainframe has full backgrounds on known felons and their M.O.s, stolen property, and everything crime related. I'm hoping their supercomputer will cough up a few 'bytes' of useful information."

"What now, Tree?"

"Now, I'll show photos of the guy who abducted Tony to Piotr. If he recognizes him, I'll get CCTV footage from the area and slap some surveillance on the Right Reverend Flood. And one of my deputies is about to become a member of his church. I'm worried about the militant rhetoric and curious what else Flood has to say to his congregation."

"Is there anything I can do to help?"

He handed me a picture of the Hispanic man in the red Civic and a close-up of the flag tattoo on his arm. "Show these around and see if anyone you know can ID the guy."

He got into his car and drove away, and I returned to the rectory feeling frustrated and far less than sanctified.

CHAPTER SIXTEEN

Sunday, March 30, 1:15 p.m.

Colleen, the patron saint of blarney and fine cuisine, had a delicious tuna casserole ready when I returned from the Church of Eternal Release. RJ was in the grumpiest mood I had ever seen, and I was grateful when Colleen agreed to stay and have lunch with us. It is pitiful, though, that an irritable little kid can intimidate an adult who is trained to manage the crises of others.

My nephew asked to ride his new bike after we finished eating. Despite the towering bank of dark clouds and the wind beating against the windowpane, I took a deep breath hoping the storm would miss us for the second day in a row, and said "Sure"—and the heavens immediately opened and drowned out any chance of playing outdoors.

RJ's mood went from bad to unbearable. Disappointing any irritable five year old is both unwise and hazardous to your mental health, so when the kiddy poop hit the fan, Colleen grabbed her raincoat and umbrella, performed a reverse Mary Poppins, and wisely flew away as fast as possible.

Falling back on my scant six months of childrearing experience, I pulled out my usual bag of tricks: building blocks, board games, Shel Silverstein poems, and Dr. Seuss books. Nothing worked, not even DVDs, which were usually a sure thing. I put a hand on his forehead to be certain his deteriorating mood wasn't due to illness, but he had no fever. I sighed. This had all the earmarks of an agonizingly long day, and I started looking forward to my next hectic shift at the hospital in the morning.

After an hour of repeated failure, I was desperate. Having trained at the feet of the master, the Wise and Devious Colleen, I resorted to a trip to the toy store, where we bought colorful stickers to decorate his new bike helmet. He continued to sulk, and by late afternoon I was ready to sell my soul for a couple Valiums. Desperate, I upped the ante to a dinner at a local Chuck E. Cheese. The pizza was mediocre and the rides drained most of the cash from my wallet, but the big costumed mouse finally got RJ dancing and smiling again.

Lousy child-rearing without a doubt, but I'm a believer in "whatever works," both in medicine and parenting. In my defense, one gets zero childcare guidance in seminary. But then again, who does? For the most part, parenting is on-the-job training and painful for all concerned.

I had finally gotten my nephew bathed and into bed for the night when Tree Macon called.

"Thanks for your help today, buddy. The *good news* is that Piotr ID'ed the thug driving the stolen red Civic as the guy in the church parking lot last Sunday. I have a deputy looking at CCTV footage from the area. Maybe we'll come up with the license plate number of his yellow sports car, or better yet, a sharper image of his face that we can run through the system. I'll stop by the church tomorrow and find out if they have security cameras. I also put a tail on Flood, but he hasn't left the vicarage since the service today. If I can connect Flood with the guy in the car, I can get a search warrant for the church and find out if he has a stash of amphetamines or drug-laced altar wine. I'd love to arrest his ass and find Tony."

"And the *bad* news?"

"The bloodwork from my volunteer at the service this morning came back completely negative. No drugs of any kind. If Flood is spiking the vino, it could be an intermittent thing. Or if he is involved in Tony's disappearance and thinks his cover is blown, he may have changed his M.O. or gone dark for the time being."

"Anything on Miriam, Angelica's missing sister?"

"Oh sorry, Jake, I meant to tell you. She was picked up a month ago near the steel plant in Lorain for suspected soliciting, but was released on a procedural snafu. Otherwise zip. Last known address was bogus. If she's still alive, she's in the wind and maybe doesn't want to be found. I'll keep an ear to the ground but don't get your hopes up."

"Did you look into Angelica's father? After she moved to the convent, she worried that he might have abused Miriam before he died."

"The guy was a boozer with a couple DUIs. Definitely not a solid citizen, but no record of abuse or neglect, though that doesn't mean diddly. A lot of abuse cases never get reported. Maybe that's why Miriam took off."

"No, that's not it. Angelica told me their dad died shortly *before* Miriam vanished."

"Most kids are independent by age seventeen. If they're street-wise enough, they can buy time before Child Protective Services gets involved. Question is, how was she paying the rent and buying food after he died. Did she have a job?"

"Not that I know of. It's hard for me to understand why a quiet, introverted kid who spent most of her free time alone with her PlayStation would suddenly go off the rails, run away, and end up on the street."

"You're a smart, well-educated guy, Jake, but you don't know squat about being a parent. RJ's young. Wait till he hits the volatile teenage years. One day they're flying high, the next they're in the dumps. Family life becomes an emotional roller-coaster. Trust me. Been there, done that, road every ride in Park Parenthood ... and didn't want the damn t-shirt. Ain't fun sometimes."

"Did you run a background check on Flood? I didn't find much online."

"Yeah. He has no arrests or priors in the system. I'll check with the local cop-shop in Arizona this week, see if they have a file on him or his previous church."

I thanked Tree, hung up, and called Sister Angelica with the update.

"My God, *soliciting*? That breaks my heart. I have to find her soon." She paused so long that I thought I'd lost the call. "I hate to ask, but I have nowhere else to turn."

"Ask what?"

"I remembered the name of a bar Miriam mentioned last time we talked. The Cavern. Sounded like she may have hung out there. I want to take her picture and show it around."

"You should have the police do that."

"No, Father. If she's breaking the law or hiding, and gets word that the police are on her trail, she'll dive deeper underground. Besides, the cops haven't made much of an effort to find her so far. I've decided to go tonight, but ...."

"But what?"

"The bar is in a shaky neighborhood, and I'm afraid to go alone after dark."

She gave me the address, and I suspected that Tree Macon wouldn't have gone there without his Glock and a SWAT team.

"Bad idea, Sister. Don't even think about it."

"Oh, I'm going! This is my sister we're talking about. I have to do what I can. But I was thinking, with your Army background and all, would you consider … going with me?"

My military training and morning calisthenics had been replaced by meditation and handfuls of Aleve for my aching joints. I wasn't sure I could protect myself in a seedy dive, let alone a young woman.

I was conflicted because Angelica was a strong-willed woman, and I suspected she would go with or without me, which was unacceptable. But RJ was asleep and I needed someone to stay with him.

"I'll have to make a few phone calls and see if I can get free. If I can't go, Angelica, *please* don't go there alone. I'll call you back soon."

Colleen was already overworked and I hesitated to ask her to babysit—but did anyway."

"I cannot, Father. I was just leaving my apartment." There was a lengthy silence, which was unusual for a chatterbox like Colleen. Finally she added, "I'm having a late dinner with … a friend."

The uncomfortable way she said *friend* screamed Y chromosome, and I felt ashamed. Although she was widowed and in her fifties, I had never considered that she might have a social life. *Mea culpa.*

I thanked her, hung up, called Emily, and asked her to babysit.

"Is this related to Tony's disappearance, Jake?"

"No, but something similar and equally depressing."

"All right then, count me in."

"Thanks, I owe you."

I couldn't leave RJ alone in bed while I picked her up, so Emily offered to come by taxi.

I called Angelica and told her to meet me in front of the convent at nine. Not what I wanted to do, but I had no choice. She was pretty, small as a minute, and would be easy prey in the wrong bar. The problem was, I was getting too old to be defending anyone's honor in a brawl, and the priesthood had dulled my aggressive edge and replaced my desire to rumble with a preference for rational discourse.

"I want you to try to look as plain and uninteresting as possible, Angelica. Downright homely if you can pull it off. No lipstick or makeup. Dress to blend in, not to impress."

She laughed. "That should be easy, Father. After all, I am a *nun*."

"I'm serious. I have no desire to get into a scuffle tonight."

When Emily arrived, I filled her in on our plan. She told me I was an idiot. I couldn't disagree, so I asked her to call Tree Macon if she hadn't heard from us by eleven.

CHAPTER SEVENTEEN

Sunday, March 30, 9:50 p.m.

On our drive to the Cavern Bar, Sister Angelica glanced over and said, "May I ask a personal question, Father?"

"Sure." I hoped it wasn't about my relationship with Emily. "Ask away."

"Being both a priest and a doctor, how do you balance the conflicting teachings of your two professions? Science is often at odds with Church teachings."

I had struggled with the question for years and had made peace with it.

"Like Albert Einstein, I seek the mind of God through science. If you accept that God made us, you must accept that He is also the God of the genome. And if God created the universe, then all the laws of science are also His creation. So I can as easily worship Him in a laboratory as I can in a Church. I know that's a simple answer to a complex question, but that's how I see it. Make sense?"

She nodded as we rolled up to the Cavern. It was nearly ten p.m. Angelica had been generous when she'd called the neighborhood "shaky." The bar was wedged between a vacant warehouse with most of the windows broken and what most likely was a chop-shop masquerading as an auto body repair business. Six decked-out Harley hogs were lined up at the door like horses at a hitching post. I'd had no desire to own a weapon since my army days, but it would have been comforting to have my old M16 along in case all hell broke out. I was tempted to grab the tire iron from the trunk, and wondered if my Ford Focus would still be in the parking lot when we came out, or scattered in pieces on the floor of the chop-shop.

As we walked into the bar, I set my cellphone on vibrate. If I received a church-related call, I didn't want my ringtone playing "Ave Maria" or "Onward Christian Soldiers." Wrong theme songs for this joint.

The Cavern was aptly named. It was dark, dank, and foreboding. The inside smelled of stale beer, puke, and body odor, and the clientele looked rough. Other than Angelica, the only other women there were the barmaid and a scantily-clad, older lady who was shooting pool.

I had dressed in a faded Cleveland Indians jersey and a pair of paint-spattered jeans. The bill of my baseball cap rode low on my forehead to mask the fear in my eyes. Angelica wore baggy sweatpants and a tattered shirt that had gone out of style a decade earlier. This was the first time I had seen her without her habit, and with her short blond curls unbound by her religious headgear, she looked like a teenager. We drew the uninvited attention of a lot of eyes, and she ran a trembling hand through her hair.

The brunette behind the bar came over with a twisted smirk that could have been either seductive or sadistic, maybe both. Her hair was short, spiky and dyed the color of clotted blood. A tattoo of barbed wire circled her biceps. Small steel barbells pierced her right eyebrow and tongue. She didn't appear old enough to drink alcohol, let alone serve it.

Angelica's request for a merlot brought a cynical snicker and produced something in a highball glass so dark it might have been prune juice. After one sip, Angelica grimaced and set the drink on the bar. I'm fond of an occasional Jack Daniel's and ordered a whiskey neat, but got something that tasted like turpentine. Definitely not Mr. Daniel's fine Tennessee mash, and I was reasonably sure that Gentleman Jack would not have been caught dead in this dive.

The bartender's dark eyes bounced between us with curiosity, narrowed, and landed on me. "That'll be ten dollars, Daddy Warbucks."

I too can do smartass. "Warbucks had less hair, and this lady ain't my daughter," I replied in a low raspy voice, trying to imitate the thugs I had seen on television cop shows.

Having anticipated the need to grease some palms for information, I'd stopped at an ATM on the way. I laid a Hamilton on the bar and she scooped it up.

I showed her Miriam's picture. "You ever seen this girl?"

"Yeah, she's been in here."

"When?"

"Can't remember." Her twisted smirk reappeared, revealing a missing upper incisor. She tapped a finger on the bar where the money had been.

I slid a twenty toward her but didn't release it. "When exactly?"

She shook her head.

I tossed another twenty down and placed my fist on top of the bills. Glancing at our reflection in the mirror behind her, I hoped to see a tough guy and his woman, but a middle-aged priest and a cute young nun stared back, both scared to death. Adding a growl to my voice, I asked again. "When and with who?"

If I had said "with *whom*," she probably would have laughed until she'd wet her pants.

"Last time must be a couple weeks." I kept my fist firmly planted on the money. She glanced at the cash, hesitated, then tilted her head toward a man drinking alone in the far booth. "See the big guy, the one built like a truck? I saw her with him once."

"He got a name?"

"Everyone calls him Mack."

"The girl in the photo was with him?"

She nodded. "That's it. Don't know nothin' else."

I retrieved my hand and Little Miss Charm pocketed the cash and walked away.

"At least she was alive two weeks ago," Angelica whispered. "That's good news."

I glanced at the man in the booth, and it didn't seem good to me. It was clear how he'd gotten his nickname. He was as big as a Mack truck, and looked about as welcoming as the chrome bulldog hood ornament.

"I haven't heard from Miriam in well over a month, Father. This gives me hope. And thanks for the money. I'll find a way to repay you."

Nuns received only a paltry stipend; at least I was paid part of my medical income.

"Forget the money. And in here, I'm Jake. *Father* might get my butt kicked." I surveyed the collection of miscreants seated around us and considered sending her out to wait in my car, but that sounded even more dangerous. "Damn it, Angelica, if I'd known what this place was like, I wouldn't have let you come."

"You couldn't have stopped me. Miriam is screwed up, but she's still my sister. Let's go say hello to our new best buddy, Mack."

She started over without me. Wishing I had brought the tire iron, I grabbed my whiskey and an empty beer bottle off the bar and caught up with her at the booth.

She said, "Mack, can we talk for a second?"

Dead eyes peered up at us from above a broken nose. His head was shaved but he sported thick, ginger-colored mutton-chop sideburns and a Hitleresque mustache.

"For you, sweet thing, I got the whole night."

Iron-pumped biceps poked out from a sweat-stained t-shirt with Willie Nelson's mug shot on the front. The words SKIN and HEAD were inked on the knuckles of his hands, and the letters A and B were tattooed on his neck, which I'd learned recently stood for Aryan Brotherhood. I thought I could see the face of death deep in his dark eyes. I was so far out of my league that I wasn't even in the same zip code.

Angelica eased into the booth opposite him as if he were her long-lost friend and lit up a radiant smile befitting her name.

I squeezed in next to her, staying close to the edge of the booth in case I was forced to jump to my feet and defend her.

Mack bared his teeth at me and growled. "Don't think I invited *you.*"

I gazed back at him and pretended to drink the last swallow from the beer bottle before plunking it down hard on the table.

"I need your help, Mack," Angelica said, redirecting his attention to her. His eyes slowly slithered down to her chest. Without flinching, she handed him a photograph of Miriam. "I'm looking for a friend. The bartender said you know her."

"I might." He eyeballed the picture, then gawked at Angelica's breasts again. "Friend, huh? You in the same line-a-work, sweetheart?"

Mack took a deep drag on his cigarette, dropped the dying butt into my beer bottle, and stared at me. "How 'bout you get me another whiskey?"

I was not getting more than two feet away from Angelica with this animal leering at her. I slid my glass of turpentine masquerading as booze across the table to him. He downed it without coming up for air.

A giant of a man in a leather Harley Davidson jacket staggered past us and plopped into a booth behind Mack. He gazed past Mack's hairless dome at Angelica, and the corners of his mouth twitched up.

My new Aryan brother ignored the biker and studied the photo for a while. "Yeah, I know her *real* good." He had drunk somewhere between way-too-much and barely conscious, and was slurring his words. "We had us ... an arrangement."

I suspected I knew what that meant. Angelica asked, "Drugs?"

His eyebrows drifted up. "You two cops?" He worked his jaw muscles and stared at us, then he chuckled. "Nah, the damn po-lice can't be that desperate." A malicious grin reemerged on his lips. "No darlin'. I don't sell no drugs. Guess again. Give ya a hint. I'm like one of them bone doctors—except I don't fix 'em. I break 'em. You don't wanna get on my bad side."

"Where can I find my friend, Mack?"

"Not sure," he replied, his breath a putrefied stench of tobacco, garlic, and cheap liquor. "Wish I knew, sweetheart."

"Is she a stripper, Mack? Hooker?" I asked. "She one of your girls?"

The grin evaporated. "Mine? You got the wrong guy. I just rent 'em." He snorted. "I love the ladies, but that ain't my line-a-work."

I suspected that no Ivy League school offered a degree in Mack's chosen field of endeavor.

Angelica tried to soothe the savage beast with another gorgeous smile, but it didn't work this time. Mack undoubtedly wanted a different kind of lip service. She pressed on. "Does she have a place around here?"

"Last I heard, a flop near 4th." He pointed at me. "You wanna know more, have this asshole get me another drink."

"No problem, I'll get you one." It was getting difficult to keep turning the other cheek with this clown. Having been in enough brawls as a youth, I reclaimed the beer bottle, lowered it under the table, and grabbed it by the neck as a weapon. It felt hard and cold, like the hand of a vengeful god. "I'll get you a *double*, soon as you answer the lady's questions."

Mack slammed a beefy fist on the table. "I said *now!*" He stood and I jumped to my feet. Half the room did the same. Rumble time.

I stepped away from Angelica and shouted to her, "Get the hell out of here." She slipped out of the booth and headed for the door.

Mack lunged at me and I swung the bottle hard at his head. He ducked away, moving fast for a drunk. I stepped back. He edged toward me, a knife in the hand that read SKIN. Hoping to keep mine, I smashed the bottle on a nearby table and waved the jagged edge in his face. He didn't seem to notice or care, slashing the air as he approached.

The biker in the Harley jacket rose to his feet holding a revolver. I nearly soiled myself. Stepping to the left, I put Mack between the gun muzzle and me. Time and my heart both stopped for a few beats.

I gave ground until I backed into the bar and could go no farther. Mack lumbered toward me and growled, joy in his heart, mayhem on his mind.

Harley man shoved his gun into Mack's spine. "Police. Freeze, motherfucker, and drop the blade."

The knife clattered to the floor, the door to the bar flew open, and an army of cops stormed in. The bartender sprinted for the rear exit, but a police woman cornered her before she made it halfway. Another cop had Angelica against the wall with her hands in the air.

I stood there like a mannequin, unable to breathe or move.

The undercover cop in the leather jacket cuffed Mack's hands behind his back, then said to me, "Drop the bottle, Father, before somebody gets the wrong idea."

I did as instructed. "But how...?"

"My boss showed me your picture and said I should keep you from dying—so don't. He's in a shitty mood."

Heavy footsteps came at me from the right. Tree Macon stopped and peered down like an angry grizzly.

"What the heck were you thinking, you jackass? The damn *Cavern Bar*? Jesus! I'm tired of bailing your helpless butt out!" He closed his eyes and massaged his temples. "Since you came back to town, I've used up an entire bottle of jackass-pirin dealing with the headaches you cause."

"Sorry, man." I pointed to Angelica, who had assumed the position and was facing the wall as a policewoman patted her down. "She's with me."

Tree stopped a passing uniform and sent him over to release Angelica from custody.

The wall clock read 10:45. In less than an hour, I'd nearly gotten us both killed.

"How'd you know I was here, Tree?"

"I came across some interesting info about Angelica's sister. When you didn't answer your cell, I called the rectory. Lucky for you, Emily knew what was going on. Wasn't sure I could get my troops together in time, so Vice loaned me an undercover guy working a biker gang in town. Good thing he got here before you decided to start World War Three."

"I don't know what to say."

"Say you'll stop being a jackass, Jake. Go stand out of the way with Angelica. When we get this under control, I got something to tell you two."

CHAPTER EIGHTEEN

Sunday, March 30, 11:15 p.m.

After nearly half of the patrons of the Cavern Bar were in handcuffs, the rest were released. The lights came on, revealing the interior to be even more disgusting and depressing, the décor a blend of medieval dungeon, frat-house party aftermath, and Soviet gulag.

Sister Angelica and I waited in the corner. A stout, balding man in a shabby suit waggled a finger at Tree and used the Lord's name repeatedly in non-biblical ways. The sheriff finally slinked over shaking his head.

"The guy in the suit didn't look happy, Tree."

"Yeah, the deputy chief just ripped me a new one for blowing the Vice cop's cover. What he's really pissed about is that I didn't ask his permission for the raid." He shrugged. "I didn't have time to go up the chain of command."

"Sorry we got you into this, buddy."

"Not like it's the first time I've ticked him off. He'll get over it. Glad you two are okay."

I introduced Angelica and she stepped forward. "Father Jake said you have something to tell us. Is it about my sister?"

"Yeah, I was talking about her with my I.T. person at the cop-shop. That's why I called the rectory and found out about your little ... adventure. Your sister was an online gamer, right?"

"According to my father, gaming was all Miriam did after I left for the convent three years ago. He said it was as if her PlayStation became her only friend. Heck, when I'd come home for a visit, she'd spend more time with that box than with me."

"Did she take it with her?"

"No, and that's one reason I'm so worried. Well, that and the fact she doesn't call anymore to let me know she's okay. The Miriam I knew would have phoned at least once a week. We were inseparable before I entered the religious life. Our father died shortly after she turned seventeen, leaving her alone and unsupervised. I'm praying you can help, Sheriff. She's all the family I have left."

"My tech guru told me there are a bunch of online gamers who are predators, messaging and befriending teens and grooming them for drugs, prostitution, slave labor … you name it. Target age group is between twelve and eighteen. But the FBI can now recover online communications from game consoles and trace them back to the sender. Her PlayStation may give us the break we need to find her."

"Thank the Lord!" Angelica said, her eyes wide with hope. "I'll bring it to you tonight."

"Two problems. First, this is cutting-edge technology and my department doesn't have it yet. Second, the FBI doesn't like to share or play nice with local law enforcement. No one at the Bureau is willing to give me access to the new technology. My calls to them got stonewalled."

"Maybe that's because you have all the charm of a rabid raccoon, Tree—unlike me."

I pointed to the scar on my wrist and waited for him to catch up. When the lightbulb went on, his face lit up. "Special Agent Novak! I forgot about her."

Keri Novak and I had both been involved in breaking up a local drug smuggling ring several months earlier, which made us brother-and-sister-in-arms. We'd both ended up briefly in the hospital, me with a compound fracture of my wrist that required surgery, her with a gunshot wound to the shoulder. She had given me her card and an I-owe-you-one promise out of gratitude for my help. I wondered if the I.O.U. was worth anything, but I would soon find out.

"When you connect with her, Jake, keep me in the loop. No more Sherlocking on your own, okay?"

"Who, me? Wouldn't think of it."

"There you go again, being a smart-ass." He glanced at Angelica. "Sister, please get this guy out of here before I throw him in the slammer. And drop Miriam's PlayStation off at my office tomorrow."

By the time I drove Angelica to the convent, returned to the rectory, and sent Emily home by cab, I was too edgy to fall asleep. Rummaging through my desk, I found Agent Novak's business card and slipped it into my wallet. Still wired from the brawl at the bar, I popped the top of a bottle of sleeping pills, reconsidered, and put it back in the medicine cabinet. RJ had occasional nightmares about his mother's death, and I didn't want to be conked out if he needed me. I picked up Les Standiford's latest novel and read until my eyelids finally lost the battle with gravity, and darkness wrapped its arms around me and held me in its embrace.

CHAPTER NINETEEN

Monday, March 31, 9:30 a.m.

After offering Mass, I walked into an Urgent Care waiting room filled with patients. I don't function well anymore without a decent night's sleep, so I guzzled coffee until my hands trembled, then pressed on against the exhaustion. Two things about my job kept me engaged: every day was different from the last, and people never failed to surprise me.

Mid-morning, a woman came in complaining of weakness, fatigue, and the onset of hair loss. When she removed her mink coat, she looked like a fashion magazine model—starvation-chic, almost skeletal. She sat her equally skinny daughter, a girl about RJ's age, in an adjacent chair. After performing a physical examination on the mother, I ordered basic blood tests, ran them stat, and asked her to wait for the results. Her blood count showed that she had the kind of anemia often associated with Vitamin B12 deficiency. She was on no medication, so I inquired about her diet and was rewarded with the first smile since she had entered the room.

"I'm a vegan, doctor, have been for years. My family is too." She patted her scrawny daughter on the head. "I'm cognizant of everything that goes into my baby's mouth. No GMOs. Only all-natural products."

The girl hopped down from the chair, and it grew obvious as she bounced around the room inspecting things that, unlike her mother, she was not the least bit fatigued. Mom seemed oblivious, so I kept one eye on the child, hoping she would not find the needle drawer or anything dangerous.

"Do you eat any dairy or eggs?"

"Absolutely not! Not the way animals are treated in this country. Besides, that stuff clogs your arteries, right? I want my daughter to grow up healthy and socially conscious. I won't wear leather or use cosmetics either."

I glanced at her coat. Apparently she made an exception for mink. I wondered where she thought the fur came from.

Her child found a dispenser full of the tongue depressors, took one, sniffed it, and popped it in her mouth. Her mother said nothing.

"I agree. Vegetarian and vegan diets can be healthy, but they require careful meal planning."

"I read, doctor, and I *know* what I'm doing," she replied as she toyed with a diamond ring the size of a grape. "Although it's a challenge sometimes with my husband and me working full-time, we do a darn good job."

"I'm sure you do. Unfortunately, essential nutrients like calcium and omega-3 fats are missing from strict vegan diets."

Her daughter found something interesting on the linoleum floor by the sink, sampled it with a finger, and tasted it. I thought that was taking an "all-natural" diet too far and guided her back to the chair, wondering what else she sampled when no one was watching her.

"Your symptoms and bloodwork suggest a Vitamin B12 deficiency." I handed her a pamphlet on vegetarian and vegan diets. "I want to test for that and get you started on B12 supplements."

While her daughter picked boogers and dined on them, Mom resisted my advice. I cajoled and we debated. When I pointed out that her hair loss would likely worsen, she finally acquiesced. I handed her a referral to see our dietician, and she took her child by the hand and left.

Never a boring day at the hospital.

After lunch, I removed Agent Novak's card from my wallet, dialed the FBI office number, and got her voicemail. I reminded her of how we had met, explained the situation with Angelica's sister, and requested her help.

I returned to work and was finishing my shift when the sheriff phoned.

"Glad you called, Tree. Did Mack-the-Knife give up any information? Could he be involved with the disappearance of Angelica's sister?"

"Doubt it. He's an arm-twister and leg-breaker for a local loan shark. The instant we busted him at The Cavern, he clammed up tight and demanded a lawyer. But we finally caught a break in Tony's case. There's been no ransom demand for him. No surprise there, 'cause his folks don't have much money."

Tree took a slurp of something, then continued. "So I stopped by Flood's church today and got the footage from their surveillance cameras. Guess what? Not only was the man with the Puerto Rican flag tattoo at the church shortly before Tony vanished, but he stopped by again yesterday. We got a full-on image of the guy's mug that I ran through the system. Name's Mateo Cruz. He has a drug history, a long rap sheet including armed robbery, and was recently released from our fine five-star, iron-barred hotel in Grafton. One of my troops is interviewing our jailhouse snitches, trading favors for info. Maybe one of the stoolies will cough up his address or known associates. Be terrific if Tony was locked up at his place, still alive. Three days into a kidnapping without a ransom note is an eternity, and a bad omen."

"With Tony and Cruz both connected to Flood's church, can you get a search warrant?"

"Already on it. Should know later today if a judge will bite. Nothing I'd like more than to analyze that altar wine and let my fingers do the walking through Flood's medicine cabinet. Got a suspicion he's got more drugs than a pharmacy. I spoke with police in Yuma, Arizona, but hit a dead-end. Flood never showed up on their radar when he preached there." Tree hesitated. "Got any interest in launching your own prison ministry?"

"Are you kidding? My plate's full as it is. Don't give Bishop Lucci any ideas."

"I'm not asking you to *do* it. Just stop in, ask about it, and snoop around. When's your next day off?"

"Tomorrow."

"It's hard for police to fly under the radar in lockup, but a priest ministering to the misguided would be nearly invisible. Maybe Flood thought that too. I could use some help, buddy. Will you stop in and nose around?"

"You're the one who told me to *stop* playing cop."

"Yeah well, I'm flexible. Grafton prison? Tomorrow? What do you say?"

I said what I always say when my best friend asks for help. "Sure. I'll see what I can do."

After he hung up, I called Grafton Prison and made an appointment to speak with the warden the next morning.

I had invited Emily to join RJ, Colleen, and me for dinner that evening and had been anticipating it all day. When my shift ended, my fatigue mysteriously vanished. I was whistling my way home in my car when Colleen phoned.

"Father, something has come up. I've been asked out to supper tonight, and I will not be able to join you at the rectory. I'll try not to be late tomorrow morning."

My, my! She has a dinner date for the second night in a row, and may come in late in the morning? Well, good for her. She had been widowed for years. Besides, I was happy to spend time with Emily without my personal chaperone in attendance.

"No problem. I'll take care of things. By the way, I'm not working Tuesday, so take tomorrow off."

"Thank you. That's very kind. But there is one other problem. I haven't yet been shopping or fixed anything for your dinner tonight, and the refrigerator is nearly bare." She paused. "I haven't the foggiest what I am going on about. I apologize. It's only for one night. Of course you'll be fine. This isn't the End Times for goodness sake! Take heart. There's some bread, baloney, and canned soup available, so you won't starve."

I didn't know what to say. Baloney sandwiches? Emily and I loved Colleen's home-cooked meals. I was a total disaster in the kitchen, and I couldn't afford to take her to a nice restaurant.

"If you prefer, Father, I believe you still have a few frozen dinners in the freezer. Just preheat the oven to 350 degrees, put the food in an oven-safe container, and bake for about 30 minutes. The instructions are on the package."

I must have hesitated too long.

"Come now, Father. I don't ask for much. I won't leave RJ till you arrive, but I must be on my way *no later* than five." I was fumbling for a cogent reply when she added, "Have you not heard? Lincoln *freed* the slaves. No later than five, Father. Surely you can fill in for me for one night."

"Of course." I'd already begun hatching a new plan. "We'll make do for dinner."

Emily had recently prepared a wonderful meal for RJ and me, and I had promised to return the favor. I'd purchased the *Cooking for Dummies* book and begun watching culinary shows on TV, but to prepare anything edible, I needed time to shop, which I didn't have. Being a resourceful man, however, I picked up a triple order of lemon chicken and fried rice at a nearby Chinese restaurant and put it in the trunk, hoping Emily wouldn't smell it.

CHAPTER TWENTY

Monday, March 31, 5:00 p.m.

The air was cool, and Emily was wearing a light sweater when I picked her up. Though she seldom wore makeup, tonight was an exception, indicating how much she looked forward to dinners away from the hospital cafeteria. I was determined not to let her down.

When we arrived at the rectory at 5:20, Colleen mumbled goodbye and took off like a jet plane. Emily appeared disappointed. I reminded her that I had promised to cook something special for her, making the entire fiasco sound like a gallant gesture on my part.

We settled into the living room with glasses of chardonnay. After RJ regaled us with riveting stories from his day at school, he ran into his bedroom and came back with a bracelet he'd made of colorfully painted macaroni on a string. His face flushed as red as his hair when he presented it to Emily. She had clearly become a mother figure to him. For a moment, the three of us felt like a family, and my thoughts wandered to the letter I had received inviting me to join the Episcopalian priesthood.

Emily slipped on the bracelet, hugged him, and offered to read one of the braille books she had bought him. RJ was fascinated by "finger-reading" and she'd begun to teach him. I had even found him in the living room one afternoon with his eyes closed, trying to read Dr. Seuss in braille. My boy never failed to amaze me.

While they were occupied, I snuck out to the car, grabbed the food from the trunk, and entered the kitchen. Not wanting the sound of our meal reheating in the microwave to give my scheme away, I warmed it in the oven. To call attention to the great effort I was making, I thawed a bag of frozen mixed vegetables on the stovetop, allowing the water to boil vigorously and rattle the pot lid.

I let the pot in the kitchen clatter away while I set the dining room table and lit candles, hoping to recreate the ambiance of a fine restaurant. Although Emily was sightless, I knew she would sense the flickering light and notice the scent of the candles. When all was ready, I placed the chicken atop the rice on my nicest dishes, turned on soft background music, and summoned my dinner guests to dine.

Supper went well. RJ kept the conversation rolling throughout the meal, and Emily asked for a second helping of chicken. As I presented them with bowls of vanilla ice cream topped with chocolate syrup for dessert, I was feeling quite proud of my ingenuity.

Emily said, "My compliments to the chef."

"Thanks, it was nothing."

She broke out in laughter. "Not *you*. Whatever nice Asian person cooked this!" She chuckled again. "Vanity, thy name is Jake Austin. Did you think I couldn't smell the meal in the car? Such blatant deceit, and you a priest!"

RJ stared at us, silent for the first time that evening.

"Hey, Em, it wasn't a lie. Simply a harmless exaggeration of my ability in the kitchen." Fortunately, she couldn't see me blush. "I told you, I'm a work in progress. I figure I should be finished about the time of the Second Coming. Have a little patience."

I had underestimated how heightened her other senses had become since her vision loss, as well as her sharp mind and quick wit. My hubris had dug a hole, and she had played me the entire meal, luring me to the edge of the pit before shoving me in. I definitely would not hear the end of my culinary shortcomings until I actually cooked her an elegant feast.

CHAPTER TWENTY ONE

Monday, March 31, 7:30 p.m.

After supper, RJ, Emily, and I assembled a jigsaw puzzle designed for young children featuring Super Heroes. Letting RJ function as her eyes, she directed him to first locate the corners and all the pieces with a straight edge. After he'd assembled the borders, she used her heightened sense of touch to actually find some interlocking pieces herself. The three of us joked and laughed, and I felt as close to heaven on earth as I could imagine.

The three of us. The phrase kept reverberating in my head. As a boy, I had lost any chance at an intact family when my father threw his suitcase into a taxi and disappeared—the day my world came off the rails and I began a journey that lead me to teenaged rebellion, drugs, and a bloody overseas war. I hadn't been much older than RJ, and I wanted to spare him those feelings of abandonment and isolation. As important as the priesthood was to me, so was giving him an intact home and a happy childhood.

"Jake, where's your head at tonight? Look, RJ and I finished the puzzle, no thanks to you!"

RJ was jumping up and down like there were springs on his sneakers.

"Sorry, I zoned out. You know what, RJ? I think I'll frame this puzzle and hang it in your room. What do you think?"

He ran over and hugged me.

"This was fun, Sport, but that's enough for today. Time to say goodnight."

"Can Emily put me to bed? Please Daddy!"

And that's exactly what happened. I watched the woman I loved tuck the child I loved into bed and kiss him goodnight. My heart was full of joy … and frustration.

Back downstairs, Emily asked for wine. When I returned with two glasses, she patted the couch next to her and I sat. After a few minutes of small talk, she slid close to me and grew serious.

"Jake, have you thought about that invitation to join the Episcopalian priesthood that Tree Macon sent you?"

"I have. A lot. It would permit me to serve the Lord and also allow us to pursue a normal relationship but … I can't do it. I'm sorry. Although our liturgies, sacraments, and beliefs are similar, and I have no problem with admitting women to the priesthood, there are a lot of differences: like our reverence for the Virgin Mary, the Pope's leadership, and different translations of the Bible. But most importantly, I was *called* to the priesthood. It's a religious vocation, not a job that you simply apply for."

She took a sip of wine. I tried to read her reaction but came up empty.

"For me, Em, it's about commitment. When I was hurtling toward self-destruction in the war, Jesus literally saved me from myself. I made a firm commitment to Him and the Church. The Episcopal priesthood is tempting, but I'm not willing to break that pledge and abandon my religion."

She ran a finger along the rim of her wine glass and it sang a soulful song. "Good. I feel the same way, but I had to ask. That's why I did what I did." She took another sip. "When we decided to explore our relationship, and I began spending more time with you and RJ, I … realized how much I loved you both, so … several months ago I filed a petition with the Church for annulment of my marriage. I should have their decision soon."

She waited for my response. I had none.

"I assumed that if things progressed between us, Jake, and marriage became a possibility, we would both want a Catholic wedding."

I was stunned, and also a bit freaked out. An annulment would force my hand. I could marry her in the Church and remain Catholic, but I would have to resign from the priesthood. I opened my mouth, but couldn't speak.

She misinterpreted my silence, and her expression collapsed. "I'm sorry, Jake. I thought we both felt the same way. That was presumptuous of me. I didn't mean to push you toward marriage. I wanted to open that door for us … just in case. Was I wrong?"

"Of course not. You know how I feel about you. I love you; I always have." I slipped an arm around her. "If I were to leave the priesthood, there's nothing I'd want more than to have you in RJ's life and mine." I touched the macaroni bracelet on her wrist. "My boy adores you as much as I do."

My mind was churning. "But an annulment is a longshot. Don't get your hopes too high. The Church is hesitant to dissolve valid unions, and you were married for over a year before the divorce. You could make a case that Everett's abusive behavior during your marriage precluded any chance for a lasting union, but I'm not sure the Tribunal judges will accept that argument."

"Well, I guess our fate is in their hands, Jake." My response had hurt her and she inched away from me on the couch, finished her wine, and called for a taxi. "It's late. I'd better go."

CHAPTER TWENTY TWO

Tuesday, April 1, 5:30 a.m.

The next morning, RJ woke me from a deep sleep at *too-early-o'clock*. April fools!

The upside was that it allowed me extra time with him before school. He begged me to make waffles with syrup for breakfast. I folded like a bad poker hand and sent him off to school with a sugar rush, hoping his teacher would forgive me. What a soft touch I am.

At morning Mass, I used my homily to encourage my parishioners to consider the Lenten season as an opportunity for self-refection, penance, and prayer. But my attention kept drifting to Emily's annulment petition, marriage, and the possibility of my resignation from the priesthood. I too had much to reflect upon and pray about. I was distracted during the entire service, and the nuns in the front pew seemed to sense my turmoil. They left after Mass without their usual greeting.

Back in the rectory, I set all the questions of my future aside, got down to business, and Googled the Grafton Correctional Institution. Located thirty-five miles southwest of Cleveland, it was a medium-security state prison housing over two thousand inmates. The short drive from Oberlin took considerably less time than the thirty minutes required to be cleared to see the warden. My Roman collar did not expedite the process. After walking through a metal detector, I was relieved of nearly all my possessions, and given a visitor badge. When I was finally led to him, however, the warden made it clear that he was far too busy to meet and handed me over to Bobby Jones, the prison chaplain.

A short, muscular black man in his forties, Chaplain Jones led me to his office and offered coffee that tasted as if it had been brewed sometime in the last century. Furnished with a gray metal desk, matching file cabinets, and two folding chairs, the room was smaller than a prison cell and almost as depressing.

Jones wore a burgundy suit over a navy clerical shirt and collar. A staff ID badge dangled from the jacket pocket below a matching blue pocket square. No drab prison attire for this man. He was all business, but with a personal flair.

A Board of Chaplaincy Certification hung on the wall behind him. Next to it, a framed needlepoint quote from Corinthians provided the only color in the room: *If any man be in Christ, old things pass away and he is new again.*

I wanted to believe that, but personal experience had taught me to be wary.

Jones caught me staring at the Bible quote, rolled up a sleeve, and pointed to a tattoo of a black widow spider on a web inked on his forearm. The image was crude.

"I did five years in Grafton for assault and battery. When I was on the streets, I was the spider, but prison was the web that trapped me like a helpless bug … then I found God. So yes, I believe all men *can* become new again."

He leaned his chair against the wall. "I was lucky. I had a degree from the community college before I fell in with the wrong crowd. In here, I volunteered to be the chaplain's assistant. When I got out, I went back to school, got my religious training, performed a lot of community service, and interned at the maximum security facility in Lucasville. Makes this place look like a five-star resort. Best thing I ever did, though, was take this job. Never been happier."

I told him I was interested in participating in a prison ministry. He considered this and took another swallow of the industrial strength coffee. His taste buds must have been in a coma.

"You should understand, Father, a chaplain's work is different from that of a church pastor. You care for a congregation's spiritual needs, but we must address *secular realities* as well. Job training, anger management, GED classes, and basic social skills. Prison is an explosive environment, and we provide a safety valve. The job is not without personal risk."

"Understood, but I still want to help." I handed him my resume. "What're my options?"

"We're always in need of volunteers." He reviewed my credentials. "We don't require any medical personnel, but as a priest, you could participate in our religious services. If you'd like, you can get involved with the death row ministries at our maximum security facilities at Lucasville and Chillicothe." He handed me a brochure entitled Volunteer Opportunities at GCI. "What did you have in mind?"

"I'm open to suggestions. I can only offer a few hours a week. Could I observe a religious service and get a feel for how things work?"

"Worship services are on weekends, but you're in luck. There's a prayer meeting run by an evangelist after lunch today. Would that work?"

"Perfect." I hoped Reverend Flood would be the evangelist-de-jour. Given his connection to Cruz, the last person seen with Tony Pagano, I wanted to observe his interaction with the prisoners.

Jones looked at his watch. "I'm free till then. Let me show you around."

We left the administration wing and he led me to the infirmary. In one room, a dental hygienist was cleaning an inmate's teeth. A prison guard stood nearby, pepper spray and a baton hanging from his belt. In another, a male nurse, who could have doubled as a bouncer at a nightclub, was cutting a cast off of a skinny convict's leg. The prisoner's arm was in a sling and his face was covered in cuts and bruises.

I raised my eyebrows and Jones whispered, "Sad story. He just got off suicide watch. Child molesters don't fare well in lockup. This one got raped in the shower more than once. Been harassed on a daily basis and still has several more years inside. He snuck past a guard and made a break for the rooftop, hoping to jump and commit suicide. When the guard caught up with him, he threw himself through a second story window. Not high enough to do the job."

We toured the small library and the prison kitchen, where inmates preparing lunch greeted Jones warmly. He ladled out two bowls of beef stew, grabbed four slices of bread, and showed me into the staff cafeteria, which consisted of metal tables surrounded by vending machines. The meal was edible, but made the hospital cafeteria seem like a fine French restaurant.

After our meal, we walked to the prison chapel. It was small and austere except for a splash of rainbow-colored sunlight streaming from a high stained glass window covered by iron bars. A vase of plastic flowers stood in one corner, a small table with Bibles and other religious items in another. As inmates shuffled in and were seated, a young man wearing black clerical robes entered from a side door. I recognized him immediately as the burly fellow who had greeted me at the church entrance the second time I had attended Flood's service.

"That's Rex Lundgren," Jones said. "He's the assistant pastor at the Church of Eternal Release. His willingness to work with convicts gives me hope. He and Reverend Flood have assembled a devoted following. I'd introduce you but I have to run to a meeting."

"No problem, I'll be fine. Thanks for the tour."

Jones said something to a guard and left. I slipped off my Roman collar, rolled up my shirt sleeves, and sat with staff members and guards in a back pew. As Sheriff Macon's jailhouse spy, I wanted to blend in.

Something nefarious was going on at Flood's church. Young Tony's overdose had led us to Reverend Flood, Mateo Cruz had abducted Tony, and Cruz was somehow connected to both Flood's church and Grafton Prison. We needed to know what was going on, and if Reverend Lundgren was involved. I wanted to see how he interacted with the inmates without him realizing he was under surveillance.

Several prisoners walked over to him, shook his hand, and chatted briefly. When the prayer meeting began, he read from Psalm 68: *God leads out the prisoners with singing, but the rebellious dwell in a sun-scorched land.* He then led the gathering in "Till All the Jails Are Empty," a hymn I had never heard before. The melody was haunting, and the power and urgency of the lyrics launched most of the inmates to their feet, many swaying to the music.

Lundgren segued into a sermon on the need to delay gratification and earn life's rewards, then to a passage from Isaiah.

"I say unto you …." He paused for effect and raised his eyes to the heavens. "He has sent me to bind up the brokenhearted and open the prisons for those who are bound."

When the service ended, I started to leave but a guard told me to stay seated. He stepped into the aisle with three others and they ushered the prisoners from the chapel. After they'd gone, I stood and was heading for the exit when Lundgren came marching toward me, a grin on his lips.

"What a pleasant surprise to see you again. I remember you from church last Sunday. I don't think we've been introduced. I'm Rex."

I shook his meaty hand and said, "Jake Austin. I'm pastor at Sacred Heart in Oberlin. I'm thinking of doing volunteer work here."

"You'll find it rewarding. Reverend Flood and I do. If you have any questions, or if I can help in any way, give me a call."

We exchanged phone numbers, said our goodbyes, and I put my Roman collar back on. A guard was waiting in the hall to escort me. The prisoner I'd seen in the infirmary was hobbling down the hallway, a walking cast on his leg. When he entered the library, I asked the guard if I could speak with the man. He said, "five minutes" and watched me from the doorway.

The inmate was seated at a table reading a magazine. Up close, his face looked like ground beef, as if he'd landed in a briar patch on his attempted suicide jump. As I approached, he eyeballed my Roman collar.

"Not another damn do-gooder trying to save my fuckin' soul. All you guys—preachers, imams, rabbis, witch doctors—you're all the same, arguing about whose imaginary friend is real. Go away, man. I'm an atheist."

"Atheist, huh. You say that as if it matters."

"I can be anything I want."

"Sure, but it still doesn't matter. If you're right and there is no God, your belief changes nothing. But if God does exist, not believing doesn't alter His greater plan, whatever that may be—though it might make a difference in *your* afterlife." I smiled. "Listen, I'm not here to convert anyone. Believe what you want." I reached out a hand. "I'm Jake Austin. I'd appreciate a moment of your time."

"That so?" He stared at my hand until I returned it to my side. "Would you appreciate my time enough to make a donation to *my* collection plate? We each got a personal account here. I wanna get connected to the new JPay system, so I can get emails and shit."

I thought about what Tree had said about predators befriending kids over game consoles and selling them drugs or sexually abusing them, and God-only-knew what else. The idea of a child molester with online access made me queasy. "You get internet here?"

"No, it's a closed system. The prison screens our emails, and it takes almost as long as snail mail." He looked up at me. "Hey man, you got questions? I got answers … for a price. What's it worth to you?"

"Depends on how helpful you are." I pulled a ten dollar bill from my wallet and waved it in front of him. His interest level rose. "Do you ever attend chapel services?"

"I did … before," he tapped his cast, "before my accident. But I could be *real helpful* for twenty bucks."

"Okay, okay. Deal."

"On your way out, tell the rent-a-cop to put it in my account. Name's Gorski."

"Fine, Mr. Gorski. Twenty dollars." I slipped the ten-spot back into my wallet. "Tell me about the preachers."

"Holy-rollers all of them, far as I can tell. But none of 'em drew large crowds like Flood and Lundgren. Even made me a believer … for a while. Though I don't think everyone *likes* being at their services."

"What do you mean?"

"Let's just say some of Flood's true believers encourage others to go. They keep the pews filled and the punks in line. One fuckin' wetback beaner told me it would be hazardous to my health *not to go* on Sundays—so I went."

"He have a name?"

"Not sure what it is. Guy goes by Duro. Means 'hard-ass' or some shit in spic lingo. Didn't want to be in the shower with that hombre. He went all Jeffrey Dahmer on my ass once and I couldn't sit for days. Probably would have chopped me into bite-sized pieces and feasted on me if he coulda. I started goin' to Flood's services so Duro would leave me alone. I stopped after he got paroled."

"What's he look like?"

"Short guy with prison pumped muscle, shaved head, and a bad attitude. Lots of tattoos. A real nasty sucker."

"Did he have a beard?"

"Nah. No beard."

"Any tattoos on his arms?"

"This is lockup, man. Who doesn't?"

"Can you describe them?"

"I donno, *tats*. Barbed wire, I think. One on his chest was a skull with fangs. That kinda shit."

"What else?" He shook his head. "I need more than that, Mr. Gorski."

"That's all I got. Not like we were BFFs, man."

"When'd he get released?"

"Don't remember and don't care. Glad he's gone. I'da been happy as warm shit if the state had given him the stainless steel ride."

"Stainless what? In English, please."

"The needle, Father. Lethal injection. Vouching for that bastard to the parole board was the only good thing Flood ever did for me."

Flood, huh. I thought about Angelica's sister and asked, "Do you play computer games on that JPay system?"

"Hell, no. This place look like an arcade to you?"

The guard at the door glanced at me, then at his watch. I was running out of time. "What do you know about Rex Lundgren?"

"Hey man, you got your money's worth already." He turned away.

"Fine, another twenty. Tell me about him."

"Can't say much about Lundgren. Only saw him a couple times. Didn't have the fire that Flood brought to the chapel. That old man could light up the room—back when I believed Jesus would save my sorry ass. It pissed me off that those two had an inner circle that kept the rest of us at a distance. I tried to talk with Flood once and Duro told me to get lost. Felt like I was in junior high, you know, trying to sit at the table with the *cool* kids."

The guard walked over and tapped me on the shoulder. "Sorry Father. Time to go."

On the way out, I requested that he take me to the Chaplain's office, where I asked Jones about the inmate nicknamed Duro.

"Yeah, I remember him. A real hard case."

"Do you recall his name?"

"Sorry, I don't. We have thousands of prisoners here, Father. His file's somewhere down in storage."

"Did he have any tattoos?"

"Lots of them."

"A flag maybe?"

His eyes widened. "Yeah, a weird-looking thing. Not one I'd ever seen before. Inked in the colors of our flag, same red and white stripes, but only one big star in the blue part." He pointed to his forearm. "Had it right here."

Bingo. Exactly like Mateo Cruz's tattoo. There couldn't be many of those around.

I thanked him and the guard led me from the bowels of the prison. I collected my personal items at checkout, asked for paperwork to deposit money in a prisoner's account, and stood motionless with the pen in my hand. The last thing I wanted to do was help a child molester. On the other hand, he had provided useful information and might in the future. I thought about poor Tony and the risk that Flood might pose to other kids, and God forgive me, I filled out the form and deposited forty dollars so a pedophile could get access to email. I hoped the officers checking messages would keep a close eye on Gorski's account.

Walking out into the cool afternoon, I savored the sweet aromas of springtime and the joyous chirping of birds. Even a few hours in lockup provided a fresh appreciation of freedom. The lazy morning mist had lingered into the afternoon, but as I walked to my car a sudden wind gust peeled away the last layer revealing a clear blue sky, and a somewhat clearer picture of the mystery surrounding Tony's disappearance.

CHAPTER TWENTY THREE

Tuesday, April 1, 2:30 p.m.

Outside Grafton Prison, I turned on my cellphone and realized I'd missed a call from Agent Keri Novak at the FBI. I played the voicemail.

"You bet I remember you, Father. How could I forget all the fun we had putting an entire drug operation out of business? The Bureau has me in Florida and I'm literally up to my backside in alligators, but as soon as I get back to the office, I'll look into your request about tracking online predators. By the way, I spoke with my source in the Marshals Service, and our mutual friend is alive and well and bored to death—meaning, staying out of trouble. I hear he's playing some gigs with a local jazz band. Talk to you soon. Take care."

I put my phone away and sighed. Our *mutual friend* was my father, who had testified against a mob boss to take the heat off RJ and me. He was in WITSEC, Witness Security protection. It was unlikely that I would ever see him again, and I was grateful for the update from Novak. I was mulling over the volcanic events that had led to his testimony and mandatory exodus when Tree called.

"I had an interesting chat with your buddy from the Cavern Bar, Maximilian 'Mack-the-Knife' Muller. I pulled his rap sheet and lo and behold, he too is a graduate of Grafton Prison's fine rehabilitation program—though definitely not with honors. When he sobered up and I pointed out that carrying a switchblade violated the terms of his parole, he became more talkative, though he denied knowing anything about Tony's abduction, Mateo Cruz, or Reverend Flood."

"What about Miriam?"

"He said, and I quote, 'Bitch works Harvard Ave. Don't know nothin' else.' Which is possible, given how little brain function Mack has. Got a plain clothes guy nosing around the Harvard area. I'll call you if we strike pay dirt."

"Any leads on Tony?"

"Not yet. Four days feels like a lifetime when a kid's missing. I cast the usual net—door-to-door interviews of neighbors, eyeballed the family for dysfunction and family friends for motives or priors, papered the area with missing person posters, got the National Center for Missing and Exploited Children involved with media outreach, and filed the case with the FBI."

"FBI? Do you think Tony was taken out of state?"

"No. I made the pitch to the Bureau that Mateo Cruz is a dangerous felon and Tony may have stumbled onto a drug ring. The Feebies will get involved early if the child is in eminent danger."

"Speaking of the FBI, Tree, I heard from Agent Novak. She's willing to help us. I also attended a prayer meeting at Grafton Prison this afternoon. One of the inmates told me Flood has an inner circle of true believers who force other inmates to attend services. A guy nicknamed Duro was one of his enforcers. Sounded like it might have been Mateo Cruz, before he grew the full beard. And guess who vouched for Cruz at his parole hearing?"

"Spit it out. I'm not in the mood for twenty questions."

"The Right Reverend Jeremiah Flood himself. I doubt that's a coincidence."

"I don't believe in coincidences. They're as rare as tweekers with teeth. Most coincidences are the smoke that tells you there's fire nearby. But Cruz as prison muscle for Flood at Grafton? Now *that's* interesting. Think I'll shake my snitches at the prison and see what they cough up."

"Could Flood be selling drugs to prisoners?"

"Nah. Not enough money in the joint to make it worthwhile, and the risk is too high. But he could be making contacts, racking up favors, and recruiting thugs. Not sure why a preacher would do that, but I'm gonna find out. Did you talk with Flood at the service?"

"No, he sent the second string, an assistant pastor named Rex Lundgren."

"Notice anything hinkey about him?"

"Not a thing. He offered to help and might even prove to be an asset."

"Okay, buddy, that helps. I'll run Lundgren through the system, see if any flags pop up. And I'll check out the nickname *Duro*, see if it's Cruz's moniker. We keep aliases and other identifying info on felons in our database. Talk to you later."

With RJ in school and Colleen on her day off, I stopped on my way back to the rectory to pick up pepperoni pizza and an antipasto salad from Lorenzo's for dinner. I was waiting for my order, wondering how in the heck I had gotten sucked into the investigations of two missing young people, when a gaggle of junior high aged girls entered. This was the after-school crowd hanging out, being cool. When they unbuttoned their coats, I saw that some were wearing clothes that promised things they should not deliver at their age. I contemplated all the unwanted pregnancies, abandoned children, and ruined lives that I had encountered, both as a doctor and as a priest. Now Angelica's younger sister might be hustling on the city streets. It felt as if I'd spent my life preaching to a deaf world. I leaned against the counter and the last of my energy drained away.

Just when I was certain my day couldn't get any more frustrating, my cell played "Onward Christian Soldiers." Bishop Lucci, no doubt about to rain down more crap on me.

CHAPTER TWENTY FOUR

Tuesday, April 1, 2:45 p.m.

"Glad I caught you, Father." Bishop Lucci sounded agitated. "Clear your calendar for a week from today, and be in my office at ten sharp."

"What's going on, Your Excellency?"

"That's the problem. I'm not certain. My friend, Stefano Demarco, is making a special trip to see me—and he wants *you* to be there."

I caught the aroma of church politics, and the reason for Lucci's agitation grew clear. The Very Reverend Father Stefano Demarco was the Superior General of my Camillian Order and a powerful man in the church hierarchy. He had assigned me here because Lucci needed priests and St. Joseph's Hospital wanted physicians committed to treating the indigent. He was on the Vatican fast-track and had acquired a great deal of influence in Rome. More importantly, Lucci had grabbed hold of Demarco's coattails, hoping to ride along with the Church's rising star to a better assignment, possibly cardinal or archbishop of a major city.

"I don't understand." I suspected I knew the answer but asked, "Why am I involved?"

"Why do you *think*, Father? This meeting is undoubtedly about your relationship with your lady friend. I did warn you, Jacob. I've tried to cover for you as long as I could, hoping you'd come to your senses and burn that bridge to your past. I suspect Stefano is wise to us both."

His Excellency was distancing himself so as not to catch any flak if my Superior General detonated my vocation. If defending me hampered Lucci's ascent to higher office, I knew what he would do. Like Pontius Pilate, he would wash his hands of my occupational crucifixion and absolve himself of any guilt.

"If you cannot tell us that your relationship with her is finished, Father, you'll be stripped of the clerical state, deprived of all rights and privileges, forbidden to celebrate the sacraments publically, and the Church will no longer provide for your material needs. At the very least, you will be ordered to a life of prayer and penance in some obscure location away from the public eye. You'll go from priest to a religious pariah." He drew a deep breath. "If you have any intention of marrying this woman, you should immediately apply for an indult of laicization and petition Rome to be released from your obligation of celibacy."

Indult of laicization—my signed resignation from the priesthood. *Defrocking*, one of the most severe punishments issued to priests.

Emily and I had been struggling with our reawakened feelings for each other since my return to town, when the lingering sparks of passion from our youth had reignited. We had kissed in December for the first time in decades—not just a peck on the cheek, the real thing—and it had shaken my resolve to the core. Now Emily's annulment was in play, and the Church was about to force our decision.

"Thanks for the warning, Bishop. I'll be there. And rest assured, I have *never* violated my vow of chastity."

But I sure as hell had been tempted. To choose between the two passions in my life, I would need the Wisdom of Solomon. Was I lying to the Church, Emily, or myself? I had some serious soul-searching to do.

A derisive grunt. "One way or another, Father, this issue will be resolved next week. Good day."

I slid the phone into my pocket, paid for the takeout meal, and drove from the pizza parlor to the rectory through a light drizzle. All the way home, I tried to decide if I had any wiggle room with Lucci and Demarco, but it appeared I would face the Inquisition next week. The rack and thumb screws were not out of the question.

I had a few minutes before I picked up RJ from school, so I replaced the wax-stained altar cloths and changed the message on the sign in front of the church to read: "Forecast: Rain ends, but God's reign continues"—my attempt at advertising. Take *that* Madison Avenue.

I picked up RJ at school, but he was unusually quiet and pensive on the way home.

"What's up, sport?"

"Nothin.'"

"Come on, something's bothering you."

He focused on his lap. "Megan said she likes me. You know, like … *likes* me." He glanced over. "Tommy says girls are yucky, but … she's funny and knows a million jokes."

"Jokes, huh. Give me an example."

"Okay." He grinned. "Knock, knock."

"Who's there?"

"Cows go."

"Cows go who?"

"No Daddy. Cows go *moo!*"

He laughed so hard I thought he would wet his pants.

"Tell you what, RJ. Anybody who knows jokes like that could be my friend."

"Yeah?"

"Darn right. I'd like to meet her. Maybe I could call her parents and ask her over for a playdate. What do you think?"

He shrugged but his smile spread from ear to ear, and just like that, the dark cloud of my impending Inquisition vanished.

We wolfed down our meals and spent the evening dodging raindrops in the empty church parking lot, practicing his bike-riding skills. Thank heavens for training wheels—the best invention since penicillin, fire, and absolution.

After I gave RJ a bath and we read *Goodnight Moon*, I put him to bed and poured a bottle of Yuengling into a frosted mug. I was pondering the unanswerable question that my Superior General would ask me next week when Tree called.

"Two things. I ran a background check on Reverend Lundgren. No flags popped up. He was a lot like you in his younger days, Jake. Rex spent time in the Air Force. He had a fondness for bar brawls that earned him the nickname *T. Rex*, and got him kicked out of Flight School shortly before graduation. Could handle an airplane, but not his temper. Honorably discharged a couple years later. Went into accounting for a while, then much like you, he got his shit together and became a preacher. After that, nothing more than a speeding ticket. No felony arrests. If he's a wolf in sheep's clothing, he hasn't been caught yet fleecing the flock."

"Guess I'm not surprised. He seemed legit. I didn't sense anything off about him at the prison chapel. And item number two?"

"You working tomorrow, Jake?"

"Not all day. I covered for another doc last week, so I'm free at noon. What's up?"

"I picked the wrong judge. She turned down my warrant for the Church of Eternal Release. The longer Tony's missing, the smaller the chance we'll find him alive. I gotta go full court press tomorrow with Flood, and I could use your help playing good cop and deflecting any biblical BS he might throw at me. What do you say, Jake?"

"I say pick me up at one o'clock."

CHAPTER TWENTY FIVE

Wednesday, April 2, 1:15 p.m.

Tree and I game-planned our approach to the interview on our way to the Church of Eternal Release. He wheeled his cruiser up to the front entrance. The parking lot was empty except for a bright red Lexus parked between a road-weary SUV and a school bus.

We headed for the church entrance and I gestured toward the Lexus. "Nice ride for a man of the cloth. And it looks like Mr. Lexus is a fan of yours, Tree. The rear bumper's plastered with Fraternal Order of Police stickers."

"Yeah, yeah. I've met Flood, and I doubt he's a philanthropist. Trust me, the guy's just trying to worm his way out of traffic tickets." Tree opened the church door and stopped. "And *nice* doesn't begin to describe that car, Jake. That's an SC 430. Top of the line. Flood's doing all right for a guy preaching in the middle of nowhere. Appears the collection basket floweth over. That baby has a retractable hardtop, goes zero to sixty in six seconds, and has a sticker price damn-near a hundred grand. I shoulda gone into saving souls, not bustin' lowlifes."

"I'm having trouble picturing the Most Reverend Tremont Macon baptizing babies and spreading the love." It was unseasonably warm out, and I rolled up the sleeves of my shirt. "More likely you'd be cuffing the sinners and hauling them off to lockup."

When we entered the church, Rex Lundgren was placing leaflets in Bibles. He gazed up at us with surprise, strode over, and shook my hand.

"Nice to see you again, Father." When I introduced Tree, he added, "I thought I recognized you, Sheriff, from the Carlisle Metro Park search. I took a dozen members in the church bus to help look for Tony. Such an appalling thing … and so devastating for his family. I assume that's why you're here. What can I do to help?"

Tree took command. "I saw the crowd here on Sunday. Quite an operation you got."

"Oh, we get by with the Lord's help."

"How'd you and Reverend Flood meet?"

"I joined him at Peace Community Church in Yuma, Arizona seven years ago. He'd built a large following but the church was failing financially. Reverend Flood is a brilliant orator, but let's just say he lacks business acumen. He asked me to help him out. I was an accountant before I entered the ministry."

"The perfect tag-team." Tree chuckled, staying in *good cop* mode. "Sounds like a match made in heaven."

"Jeremiah calls us the 'dynamic duo' but in reality he's Batman, and I'm Robin the bean-counter and fund raiser. Works well though, and it's allowed us to build a thriving congregation. I feel blessed." He noticed the tattoo on my forearm. "Were you in the service, Father? I was Air Force. Loved flying those beautiful birds above the clouds."

"I served in the Army and never wanted to get any higher than the seat of a barstool."

We exchanged *Hooah* battle cries, then Tree got down to business. He handed Lundgren two photographs, one of Mateo Cruz's face and one of his Puerto Rican flag tattoo. "You know this man? He a member here?"

I watched Lundgren closely for any hint of surprise or recognition, but he merely shook his head. "Definitely not a member." He handed the pictures to Tree. "Don't think I've ever seen him or the tattoo."

Tree nodded at me, and it was my turn. "Why'd you and Flood leave Arizona?"

"To tell the truth, when his wife passed away, Jeremiah … lost focus. She was his rock. It hurt him to even be in the church they'd built together, and living alone was unbearable for him. I moved into the vicarage for company, but it wasn't enough. The man simply needed a new start. I tagged along to help him out. When he's completely back on his feet again, I'll seek out my own ministry."

"I'm sure he appreciates your support," I said. "I know how lonely the religious life can be. One question, Reverend. When I attended services here, I noticed the front pews were reserved. That's quite unusual. What's that about?"

"Oh, The Blessed? That was Reverend Flood's idea, a stroke of genius actually. Members who are firmly committed to our ministry are given a special place of honor. Sets a high bar for the rest of the congregation, a goal to strive for."

By the way The Blessed were decked out in their Sunday finest and treated with deference, I suspected that their 'commitment' was largely financial in nature.

Lundgren continued. "Most of the folks I brought to the park to look for Tony are members of that group."

"Your help in the search was appreciated." Tree's radio squawked, but he ignored it and lowered the volume. "Have you noticed any change in Reverend Flood's behavior since you moved here?"

Lundgren furrowed his brow. "What do you mean?"

"Any change in his attitude or performance since you arrived?"

The furrows deepened. "Well, he's not quite the old affable, laid-back Jeremiah I first met, still a bit jumpy and irritable, but moving here has been good for him. He's much more energetic and engaged." Lundgren hesitated, gazing up at the rafters. "Though I must say, he's been in the dumps since Tony went missing. Nothing I do seems to help. I'm worried he'll fall back into a deep depression."

Tree gave me a nod, and I said, "Well, his sermons haven't lost any fire. He can certainly raise the roof when he wants. Is he around?"

"He's in his office, through that door." Lundgren waved a sheaf of papers. "I better get to work. Nice speaking with you both, and may God guide you in your search for Tony."

Reverend Flood's office door was open and he was seated at his desk. His expression darkened when he saw us. He set his coffee cup down, slipped something into a top desk drawer, and invited us in.

We took the two chairs he offered. Having met before, Tree got down to business.

"We are actively continuing our investigation of Tony Pagano's disappearance." Flood's eyebrows rose at the word "we" and he glanced at me. "Nothing to report yet, but I finally got a chance to talk with Reverend Lundgren today. You two make quite a good team."

Vintage Tree, playing the good cop but pitting the two suspects against each other.

"I think so. How may I be of service?"

Tree reached into his shirt pocket, pulled out a surveillance photo of Mateo Cruz and laid it on the desk as if playing his trump card. "Know who this is? He a member of your congregation?"

Flood studied it. "No, never saw him before."

"That right? I'm sure he's been here." Tree slapped another picture down. "Maybe you recognize his tattoo?"

Flood picked the photo up with a shaky hand and frowned. "I recognize the flag. My grandmother was from Puerto Rico." He set the picture down, sniffed, and blew his nose. "Sorry. I hate pollen season. Can't wait for spring to end." He examined the picture again. "If I'd seen this man or that tattoo before, I'd definitely remember. Sorry, I have no idea who he is. But if he's the one who took Tony, I hope you bring the wrath of God down on him, Sheriff. I know Tony better than most of the youth here, and he's a fine young man."

"Huh, no idea who the man in the photos is? I find that hard to believe, Reverend. His name's Mateo Cruz. Ring any bells?" The muscles in Tree's jaws contracted as the "good cop" left the building. "His yellow sports car was parked in your church lot recently, and your organist ID'd him. Look harder."

"The church is filled with worshipers on Sundays and the parking lot's always full. I don't know all of my congregation personally." Flood laid his trembling hands in his lap, out of sight. "As I said, I don't recall this man."

"Were there lots of people at Cruz's parole hearing too? You should know. You vouched for him and supported his release from Grafton. Don't play games with me Reverend."

Flood studied the picture. "This man looks more like Che Guevara than Mateo." He scooped up Cruz's photo again. "I guess this could be him. He didn't have the beard back then, and I haven't seen him since his parole hearing." He set the picture down. "Mateo came from extreme poverty and a broken family. He attended services and Bible study regularly, and seemed to be turning his life around. Worked on his GED and took classes in auto repair. He wanted to make something of himself, and I felt he deserved a second chance."

"So you knew Cruz's upbringing and his hopes and dreams, but didn't recognize him when he walked into your church? That's your story?" Tree pounded a fist on the desk. "Lots of folks from poverty and broken homes never commit armed robbery. Are you covering for this man? Where is he?"

Flood sniffed again, grabbed a tissue and wiped his nose, then stood and gestured toward the door. "What are you implying, Sheriff? I think you should leave."

Tree had no real evidence and was losing his cool. I decided to step in. "Please bear with us, this is important." I tapped the photographs. "We're positive Cruz was in contact with Tony, and we're trying to figure out their connection." Tree glared at me but I continued. "Did Tony ever mention his name?"

Flood sat down again. "Not that I remember."

"Cruz has been seen driving both a red Honda and a yellow sports car. If he shows up, Reverend, please give the sheriff or me a call." I handed him my card and changed the topic. "Oh, I also have a church related question. I'm thinking of starting a group for young people—something special to keep teenagers engaged. Do you and Reverend Lundgren have a youth ministry?"

"We do. Rex is not involved, he's ... young and never been married or had children. He doesn't yet understand how to relate to them. I had a wife and young child, so I'm comfortable with kids." I noticed the word "had" but didn't interrupt. He stopped and blew his nose again. "I run a Saturday church camp for ages ten to eighteen. We take the bus and go hiking, canoeing, and camping—kind of like Boy Scouts with Jesus as the troop leader. Tony was my right hand, that's how I got to know him. Don't get me wrong, Rex is a huge help. He's in charge of church finances and fund raising, and runs special programs for our most active members and donors."

"I think he mentioned them. The Blessed?"

"That's Rex's name for them, but yes. Before every service, he holds a special prayer meeting for them. They're well attended and well received. Thank God that Rex came up with the idea. I don't think we would have survived financially without their support."

I was trying to think of my next question when Tree abruptly resumed command of the conversation. "I appreciate your help, Reverend. Thanks for your time." He stood, his expression dark and cold. "We'll be in touch."

We walked in silence to the police cruiser and got in. Tree fired up the engine and gave me the *stink-eye*. "Don't ever interrupt my line of questioning again."

"When he told you to leave, Tree, your interview was over. Without a warrant, you were done. I was buying time. Besides, you were losing it. I thought I'd have to take your gun away before you shot Flood."

"Bull. I wasn't losing it, just revving up. With Tony missing for five days, the odds of finding him alive are dropping. We're running out of time and can't afford to screw this up. Flood's looking better and better to me. You notice his sniffing? Allergies my ass. I'll bet a week's salary he's putting more than nasal spray up his nose. My sniffer's *not* broken, and I smell a druggie and a perp."

Tree gunned the engine, threw a patch of gravel, and we tore out of the church parking lot. Silence filled the cruiser. When he turned on to Route 58, he added, "Sorry, buddy. I'm just worried. Tony's clock is running out of ticks. Linking Flood to the youth ministry and Tony was a good move, Jake. Thanks."

"I wonder if Cruz really had no beard in prison, or if Flood was playing us."

"He was telling the truth about that. I've seen Cruz's mugshot. No beard back then." He slapped the steering wheel. "But did you catch the discrepancy? I love it when folks contradict each other. Means someone's lying. Lundgren said Flood started The Blessed, and Flood said it was Lundgren. And those 'special prayer meetings' they offer The Blessed sound a lot like perks in exchange for donations. One hand on the Bible, and the other lifting the donors' wallets. As a wise man once said: *Follow the money."*

CHAPTER TWENTY SIX

Thursday, April 3, 2:00 p.m.

My Thursday morning shift in Urgent Care was routine. Then came the afternoon. To paraphrase Forest Gump, life and practicing medicine are both like a box of chocolates—most patients are sweet and a delight, others present unexpected surprises, but a few are just plain nutty at their core. Sometimes it boggles the mind.

The afternoon transformed into one of those days at the hospital when patient folly reached new heights. I should have known I was about to hit the "patient daily double" when Nurse Ochs handed me a chart, chuckled, and walked away.

I opened the chart and read the last entry. This middle-aged man had presented a week earlier in the emergency room with a scrotal abscess, but had left before the surgeon arrived because he had "important shit to do."

I sighed, entered the examination room, and greeted my patient. A biker sat on the examination table. He had removed his pants and underwear but was wearing his leather jacket. All his visible skin had been heavily inked, resulting in a high tattoo-to-tooth ratio. He was gently massaging a scrotum the size of a softball. I briefly considered a career change, then slipped on gloves, performed a quick exam, and telephoned Dr. Glade. He was a semi-obnoxious human being but an excellent surgeon, and over time we had reached something approaching friendship.

I explained the need for an emergency operation to my patient and said the surgeon was on his way and would arrive any minute.

"This crap didn't help." My patient tossed me an empty antibiotic bottle, stood, and picked up his underwear. "Ain't got time to hang around. Give me something for pain, Doc. Somethin' strong. I got shit to do."

Apparently the *shit* requiring his immediate attention was an ongoing crisis. His abscess had doubled in size since his last visit, and I didn't want to be on duty when he returned again next week. His breath suggested that he had already made an unsuccessful attempt to self-medicate with booze, and by the way he wobbled, his alcohol level had surpassed his I.Q.

I wondered if he was making the rounds at all the hospitals, stockpiling narcotics. "Give me somethin' strong for pain" probably meant opioids. But the terror in his eyes at the word "surgeon" suggested that his bad-ass biker demeanor was a ruse to cover the fear of an operation on his manhood.

He was putting on his briefs when Dr. Glade charged in. He took one look at my patient's groin and said, "I'll take it from here, Jake." I walked to the nurses' station shaking my head, certain that I had now seen it all. I was staring at the wall clock, willing it to jump to the end of my shift, when the second of the "daily double" arrived.

A man dressed in full camouflage carrying a garbage bag ran past the receptionist and up to me. "What kinda snake is this? I was splitting logs when it bit me."

His left hand was swollen to the size of a catcher's mitt with a pair of puncture wounds near the wrist. He had used his belt as a tourniquet above the wound. The top of the bag was tied shut but something inside it was thrashing around. All the nurses scattered except for Ochs, who was on the phone to security.

I didn't give a rat's ass whether it was a copperhead or a swamp rattler, I just wanted the damn thing gone. And I couldn't imagine how or why he'd captured the snake in a bag.

Opening the janitor's broom closet, I popped the lid on a large plastic trash can and said, "Sir, set the bag in here. Gently!" When he did, I slammed the top back on the can, set a gallon jug of soap on it to weigh it down, shut the door, and used a patient gown to seal the crack at the bottom.

I sent Nurse Ochs for polyvalent antivenom, which is effective on all types of viper bites. As I led the man into an exam room, the security guard arrived and I explained the situation.

He shook his head. "Every time you're working here, Doc, I get crazy calls. I'm beginning to think *you're* the problem."

I had cleaned the wound and was evaluating my patient's symptoms when Nurse Ochs returned with the snakebite serum, which I administered.

Because antivenom can have unwanted side effects, I admitted our backwoodsman for overnight observation.

By then, Urgent Care was filled to capacity. I commandeered a second resident, and together we managed to clear the waiting room. My blood pressure had reverted to normal by the end of my shift, but then my cellphone played "I Shot the Sheriff."

"Brace yourself, Jake. We found Tony in an abandoned house last night, not far from the park we searched in LaGrange. He's dead."

The world around me fell away, and I went mute. Tree filled the void.

"I rammed a stat toxicology screen through. He OD'd on meth. Had a bunch of needle tracks in his arms, as if he'd been shooting up for weeks."

I remembered the kind and gentle young man I'd met ten days earlier. My eyes filled with tears, my mind with rage. "That's crap, Tree. When I spoke with Tony at his house, he was wearing a short-sleeved shirt. He had no needle marks."

"Yeah, the coroner said none of the tracks were old. It's a murder, set up to look like an accidental overdose. I don't give a damn about warrants and protocol. I'm on my way to that church to kick ass and take names."

"I'll meet you there."

"No way, Jake. I may not play nice and don't want any witnesses. Stay out of this."

CHAPTER TWENTY SEVEN

Thursday, April 3, 5:40 p.m.

Stay out of it, my ass! I had been involved with Tony from day one and was mad as hell. I wanted to be there when Tree slapped the handcuffs on the man who had killed an innocent teenager for accidentally stumbling upon altar wine spiked with amphetamines.

I told Nurse Ochs I had an emergency and needed to leave Urgent Care a few minutes early, then drove like a maniac to the Church of Eternal Release, parked next to the sheriff's cruiser, and rushed inside. Tree was in the church foyer. When he broke the tragic news about Tony, Lundgren slumped onto a church pew and wept uncontrollably.

Tree was not happy to see me. "Forget it, Jake. This is police business."

"I thought I could help."

"Help would be great. Can't wait till it arrives. Now go home." He turned his back on me.

"No way! It took *both* of us to get Tony to the hospital alive, and I've been at your side ever since. I'm not leaving. You can arrest me or get on with it. Up to you, Sheriff."

Tree shook his head in disgust and redirected his attention to Lundgren. "I have more questions. Don't leave the premises until I talk to Reverend Flood. Where is he?"

"No idea. I just returned from ministering to one of our members," he blubbered. "His car's parked by the vicarage, so Jeremiah's probably there."

The doorbell produced no response, but the vicarage door was unlocked. Tree announced himself, and we entered and searched the residence, but found no sign of Flood. All the furniture was old and the rooms were unadorned, almost Spartan, surprising given Flood's flamboyant style and expensive car.

We reentered the church and knocked on Flood's office door. *No reply.* It was locked, so Tree asked Lundgren to open it.

The lock on the doorknob clicked when Lundgren turned the key but the door still wouldn't open.

Lundgren shrugged. "He's a private man and his office is his castle." He pointed to the deadbolt above the doorknob. "Jeremiah must have thrown the bolt from the inside, Sheriff. If he wasn't in the vicarage then he has to be in there. I'm worried. This is so unlike him, though … he hasn't been himself the last few days."

Tree knocked hard with a fist. *No response.* "When'd you last see Flood?"

"Yesterday. We discussed church finances in his office late afternoon. He was … acting strangely, very nervous. Said he wasn't feeling well and asked me to run the seven o'clock church service. He's never done that before."

Tree said, "You two stay here while I go outside and try to jimmy a window." When he returned, he motioned us to the side of the hall. "Windows are all locked and the drapes are drawn. I don't like this." He pounded on the door again. "Reverend Flood, you okay?" *No reply.* "Police. I'm coming in."

With that, Tree drove his size thirteen boot and then his shoulder into the door, using his two hundred and fifty pound body as a battering ram. On his second attempt, wood splintered and the door burst open.

The Reverend Jeremiah Flood hung motionless from a rope tied to a ceiling rafter. His eyes bulged and his purple tongue protruded from his bloated, blue face. His desk chair was toppled over nearby.

"Call an ambulance, Reverend, then wait in your office. Follow me, Jake." Tree rushed into the room. "Grab his legs and hoist him up." As I did, the sheriff set the desk chair upright, climbed on it, and cut the rope with his jackknife. With Tree holding the rope and me supporting Flood's legs, we lowered him to the floor. Tree loosened the hangman's noose around his neck. "Put on your doctor hat, Jake."

I knew from the instant I touched his cold, cyanotic skin that Flood was long gone. I went through the motions anyway, stopped, looked at Tree, and shook my head. Flood's eyes and lips were stippled with tiny ruptured blood vessels. The rope had left a blue-black bruise around his neck. Post-mortem lividity gave his gravity-dependent lower legs and arms a dusky color from hanging vertically.

The room showed no disarray or evidence of a struggle. Unlike Flood's living quarters, his office was surprisingly upscale, decorated with masculine furnishings and wood-paneled walls.

Tree directed me to stand outside of the office, called for a CSI team, and requested the coroner. I watched Tree from the doorway as he slipped on latex gloves and examined Flood's desk. A laptop was open, its screen dark. When Tree jiggled the computer mouse, it lit up. I could see a Word document on it but was too far away to read it.

He began opening desk drawers. When Tree came to one on the right, he took a photograph with his cellphone, briefly removed a small plastic bag containing a white substance, inspected it, then set it back in the drawer.

Exhaustion draped me like a wet blanket. I'd seen far too much death and violence in my lifetime. This whole fiasco was so unnecessary, so senseless. First Tony's accidental overdose, his subsequent abduction and death, and now Flood's suicide. The connection was obvious, the scenario clear.

When Tree snapped on the desk lamp, a piece of metal on the carpet near the doorjamb reflected the light. I pointed to it. "What's this, Tree?"

He came over, looked at it, and told an approaching deputy to place a yellow evidence marker next to it.

"Nice catch, Jake. It's a metal screw."

"Why evidence markers? This appears to be an obvious suicide."

"Standard policy. A suicide is always considered a homicide until we prove it isn't. You'd be surprised at the number of apparent suicides that are staged, though not many hangings are actually murders." He gazed down at Flood's body, lowered his voice, and added, "*This* one, however, might be a homicide, but I got a shitload of work to do now to prove it. Go home, Jake, and play with RJ. Life's too frickin' short."

I turned to leave as the county coroner and her assistant came charging down the hallway. I stepped to the side and let them enter Flood's office. Dr. Gerta Braun had a reputation as a smart, no-nonsense, tough-as-nails pathologist. She had been the county coroner for decades, as her white hair and the thatch of crow's feet around her eyes could attest. I decided to stay and watch a master class in crime scene investigation.

Braun gloved up. "What do we have, Tree?"

"The Reverend Jeremiah Flood, last seen alive around five last night. I cut him down. The guy was reportedly depressed, and it appears he has cocaine in a desk drawer. There's a suicide note on his computer."

After her assistant took some photos, Braun studied the body, and stood. "Well, that's interesting. I haven't seen one like this in quite a while. Look at the marks on his neck, Tree. The rope left a thick bruise in the shape of a 'V' as you'd expect with a hanging. But there's a second, deep horizontal mark that's not V-shaped."

Tree circled the body, then dropped to one knee for a closer inspection of Flood's neck.

"The horizontal furrow usually indicates the victim was strangled, Tree. We see petechial hemorrhage in the eyes and mouth with *all forms* of strangulation. The absence of finger impressions on the neck suggests a garroting rather than manual strangulation. The depth of the thin groove indicates that our victim was garroted using a wire or thin cord, then strung up to simulate a suicide and obscure the ligature mark."

The coroner continued her examination, using a body cavity thermometer to determine time of death. She scribbled in a notebook and motioned her assistant to bring in a stretcher.

"I'll call you after the autopsy, Tree, but two plus two always equals four. That's what I love about science. Facts are true whether you believe them at first or not. $E = mc^2$ is not optional. I'll bet you a bottle of single-malt scotch that this is a homicide—and premeditated. Hangings in depressed people are usually spontaneous. They grab a belt, a lamp cord, or something readily available. In this case, someone took the time to buy a rope and tie a perfect hangman's noose."

"I got tired of losing my money and stopped betting against you years ago, Gerta." Tree noticed me lurking near the office door and said, "Go home, Jake. Now. I mean it."

I took one last look at Reverend Flood's corpse. A heavy gloom swept over me and I trudged to my car. Tree's job and mine too often forced us to confront both suffering and the darkness of the human soul. I was more than ready to forget what I had witnessed and spend a few hours with a five year old whose world offered a lot more light and hope.

CHAPTER TWENTY EIGHT

Thursday, April 3, 6:15 p.m.

On the short ride back to the rectory, I tried to make sense of the scene in Reverend Flood's office. A room with locked windows, the only door deadbolted from the inside, an apparent suicide, and yet the coroner suspected murder. It made no logical sense, and I merely succeeded in giving myself a headache.

When I arrived home, I compartmentalized the unwholesome parts of my world as I'd learned to do since becoming a physician and had perfected since my nephew entered my life. It was the only way to function without being overwhelmed.

After releasing Colleen from child-care duties, RJ and I gobbled up some leftover pizza and spent the last waning daylight at the playground. As a velvet dusk began to descend, my mobile awakened and area code 703 appeared on the screen. I recognized it from the phone call I'd made to Quantico.

"Hey Father, it's Keri Novak. Hope it's not past your bedtime there. Sorry, I'm out in the City of Angels, and my body clock is all screwed up. I have some info that might help with that missing girl you told me about. You interested?"

"Fire away, Agent. I'm all ears."

"I don't know squat about computers, but I've made an FBI connection. Agent Gates is the head of the Bureau's geek squad and their leading expert on the online recruiting of victims. And you, Father, are in luck. He's lecturing at a law enforcement seminar at the Hyatt Regency in Columbus tomorrow. He's a bit of a rock star, but I managed to get you and Sheriff Macon front-row tickets to the show and backstage access to the man himself. Interested?"

"Interested? Heck, yes." One of the two missing teenagers was dead, and I would have done anything to recover the other safely. "If you weren't two thousand miles away, Agent, and I wasn't a priest, I'd kiss you."

I glanced at my nephew, who was dangling upside-down by his legs, high up on the bars of the jungle gym. The kid was half-chimpanzee. Visions of emergency rooms danced in my head and I was about to holler to him when RJ righted himself, dropped to the mulch-covered ground, and dashed to the slides.

I regrouped mentally. "Sheriff Macon and I are in. What do we need to do?"

"Show up before he leaves the conference at noon. Give him my name. He's expecting you. And forget the collar and Bible. Try to look like police."

"Will do. Thanks, Keri. I owe you one."

"Nah, we're even. Let me know if I can help. Gotta run, Padre. Later."

RJ and I strolled back to the rectory under a night sky brimming with stars. I wrangled him out of the bathtub, read him a story, and put him to bed, then called Emily. It was time for a little pleasure before business.

"Hi Em. I was hoping you could join us for dinner tomorrow night."

Over the past few weeks, she had been hesitant whenever I'd suggested we spend time together. She seemed more distant and each time I approached the topic of "us," she would deflect the conversation. I had assumed that the futility of exploring a relationship with a priest had finally reared its ugly, but rational, head. Her application for annulment, however, had raised my hopes again. The last time I invited her to join me, she'd said she couldn't because she had a doctor's appointment. I wondered if that had been an excuse, so I asked, "Are you feeling any better?"

"I, ah ... I'm okay. Dinner would be nice. I've been meaning to speak with you anyway. Six o'clock all right? I'll come by cab."

"Great. See you tomorrow," I replied and hung up. Not so great—*Been meaning to speak with you* had an ominous ring to it.

Tomorrow night was out of my control, but the morning wasn't. It was time to get down to business. I called the sheriff.

"Tree, are you free tomorrow?"

"You asking me out? I told you that celibacy thing wasn't healthy. Besides, you're not my type. What's up?"

"Agent Novak called." I gave Tree the bullet points. "We need to get to the conference by noon, but I have to say Mass in the morning. Can you pick me up at nine thirty? We may have to break the speed limit to get to Columbus before Agent Gates leaves. Are you up for some Indy 500 action?"

"Tomorrow? I don't know. I got a lot on my plate." He filled my ears with silence for a moment, then said, "I guess I can rearrange my schedule and leave my number two in command for a few hours. Okay. You're on, buddy. I always wanted to drive at Indy. Bring your crash helmet."

CHAPTER TWENTY NINE

Friday, April 4, 6:00 a.m.

I awoke early on Friday, opened my Breviary, and said Lauds, the morning prayer that reminds us daily that Jesus Christ brought light into a gloomy world.

After Mass, I dressed in a sport coat and hopped into the sheriff's cruiser. Tree was decked out in his uniform and wearing his game face.

"Did Sister Angelica drop off Miriam's PlayStation?" I asked.

"It's in the trunk."

When I inquired about the progress on Reverend Flood's death, he growled, took a sip of coffee, and slid a Best of Motown CD into the player. Isaac Hayes' funky "Theme from Shaft" filled the car as we headed south. When Tree was in a mood, he could also be a "bad mutha," so I opted not to prod Sheriff Grizzly with a bunch of questions.

Friday traffic was heavy and orange construction barrels littered the road, putting us behind schedule. When we took the entrance ramp onto the Interstate, Tree lit up the light-bar flashers on the roof, gunned the engine, and the world flew past my window all the way to Columbus.

As we cruised down North High Street, I decided to prod the grumpy old bear.

"I received a letter of invitation to the Episcopal priesthood in the mail, Tree. I didn't realize you Baptists were so friendly with their denomination."

The big guy grinned. "Got no idea what you're talking about."

We parked in the Hyatt Regency lot and trotted through the lobby into the conference room as the audience was applauding Agent Gates' lecture. I had met several FBI agents while working with Keri Novak, and Gates' appearance did not fit the stereotypical clean shaven, buzz cut image.

His hair was long and his beard full. He wore the standard black suit, but had jazzed things up with neon red socks and a Mickey Mouse necktie. *A nonconformist making a statement?* I doubted that Quantico approved, but if you're an important enough cog in the FBI's machine, the honchos probably turned a blind eye.

He was packing up his laptop when we intercepted him. Up close, Gates was slim and looked young enough to be in high school. A colorful tattoo peeked over the top of his shirt collar that was definitely not Bureau issue. We introduced ourselves and he extended a hand.

"Gates. Brian, not Bill. Don't have his money or his clout." He studied me and his pale eyes lit up. "Ah yes, the infamous Father Jake. The priest who's ready to rumble. Agent Keri Novak told some interesting stories about you. I heard the two of you went all *Eliot Ness* on Big Angie's gang. And I thought *I was* the odd man out." He eyeballed my sport coat. "Incognito are we, Father?" He laughed. "Hanging out with Keri? Wow, you're a braver man than I. With or without her Glock, she scares the hell out of me." He closed his briefcase. "What can I do for you two?"

Tree took the lead. "Miriam Riley is a teenaged girl who's been missing for two months. It seems that overnight she went from an introverted gamer to a working girl turning tricks on the street."

I showed him the before and after pictures Sister Angelica had given to me: the fifteen-year-old princess in a frilly dress at her birthday party, and the surly seventeen-year-old rebel with fluorescent-green hair and angry eyes.

"Because of the troublemakers she hung out with in high school," I said, "law enforcement was quick to write her off as a runaway, but we're not buying it. She disappeared without taking her computer. I'm worried she was abducted."

"An avid gamer without her computer? You're right to worry. Unfortunately, I've heard similar stories before. How do I fit in, Sheriff?"

"Miriam spent a lot of time on her PlayStation. I've heard online gaming can be used to seduce kids into the world of drugs and other illegal activities, and that you've come up with a way to trace the scumbags who are preying on children. True?"

"You heard right. We're in the early stages of software development and have had some success. Ever since PlayStation and Xbox were released with the ability to communicate, we've stumbled into a sewer full of online predators. They make friends with teenagers, convince them to run away from home, and recruit them for gangs, drugs, or prostitution. Kids usually don't tell their parents because … well, fellow gamers are *cool* and they consider their folks ancient, out-of-touch, and anti-fun. In fact, if caught messaging, teens often *defend* their online friendships."

Gates grabbed his laptop and briefcase and began walking toward the exit, flanked by Tree and me. "We're recovering online communications from game consoles and tracing them back to the sender. When we're successful, we explore *the sender's* connections to other youngsters and can often shut down an entire network. The highlight of my day is watching a perp shoved into the back of a police cruiser. Some kids we get to in time, others … that's where Keri Novak's team comes in."

"What's her role?" I asked.

Gates snickered. "I know you're a kick-ass priest, but you don't want anything to do with *her* operation, Father. She calls it S.O.K. Save Our Kids. If I was involved with selling drugs to children or hurting them in any way, I wouldn't want to cross paths with Keri. She lost her son to an overdose, so it's *personal* for her. She's spent years busting dealers, but she created S.O.K. to rescue victims instead. She never caught the dealer whose drugs killed her boy and never quite got over his loss, so S.O.K. is half therapy for her and half revenge. God have mercy on the bad guys, since Keri sure-as-hell won't."

He stopped, yanked off his necktie, shoved it in a coat pocket, and lowered his voice. "She's recruiting a strike force of former CIA, Special Ops guys, and Vice operatives, and is training them to covertly extract trafficked victims all around the world. But listen gentlemen, this is all hush-hush. Her operation and mine are not ready for public consumption. We want to catch as many perps as we can before the word gets out. I'm only telling you 'cause Keri asked me to help. Mum's the word. Got it?"

"Got it." Tree smirked. "Cross our hearts and hope to die—or worse, become sleazy defense lawyers," he said, making the appropriate gesture over his heart. "How do I go about examining Miriam's game console? Is there a program I can get for my tech person?"

"Not that simple. Our proprietary software is nowhere near ready for distribution. Did you bring the girl's console?"

"It's in the trunk of my cruiser."

"Get it and I'll see what I can do, Sheriff. For Keri, I'd go through a stone wall. But as I said, we're in the early stages of development. No promises."

I shook his hand, thanked him, and gave him our contact information while Tree grabbed the game console from the car. When our meeting with Agent Gates was finished, I felt something I hadn't felt for a couple weeks—hope.

CHAPTER THIRTY

Friday, April 4, 1:00 p.m.

As we walked through the lobby toward the Hyatt parking lot, Tree said, "Mind if we stay for the rest of the conference? I'd like to hear what else the Feebies are working on."

"Sorry, I can't. Colleen's already logged too many hours babysitting RJ, and Emily's coming over for supper."

A smile spread across the big man's face. "My, my. Jakey's got a hot date!"

"Oh, grow up. It's just dinner." I climbed into his cruiser and slammed the passenger door harder than necessary.

On the drive north, I phoned Sister Angelica, told her we had delivered her sister's game console to the FBI expert and that I would keep her posted. After I hung up, I asked Tree, "Anything new on Reverend Flood's death?"

"A couple things. The altar wine for the congregation was stored in the church vestry, but a locked cabinet in Flood's office also contained a large amount of wine, and guess what? Only his special stash contained amphetamine, and plenty of it—enough that a one ounce Communion cup could deliver a nice buzz. The key to the wine cabinet was on Flood's keychain."

"Was there amphetamine in Flood's system on the autopsy?"

"Cocaine but no speed. The coroner found damage to his nose, a sure sign he'd been a regular user for at least a couple years."

"What the heck was his game? Why drug the Communion wine?"

"Not sure, Jake. Maybe leaving his congregation happy after each service so they'd keep coming back for more."

"Hooked on heaven? Addicted to church? I thought I'd seen everything. But why?"

"Think green, Jake. You saw the crowd. If a little buzz from the wine could get them all attending Church twice a week, that's a lot of cash filling the collection baskets. That group in the first few pews, The Blessed, looked especially well-to-do and capable of generous donations." He drummed his fingers on the steering wheel. "And the unsuspecting worshipers have no reason to be suspicious of their satisfying *religious* highs after church. Pleasure without guilt, the ultimate joy. Maybe Flood had a serious coke habit and financed it with the collection plate money. It's enough to make me an atheist."

"Wrong perp. Don't slap the handcuffs on the Almighty, Tree. God's love is pure, but organized religion can at times be a dirty bride, and some clergy are flat-out harlots. All barrels contain rotten apples, including law enforcement."

The cruiser sped north on I-71, shrubs and trees flying past my window as I tried to make sense of the senseless.

"An innocent kid dead, all over money and drugs. That's crazy! What did the suicide note on Flood's computer say?"

"It was short, vague, and not so sweet. 'Coke is the devil's spawn. God forgive me!' The fingerprints on the computer were all Flood's, but that's no surprise."

"So, let me get this straight, Tree. Tony Pagano accidently stumbles onto the drugged wine and Flood needs to eliminate him. Flood knows Mateo Cruz through Grafton prison. Cruz abducts and presumably kills Tony. When we pressure Flood, he realizes the jig is up and kills himself." I paused and considered what we knew. "That all seems clear, Tree, so why'd the coroner suspect it wasn't a suicide? I understand that two different marks on his neck suggests murder—but locked windows, a suicide note, a room dead-bolted from the inside. What else could it be?"

"Oh, it was a homicide, Jake. The autopsy proved that the deep horizontal furrow below the rope mark on his neck was made by a thin ligature that actually strangled him. Gerta found fractures of both his thyroid cartilage and that tiny bone … what's it called?"

"The hyoid."

"That's it. Hyoid. The coroner said it's unusual to fracture both of them in a suicidal hanging. No, Flood was garroted from behind by a thin cord, then strung up to make it look like suicide. He had a baggie of cocaine in his desk drawer and plenty up his nose, but there was only a small amount in his bloodstream. Meaning, it was put up his snout after he'd died."

"It still doesn't make sense. How'd the killer leave the room? Is there a secret door or passage?"

"Nope. We checked. That was our first thought, and we went through the place with a fine-toothed comb. Even reviewed the architect's blueprints and inspected the ceiling."

"Then how the heck did the killer exit the room after locking the deadbolt from the inside? With no slot in the lock's faceplate on the outside of the door to insert a key, he couldn't have locked it from the hallway."

"You're getting warmer, Jake." He was playing cat-and-mouse with me—and he was purring.

"All right, I admit it. You're a genius, Tree. So, explain things to your simple-minded disciple, All-Knowing Grand Poobah of Justice."

"You're right, the office door couldn't have been locked with a key from the outside." Tree swerved around an old man in a Lincoln Continental doing forty miles per hour in the passing lane. "Did you notice anything strange about the lock itself?"

"No, I was busy helping you cut a dead man down from the rafters. Come on Tree, give. Quit toying with me. What's the answer?"

"Remember Flood's office? The décor in the room was well designed and coordinated. Wood paneling on the walls, masculine furnishings, and the fixtures were all brass, including the doorknob.

"Okay. So?"

"What color was the deadbolt, Jake?"

"Brown, like the other brass things in the room."

"Correct. And what color was the lock's faceplate on the outside of the door?"

"Silver, I think."

"You're right, it was chrome."

"Why's that important?"

"You ever put a deadbolt in a door?"

I shook my head.

"That's not how lock sets are sold. They have the same metal throughout, never a chrome faceplate on one side and a brass one on the other. Actually, it took three of us to figure it out, Jake. You noticed the brass screw on the carpet near the doorjamb. Didn't seem important until the CSI gal dusting for fingerprints pointed out that one of the screws on the brass deadbolt was chrome and didn't match. Sharp-eyed lady that one."

Traffic bottle-necked at a road construction site. Tree put on his lights and siren, and edged along the berm past the slowdown, then continued.

"The jigsaw pieces began to fit together when I examined the lock. It's not the kind that you turn by hand from the inside after the door is closed. Those are privacy locks. Flood's door had a spring-latching deadbolt, which is tapered on one side. After you release it, those automatically lock when you close the door, but they *always* have a key slot in the outside faceplate, so you can get back in if you accidentally lock yourself out."

"Still lost here, Tree. Wouldn't Flood have chosen a privacy lock for maximum security? He sure as heck didn't want anyone to unlock the door and come in when he was snorting coke or spiking wine with amphetamines."

"True. He definitely wanted to keep folks out of his office while he was drugging, but you're missing the point, Jake. A spring-latching deadbolt *is secure* if you are the only person with a key to the lock—and Flood had the key for that lock on his keychain. But the faceplate on the outside of his office door had no key slot."

Tree skirted an ambulance and a police cruiser at the scene of a three car pileup near the Ashland exit, then chuckled. "Try to keep up, buddy. Here's your final exam in sleuthing. A chrome screw was inserted through a brass deadbolt to fasten it to the chrome faceplate on the outside of the door. What does that tell you, Sherlock?"

Let there be light—and everything became clear. "My God! So all the killer had to do was replace the keyed faceplate with a keyless one—but in his hurry, he dropped one brass screw, couldn't find it on the brown carpet, and had to replace it with a chrome one."

"Bingo. The faceplates are interchangeable, and it would only take a minute to switch them. After our perp killed Flood, he simply released the latching deadbolt, wiped his fingerprints away, and the lock automatically engaged when he closed the door. He knew that when the police arrived, it would appear that the office had a *privacy* lock that had been secured from the inside, and we'd break it down to get in. Once in the room, everyone would focus on the corpse, and no one would pay attention to the lock itself."

"One problem with that, Tree. If the killer went to all that trouble, why not replace the faceplate with a matching one made of brass? Why risk drawing attention to it with chrome?"

"Ah, very good little grasshopper," Tree said in an Asian accent. "You have learned much sitting at the foot of the master." He laughed. "You're right. A crucial mistake—but most killers make at least one. And if you and my tech hadn't pointed out the two different screws, I might never have given the lock a second thought. Our killer bought the keyless faceplate from the manufacturer that made the lock, so the two sides would fit together properly. I'm sure he *tried to purchase* a matching one of brass, but the company stopped making the brass version a year ago. He had no choice but to go with chrome."

We left the interstate and crossed into Lorain County, where early rush-hour traffic came to a hot-tempered boil that thickened and congealed, and movement slowed to a crawl.

"Somebody went to a lot of trouble, Jake." Tree slapped the steering wheel with the palm of his hand. "Definitely *premeditated* murder. But that lock may be our killer's Waterloo. Psychopaths usually overestimate their own brilliance. Our perp wasn't smart enough to wipe down both sides of the faceplate. When I disassembled the lock, guess what I found? A partial fingerprint on the *inside* of the faceplate! Not enough of a print to definitely match anyone in the Automated Fingerprint Identification System, but when I make an arrest, it will put the killer on death row."

Traffic thinned as we approached Route 58. Tree moved into the left lane and gunned the cruiser.

"With a history of drugs and violence, Tree, Mateo Cruz has to be the prime suspect. Flood spoke on his behalf at his parole hearing, and probably ordered him to abduct Tony to silence him. The two of them were tight. Maybe Cruz was afraid Flood's cocaine habit was getting the best of him and he might let something slip to the police. Or maybe Flood was getting cold feet and wanted out. I'd give Cruz a hard look if I were you."

"First I'd need to find that mook, and second his fingerprints in the AFIS system *are not* a match with the print on the faceplate. But I bet he knows whose prints *do* match. Be nice to grill Cruz's ass for a few hours in interrogation." Dark clouds blanketed what was left of the afternoon sun, and Tree flipped on the headlights. "There were hundreds of fingerprints in Flood's office, mostly parishioners, but none belong to Cruz, so I got no proof he was involved in Flood's murder—but his ass is already mine for the kidnapping and murder of Tony."

Tree hesitated. "I'm wondering if Virgil Pagano could have suspected that Flood was connected to the amphetamines and his son's overdose at the church. He went bat-shit crazy when we notified him of Tony's death. You've interacted with him more than me. You think he's capable of murder?"

"Virgil definitely has a temper, but he's extremely religious. I can't see him as a killer, but who knows? If he killed Flood out of anger and revenge for Tony, I doubt that he would've taken the time to premeditate anything, let alone tamper with the deadbolt."

"Good point. He probably would have stormed in with a shotgun and done the deed."

"And most likely called the police to turn himself in afterward. No, Tree, I can't see it."

"I suspect you're right." A silver Corvette swerved in front of us and Tree hit the horn. "Jesus, it says SHERIFF on the side of my cruiser! Are these frickin' idiots blind? I'd arrest his ass if I hadn't had my quota of bullshit for the week. This case, and the loonies on the road, are giving me a headache. There's aspirin in the glove compartment. Grab me a couple."

I gave him two and he swallowed them dry. "The thing is, Jake, the church was full of people around the time that Flood died. Coroner estimates the time of death between four and eight p.m. At seven, Reverend Lundgren was leading Wednesday's prayer service, which means Tony's father was probably there along with a gazillion other people. I already looked at the camera footage from the church and didn't see Cruz in the crowd of worshipers."

"I'm positive Flood wouldn't have a security camera inside his office, but are there any outside it?"

"There's one in the hallway, but the surveillance system is old and re-records every twenty four hours on a single tape. I pulled the video cassette after the coroner arrived in Flood's office, about quarter after six."

"Who does it show entering Flood's office on the night of his death?"

"Absolutely no one. By the time I got my hands on the video, it had already taped over everything that happened on the day of the murder. It shows you and me entering to cut Flood down, and the coroner coming in to begin her examination of the body the next day. That leaves more than a two hour window from four till after six on the night Flood was killed with no video in the hall. I can't even confirm Lundgren's meeting with

Flood in the afternoon. The tape after that shows only an empty hallway. I got my lab rats trying to reconstruct images from the missing hours, but I'm not hopeful."

"So you can't ID Flood's killer from the video tape? Damn."

"Yeah, double damn. Now I've got not one but *two* related murders, Tony's and Flood's, and no hard evidence."

Tree drove up to rectory, dropped me off, and left me standing there with my own throbbing headache, and more questions than answers.

CHAPTER THIRTY ONE

Friday, April 4, 6:00 p.m.

The instant I walked through the door, Colleen hurried from the rectory. I suspected that I might not be the only person tonight with what Tree had called *a hot date*. She had left us a taste of Ireland, however, warming in the oven—corned beef and cabbage. I popped the cork on a bottle of pinot noir to let it breathe and joined my nephew in the living room.

Punctual as always, Emily arrived by cab as RJ finished an in-depth summary of his day at school. When I answered the front door, he ran up and gave Emily a hug. Their growing bond was undeniable and a joy to witness. The more often she came to supper, the more it felt like a family gathering—and I loved the feeling.

After our meal, we settled in at the kitchen table for a game of cards. RJ had pestered me until I purchased a *braille* version of Old Maid, so Emily could play. The two of them teamed up to repeatedly dump the spinster card on the ineligible bachelor priest, much to their combined glee. After RJ's bath, Emily helped me put him to bed. We retired to the living room, which looked as if a bomb had exploded in a toy store. I guided her safely past the rubble, entered the kitchen, and poured her another glass of wine.

When I reentered the living room, she was standing behind a vase filled with fresh spring flowers on an end table. I said, "Em, here's your glass …" then froze. I couldn't find the words or take another step. In her simple white dress, she looked like a bride holding a bouquet, and all of the could-have-beens and should-have-beens came roaring back to me.

"What's wrong, Jake? Are you okay?"

I was not. I stared a moment at the ghost of relationships past—a ghost of my own creation.

"I'm fine. I was just thinking how lovely you look tonight."

She blushed and sat on the couch. I joined her, but she slid a foot farther away. As she filled me in on the latest hospital gossip, my mind wandered back to December, when our relationship had rekindled and we had kissed for the first time in years. The memory and the taste of her lips had lingered fresh and sweet, like a juicy apple dangling from a low branch in the Garden of Eden.

That kiss had been an implicit promise to explore our renewed relationship. Her request for an annulment was another giant step in that direction. I guided the conversation to our early years together in school, when the idea of a *forever us* appeared inevitable, hoping to ease into the subject. She smiled as she recounted the night we'd danced to "our song" at the prom, then suddenly went silent. I read what I thought was longing in her eyes and leaned in for a kiss.

"Jake, no!" She pulled away, an expression of surprise and dismay on her face. "I ... I can't. We can't. I think we should ...." She turned away. "May I have more wine please?"

She'd already had more than she usually drank. "Really?"

"Yes, really. It's not as if I'm driving home."

I refilled her glass. "What's going on with you? With us?"

"This can't continue. Things are impossible now, Jake. Maybe I should leave."

Her words struck me like fists.

"Not till you tell me what the heck is going on, Em. I thought we both felt the same way. This doesn't make sense. Please help me understand. Is there someone else?"

"No, no one else." She took a sip. "There never has been. But this isn't about you."

Isn't about you—words that usually led to *goodbye*. It sure seemed like it was about me. I waited for an explanation that didn't come.

"Then tell me, Em. What the heck *is it* about?"

She hesitated. "Remember when I canceled our lunch plans a couple weeks back? There was a spot on my mammogram. I had a biopsy and it came back ... positive." The moment expanded around us, her words echoing in the surrounding silence. She downed the last of her wine. "I have cancer, Jake. Dr. Glade will do surgery on Monday, remove the tumor, and probably perform a total mastectomy."

It felt as if the floor had suddenly disappeared and I was plummeting. "I'm so sorry, Em. I don't know what to ...." I tried to give her a hug, but she stood and pushed me away.

"Em, I love you and want to help!"

She raised a hand to silence me, removed her phone from her purse, and called for a cab. "I won't put you through this, Jake. You went through hell with your sister's illness, and you understand *exactly* what lies ahead for me. I was broken enough with my blindness, but *this*? I can't do this to you. Our childish dream of happily-ever-after is over. I don't know what the future holds, and I have to concentrate on me, on my recovery. What I need now is a friend and your prayers."

"Wait! You can't just shut me out. I'm *already* involved."

"This isn't up for discussion. I'm sorry, Jake ... but I wanted to tell you in person." She extended her red and white cane. "The taxi's on its way."

"Let me walk you—"

"Don't bother. I'll meet it outside."

She marched out of the door and left me alone, so very alone. After a few seconds, I shook off my self-pity, ran outside, and stayed with her under a starless sky until her cab arrived. Only a lone whip-poor-will spoke, and he sang the same sad song all night long outside my window.

CHAPTER THIRTY TWO

Saturday, April 5, 11:00 a.m.

I slept fitfully on Friday night, and my morning shift at the hospital was mental chaos. Thank the Lord that I had a competent resident working with me, because I was damned-near useless.

I'd just been to hell and back with my sister's leukemia, and the possibility of a return trip with Emily cast a shroud over my roiling thoughts.

I was completing my notes on a patient's chart when Nurse Ochs walked over.

"Doctor, Mrs. Hudson is in the waiting room. She wants to speak with you."

I had first met her months earlier when she had come to Urgent Care with the onset of numbness in her cheek, blurred vision, and painful eye movement. When I noticed muscle spasms in her left leg and found weakness on physical examination, I'd ordered the usual battery of tests. The MRI and other results had suggested multiple sclerosis, and I had referred her to Dr. Taylor in Neurology, who'd confirmed my diagnosis and begun treatment. I had nowhere near the expertise that Taylor had and couldn't imagine why she would want to speak with me now. But it was better to focus on her concerns than on my own.

"Fine. Please put her in an exam room, and I'll see her shortly."

As Nurse Ochs led her past me, I was shocked at the way her condition had worsened. In less than a year, her gait had become unsteady, she had a left foot drop, and now leaned heavily on a four-pronged walker. The deterioration was heartbreaking.

When I entered the room, she was weeping softly.

"What can I do for you, Mrs. Hudson?"

She wiped her tears with a tissue and looked up. "Dr. Taylor's prescribed physical therapy and all the usual medications, but nothing seems to work. I keep getting worse. Don't get me wrong, he's a good doctor, but he's not … creative. He won't challenge the status quo. You struck me as a man who might."

"I don't understand. You've lost me."

"I've been living on the computer since my world unraveled, reading all I can about MS. Have you heard of the drug Previax?"

"I've read about it in medical journals but never prescribed it. It shows promise."

"It's been available in Europe for years, but it was finally approved by the FDA last month. Dr. Taylor gave me a prescription, but my insurance won't pay for it. It costs over nine thousand dollars a year, and that's only if I pay cash! MS cost me my job, and my husband's a truck driver who was laid off. We're having trouble just putting food on the table as it is. Nine thousand bucks? We can't afford Previax, Doctor. We'll lose our house, everything. And I have my daughter to consider. I'd sooner die than put her on the street." She took out her phone and showed me a photo of her husband and six year old daughter. Her child had a luminescent smile and curly red hair like RJ's. "I'm not willing to bankrupt my family's future for a longshot on mine. Do you have children?"

A complex question. "I do. I'm raising my nephew. He's about your daughter's age."

"Then you understand. Will you help me?"

"How?"

"The medicines I've taken so far haven't helped, and I'm desperate. I have nothing to lose at this point and want to try Previax. My insurance will cover the cost if I have one of these specific symptoms." She handed me a list. "I don't, and Dr. Taylor refuses to say I do. He can't without putting his medical license at risk. I get that and don't blame him, but I was hoping…. I know this is a big ask, doctor. Would you be willing to help me?"

Big ask indeed! I had my own child to support and couldn't afford to lose my medical license either.

She pointed to the list. "I've read about this symptom and can fake it. All I need is a signature." She produced an insurance form from her purse and held it out to me. "It's all filled in."

Once again, the dream of modern medicine crashed headlong into the reality. I plopped onto the desk chair and pondered the economic-scientific paradox: potentially lifesaving advances that were too costly for most patients. Dear God in Heaven!

A framed copy of the Hippocratic Oath hung in my study next to my medical degree. *First do no harm* was the primary directive. If I falsified this form, I'd be cheating the insurance company. And if I got caught, who would I be harming? RJ and myself. If I didn't sign it, who would suffer? Mrs. Hudson, her husband, and her innocent child.

Given time, it was likely that Previax would be approved for more indications. But time was exactly what this poor woman didn't have.

I had once seen Tree Macon twist the law and the truth to put a killer behind bars, and it had diminished him in my mind forever. I didn't want to be that guy. I looked into Mrs. Hudson's pleading eyes and ran a hand down my face.

What to do? I *did* know one thing for certain. If I could have saved my sister, I would willingly have done anything without a second of regret. And if a lie could save Emily now, I wouldn't even hesitate.

I grabbed the form, signed and dated it, and handed it back to her. Not a sound medical-legal decision, but a compassionate one. Sometimes a *good* lie was the kind and decent thing to do. If there was hell to be paid, then I would pay it.

Mrs. Hudson hobbled closer and kissed me on the forehead. "If Dr. Taylor asks, I'll tell him we got a loan from a relative. And I promise you, Doctor, if the insurance company finds out and comes after you, I will swear on a Bible in court that I forged your signature. I won't let you take the fall."

Fall? I had been falling from grace in the Church's eyes since the moment I was reunited with Emily. Now I'd committed fraud. Who the hell had I become? Only the knowledge that I'd be helping this poor woman and her family convinced me that my moral compass was still pointing toward true north.

After Mrs. Hudson left the room, I placed my head in my hands and savored the healing silence—until my cellphone banished it.

CHAPTER THIRTY THREE

Saturday, April 5, 11:30 a.m.

When I answered my phone, Tree Macon asked, "Are you working at the hospital today?"

"Until one. Why?"

"I need a favor. Remember my question yesterday about Virgil Pagano being capable of murder? Well, I spoke with Reverend Lundgren today, and he told me Virgil stormed into Flood's office Wednesday morning and slammed the door. He heard a lot of shouting, but didn't know what was said."

"So you're wondering whether Virgil may have returned that night to avenge his son's death? He's definitely big and strong enough to overpower Flood, strangle him, and hoist him up with a rope to make it look like suicide. He does have an explosive temper, but I find it hard to picture him as a cold-blooded killer, Tree."

"Maybe Tony told him about the drug-laced wine or he figured it out, and Virgil went off the deep end when his son was killed."

"I suppose. If the man Virgil put all his faith in at the church was behind his son's death, he might not have been willing to wait for the Lord to settle the score in the afterlife."

"Problem is, I can't totally rule Virgil out 'cause Tony's death gives him motive for revenge. I got no hard evidence against him and need to know what they fought about. Since the security tape recorded over whatever happened at Flood's office before six-fifteen that night, I can't even confirm that they argued. What are you doing after work?"

"Going to the cemetery to put flowers on my sister's grave, then home. Why?"

"Tony's funeral was this morning. There's a reception at the Pagano house this afternoon. Would you stop in and snoop around, buddy, and see how Virgil's reacting to Flood's death? Find out what they fought about. Scout the landscape for me before I have to charge in and go all mano-a-mano on a grieving, possibly innocent, father. Flood's death and Tony's are linked, and I want someone locked in the slammer, as you priests say, *for ever and ever, amen.*"

Considering how hostile my first two encounters with Virgil had been, I hesitated. He would not be the least bit forgiving if he caught me nosing around at his home. I wanted to refuse but two people were dead, and my best friend was asking for my help.

"Sure, Tree. I can visit the cemetery another day. I'll see what I can find out."

When my shift ended, I hung my white coat in my locker and drove to the Pagano's farm. Virgil must have recently fertilized his fields because the air had a pungent odor—appropriate, considering that life was fast becoming a shit-storm for me, Emily, Angelica, and the Pagano family.

Inside the front door, dozens of people milled around. I recognized some from Flood's congregation. Soft gospel music floated through the living room. The dining room and kitchen tables were covered with casserole dishes and desserts. The aroma of freshly brewed coffee filled the air. Edna Pagano spotted me and came over. Her hair was disheveled and her makeup streaked with dried tears.

"I'm so, so sorry, Mrs. Pagano." I wondered if there was ever anything appropriate and healing to say to a grieving mother. "Tony was a fine young man. He'll be missed. I'll be praying for you and your husband. If there's anything I can do...."

Short of resurrecting the dead, I couldn't imagine what that might be.

"Thank you for all your kindnesses, Father. Can I get you something to drink?"

"Coffee would be nice." She led me to the coffee pot and handed me a cup.

"Now we've lost Jeremiah Flood," she said, her expression wilting. "He was our shepherd and we all feel lost. Thank heavens for Reverend Lundgren. I know God has a grand and mysterious plan but...." A tear rolled down her cheek. She looked over my shoulder, raised a trembling hand, and waved to a new arrival. "If you'll excuse me."

I wandered through the crowd eavesdropping on conversations, overhearing accolades for Tony but not a negative word about Flood. Rex Lundgren stood near the living room window surrounded by a well-dressed crowd, presumably members of The Blessed. Staying out of his line of sight, I strolled over and listened. A nervous little man in a silk suit worth more than my car was making a pitch to add a special Friday evening prayer meeting, and Lundgren seemed receptive to the concept.

The conversation had shifted to fund raising when I noticed a woman step out of a bathroom into a hallway. Across from it, a door was cracked open and I glimpsed a poster on the wall of four young men dressed in black. *A teenager's bedroom?* I headed toward it as Mahalia Jackson's soulful rendition of "Move On Up A Little Higher" floated through the gathering.

A voice from behind stopped me. "Didn't expect to see you here."

Virgil Pagano approached me warily, looking as if he had aged a decade overnight. With his left hand wrapped around a glass of bourbon, he extended the other and shook mine.

"Sorry if I was rude before, Father. I know you mean well. Thank you for what you did for our son, and for coming today. Tony was the best thing that ever happened to Edna and me."

He lowered his gaze and recounted some of his son's accomplishments at the church and in school. When he downed the last of his drink and rattled the ice in his glass, I said, "And it's so sad about Reverend Flood."

Virgil's eyes narrowed. "I can't understand how a man of God could take his own life, Father. Not for me to judge, but ...." He crunched an ice cube. "Rex Lundgren's a fine man, but no one can ever replace Jeremiah. He built our congregation from a handful of followers, and raised enough in donations so we can soon break ground on our own Christian school." His eyes wandered down to the floor. "Tony would have loved going there."

"I admired Reverend Flood's youth ministry. Even as an outsider, it was obvious to me that he cared a great deal about children. Now he's gone. What a loss. I was told he had an argument with someone in his office the morning he died, possibly about the school project. Any idea who that might have been?"

"Nope. I wasn't at the church Wednesday." Virgil glanced at the bar. "Excuse me. I need a refill," he added and walked away.

He wasn't at the church? Either Virgil was lying, or Lundgren was; interesting.

I had other questions but decided not to push too hard. Maybe I'd have another go at him after he finished his next drink. I stepped into the bathroom, locked the door, and rifled through the medicine cabinet looking for prescription bottles, but found none.

I flushed the toilet, ran water in the sink, then slipped across the hall into Tony's room, leaving the door ajar so I could hear if anyone approached. I didn't want to be caught snooping around a dead child's room and had to hurry. Once again, helping Tree was turning my hair gray and eroding an ulcer in my stomach the size of a golf ball. The sheriff owed me big-time.

I was standing in a typical teenager's room. The wall poster was of a contemporary Christian band named 4Him. Nothing unusual jumped out at me.

I searched Tony's desk and peered under his bed, finding nothing. A cursory examination of his dresser was unremarkable. Clean clothes were neatly hung in his closet and the dirty ones were in a hamper. The room probably hadn't been touched since his death. I was about to close the closet door when I spotted something at the back of the top shelf. I reached up and removed two shoeboxes. The top one contained new sneakers. The bottom shoebox contained a Playboy magazine hidden under a circular advertising local concerts and entertainment. Tony had highlighted some upcoming events in red.

A typical teenaged boy's bedroom, true, but I didn't want Edna Pagano to stumble upon a girly magazine. The poor woman had suffered enough without tainting the memory of her son. I also wanted to see what items in the circular had caught Tony's attention.

Someone coughed in the hallway and I froze. I'd already been in the room too long. The question was how to get the magazine and circular out of the house. A priest carrying a rolled-up Playboy might draw unwanted attention and cause considerable embarrassment.

I tucked them both into an empty manila folder from Tony's desk and peered out of the door; no one in sight. My nervous system was on overload and my hands were trembling.

Enough skullduggery for one afternoon! I stepped into the hall, strolled into the kitchen, nodded to a couple near the coffee urn, then slipped out the back door and drove to the rectory feeling like the wheelman at a bank heist.

CHAPTER THIRTY FOUR

Saturday, April 5, 3:30 p.m.

I parked at the rectory and slipped the folder containing the Playboy and circular under the driver's seat, then locked the car door. I didn't want Colleen, the Queen of Gossip, to catch me with erotica and have to stumble through an explanation.

When I walked through the back door, she joined me in the kitchen.

"How's my little man doing today, Colleen?"

"Fine until an hour ago when a mood descended on the lad. Missing his dear departed mother, he is. 'Tis natural at his age, especially so soon after her passing, but it pains the heart to watch. I've not been able to put a smile on his face."

"Thanks for trying."

Living with the eccentric uncle that every family seems to have certainly didn't make it any easier on my nephew. Neither did my dual roles at the church and hospital. The alternative, however, was foster care or an orphanage and frankly, my life would have become a pale facsimile without him.

It truly does take a village to raise a child. Thank God mine was populated by Colleen, Emily, and Tree. Most folks were stuck with the family they were born into. I was fortunate enough to have *chosen* mine. They helped me bring stability to RJ's life—but Colleen not only functioned as a grandmother figure for RJ, she was definitely the *mayor* of our village.

"I'll take over, Colleen. Enjoy the rest of your day."

"That I will, Father, but I've not yet prepared supper."

"Not to worry. I'll handle it."

I left all thoughts of abduction and murder behind, walked into the living room, and immersed myself in the wonderful world of my favorite preschooler. RJ was hunkered down on the couch with his Winnie the Pooh stuffed animal watching cartoons. He barely said hello.

"How was your day, RJ?"

He shrugged.

"Want to go outside and play catch?"

"Nah."

"What would you like to do this afternoon?"

He hugged Pooh to his chest. "Nothin'."

I had recently taken him to Chuck E. Cheese for games and pizza in order to raise his spirits, so I needed to pull a new rabbit from my parental hat.

"How was *Pooh's* day?"

Another shrug, so I pointed at my nephew's best friend, who smelled like he should spend time in the washing machine. "You know what might cheer up this bear, RJ? That Winnie the Pooh movie you've been talking about. Want to go? What do you say?"

His eyes widened and he jumped to his feet. "Can Pooh come?"

"You bet, buddy. He's the star of the show!" I checked my watch. "If we hurry, we can make the next showing."

RJ, Pooh Bear, and I hustled to the Apollo Theater and settled into our seats with a giant tub of popcorn. When Pooh's likeness appeared onscreen, the smile I had come to love lit my nephew's face. Thank heavens for Disney movies!

While RJ laser-focused on the show, I shifted my attention to Emily's cancer and her upcoming surgery. I was so wrapped up in my own concerns that I didn't realize the movie had ended until my nephew and the other children in the theater began clapping and talking.

By the time the credits rolled, RJ was his usual bubbly self again. He asked to stop at McDonald's for a Happy Meal on the way home, which was not my preferred choice for fine dining, but what the heck.

At the restaurant, he was all giggles, waving at classmates, joking, and rambling on between bites about someone at school named Joshua. We reversed roles as I continued to fret about Emily, sliding into my own depression. With her surgery scheduled for Monday, there wasn't a thing I could do for her except worry and pray.

My concerns must have bled through because RJ asked, "Are you okay, Daddy?"

"I'm fine. Sorry, sport, I just have things on my mind."

He cocked his head and frowned. "Can I help?"

I chuckled. Who was the adult now? I'd undertaken my nephew's care to help him recover from the loss of his mother—but his presence in my life had become healing for me as well. I was beginning to think of him as my personal, miniature Atlas, lifting me up when life weighed me down. "You've already helped, RJ, by keeping me company—and by being such a terrific kid."

I leaned in to kiss him on the forehead, but he glanced over at a classmate and jerked away. "Stop! I told you. No kisses! I'm a big boy now."

It appeared we were growing up together.

We topped the evening off with an ice cream cone at Gibson's Bakery. After I'd tucked RJ into bed, I tried for a goodnight kiss but was again confronted with a frown and a headshake.

"Kisses are only for *mommies*."

News to me. "Fair enough, buddy. How about hugs?" I picked up Pooh Bear from the chair. "Would it be all right if I gave Pooh a hug?"

RJ considered this, then nodded. "Hugs are okay." And he reached up and gave me one.

After he was asleep, I brought the folder from my car into the kitchen. The Playboy cover showed more nudity than I'd seen in a long time, so I tossed it into the wastebasket before I could be tempted to sneak a peek at the centerfold. *Lead us not into temptation.*

On the circular, Tony had highlighted an upcoming school play and a rock concert in red ink. Images on the band's website showed a disheveled troupe of degenerates partying hard. By no stretch of the imagination, could they have been classified as sound Christian entertainment. *Early teenaged rebellion?* I thumbed through the rest of the brochure to see if any other events had caught Tony's attention. Nothing else had been circled, but I noticed a familiar address in the advertising section: The Fantasy Salon, on Harvard Avenue near Fourth Street, the last known location of Angelica's sister.

The ad read: "Full body massage & more! Gentlemen, try our Endless Bliss package. Uninterrupted and private. Your place or ours. Satisfaction guaranteed. Restraints available."

Endless Bliss? Restraints?

The two women pictured in the ad were showing nearly as much skin as a Playboy centerfold and looked as if they would be comfortable hanging naked from a pole in front of a room full of drunken, leering men. A legitimate massage parlor was unlikely, and definitely not in that part of town. I doubted that their clientele included any "gentlemen."

I called Tree on his cell. "Two things. I went to the reception at the Pagano's house after Tony's funeral. If Virgil killed Flood, he should get the Oscar for best actor. I didn't catch a whiff of guilt or deceit."

"Did he confirm having an argument with Flood?"

"No, he denied being at the church at all that day."

"So either Virgil or Lundgren is lying."

"Correct. Virgil did say that Flood has raised enough money to start construction on a Christian school, so there's a pile of cash stashed somewhere. Tony's mother, of course, was distraught, and I didn't have the heart to question her. I did, however, snoop through Tony's bedroom but couldn't find any connection to either Flood or Mateo Cruz."

"You said there were two things, Agent 007. What else?"

"Do you know anything about the Fantasy Salon on Harvard? I suspect they're offering more than deep muscle massages."

"Expanding your horizons, Father? Yeah, I'm all too familiar with that joint. Question is, how do *you* know about it?"

"Don't ask. It's located close to where Angelica's sister was last seen. Can you check it out? I'd go myself and show her photo around, but...."

"Yeah, Jake, that worked so well at the Cavern Bar that you almost got yourself sliced and diced. Don't even think about it. You may be on to something though. There are more sex-related shops in that neighborhood than convenience stores. Prostitution is a slippery slope. Pimps usually ease the newbies into the life at strip clubs and massage parlors. I'll give Miriam's picture to the Vice guys working the area and get them to keep an eye out for her." It sounded as if Tree took a gulp of something before he continued. "The results of the background check on Mateo Cruz were interesting. He was in Yuma, Arizona at the same time as Flood. I couldn't find a direct connection between the two, but Flood vouched for Cruz at his parole hearing—and a year later, Cruz kidnapped Tony. His link to Flood is not proof of anything, but circumstantial evidence is still *evidence*."

"Maybe they worked together back in Yuma, Tree."

"Possible, but *maybes* aren't admissible in court. With a Lexus worth a hundred grand and money rolling in for the school, though, it makes sense that Flood might want Tony out of the way because of the heat my investigation into the drugged wine incident caused—but who wanted Flood dead?"

"You said it yourself, Sheriff. Follow the money. Who's number two in the organization? Sounds to me like it's Cruz. We know he did Flood's dirty work."

"Could be. But I can't totally rule out Rex Lundgren or Virgil Pagano. Patience, buddy. Time will tell. This old hound dog is on the scent."

CHAPTER THIRTY FIVE

Sunday, April 6, 2:00 p.m.

For a change, the pews were filled for morning Mass, my homily hit the mark, and the collection baskets overflowed. Although a baby wailed throughout the service, that never bothered me. I had always believed it was better for babies to cry during my sermon than for parishioners to snore.

After the service, I changed into jeans and a Cavaliers sweatshirt, and RJ and I spent the day perfecting his bicycling skills. Thank the Lord for training wheels. He was finally getting the hang of it, and I'd relaxed enough to admire a beautiful cobalt-blue sky dappled with marshmallow clouds when my mobile chimed, and I heard a question I had never been asked before.

"Will you accept a collect call from the Grafton Correctional Institute?"

Against my better judgement, I said I would.

"You and me spoke in the library, Father. I answered a bunch of your questions." Images of the child-molesting weasel with the broken leg came to me as he spoke. "Thanks for putting the cash in my account. Didn't think you'd cough it up."

"I remember. What can I do for you, Mr. Gorski?"

"Been askin' around. Heard some interesting shit. We should talk again later this afternoon. Be helpful to *both* of us. Bring your check book. You're on my approved visitor list. See ya soon." Click.

Damn. Not how I wanted to spend the Lord's Day—with a pedophile. Colleen said she could watch RJ until dinner, so I dropped him off at her apartment and headed to the prison.

After surrendering my phone and personal belongings at the entrance, I was led into a visitor's room with six gray metal tables bolted to the floor.

The word *grim* best described both the décor and the mood of everyone there. At the far end of the room, an older woman was talking with an inmate who was shackled to a table. A guard stood nearby.

I sat at the first table and an officer led Gorski in. Although some of his cuts and bruises were healing, his leg remained in a cast.

"You asked me about that spick bastard, Duro, Reverend Flood's enforcer. The guy who filled the pews and kept the punks in line. Been talkin' to anyone who knew him. Heard some interesting shit, Father."

"I'm listening."

"His name's Mateo Cruz," he said, a cat-who-ate-the-canary grin on his lips. "Twenty bucks."

"I already knew that. No cigar … and no cash."

The smile faded, then returned. "Okay, there's more. I told you about big crowds in the chapel, right? Looks like Flood was sneaking drugs into the chapel, stashed in Bibles and other religious shit. That's why Cruz wouldn't let me anywhere near Flood."

"Flood's dead. Old news. Strike two. Try again."

"Yeah well, I'm guessing you don't know Cruz grew up with that other preacher, name of Lundgren. Buddies in school, those two. Real tight."

"Much better, Mr. Gorski. Cha-ching. Anything else?"

"Nah, but I'll keep digging." He handed me a piece of paper. "My email, and a phone number to reach me through the prison goon squad. A Robocop will come get me if I can talk with you. Been a pleasure doing business, Father. Hope to see ya soon."

I was overwhelmed by a desire to rush home and take a shower, and left before I had to breathe anymore of the same air as Gorski.

From the parking lot, I called Tree. "I'm at Grafton Prison. Flood was sneaking drugs into the prison chapel in Bibles. Why would he do that? Inmates don't have money. What was in it for him?"

"Maybe he was recruiting talent, like Mateo Cruz. It's hard to recruit thugs from church."

"That's not all. Here's the real shocker. Cruz and Lundgren grew up together and were pals."

"Well, well. That casts a different light on things. Two's company, three is maybe … a gang. Time to concentrate on Lundgren, turn over some rocks, see what crawls out. How'd you find all this out?"

"I have my own personal snitch here, and he's already bled me for sixty dollars."

"Fear not. As the Grand Poobah of Law Enforcement, I hereby dub thee my confidential informant. Your check for services rendered will go out tomorrow. It's good to be king—but I'm shooting for emperor." I heard voices shouting. "Sorry, Jake. Gotta run. Call me if you come across any more info."

I phoned Sister Angelica and told her that Tree had assigned Vice cops to keep an eye out for Miriam near Harvard Avenue and added, "Please don't go there yourself. That area's too darn dangerous."

"Don't need to go, Father. I've already been." A pause. "Don't worry. I took a couple of football players I went to high school with. We showed Miriam's picture around but no one admitted to seeing her. We also papered all the restroom stalls in the bars with stickers for the Human Trafficking Center hotline."

"Defensive linemen are definitely a much better choice of body guards than an aging priest."

"Have you heard anything from the FBI about Miriam's game console?"

"Not yet, but I'll let you know when we do. Stay safe, Angelica. Bye."

I picked up RJ and took him to the park until bedtime. As I tucked him in for the night, I thought about Gorski the pedophile and Cruz the kidnapper, and wondered if anyone was truly safe anywhere. These days, it didn't matter whether you lived in Gotham or Mayberry—scum always floated somewhere near the surface. I watched RJ's quiet breathing from the doorway and whispered a prayer for the safety of all children.

CHAPTER THIRTY SIX

Monday, April 7, 12:30 p.m.

I was on my way to the hospital cafeteria when I spotted Gavin Glade, dressed in his usual blue scrubs. Emily had been first up on his morning surgery schedule. I had worried and prayed for her all weekend. A mastectomy was a major procedure, and cancer a wily and relentless disease. I wanted an update. I waved to him and walked over.

Although we got along as colleagues, we weren't pals. Besides wielding a scalpel, slicing up others with innuendo was his stock-in-trade. He knew Emily and I were close friends and had undoubtedly heard the unfounded rumors about our supposedly torrid relationship, so he rarely missed the opportunity to goad me about my wild sex life just to watch me squirm.

"Hey Gavin. How'd things go with Ms. Beale?" I tried to sound casual but braced for a hassle.

His eyes narrowed and he frowned. "Come on, Jake. I can't divulge patient information. HIPAA laws, you know." Glade could be a real jackass at times. He started to walk away, then gazed at me. "But if I *could*, you'd see a big grin on my face as I waltzed into lunch." He lit up a smile and strolled into the cafeteria.

A bit of a dickhead, true, but an excellent surgeon. I could live with that.

I ate my meal and returned to Urgent Care. My shift was uneventful and when it ended, I checked again on Emily's status. She was stable and had been transferred from the Recovery Room to the surgical floor. Although I wanted to stop in and see her, it was likely that she was groggy, in pain, and probably didn't want any visitors other than her father. And God-only-knew what additional hospital gossip a visit from me would spawn.

Before I left for home, I stopped in the physicians' lounge, fired up the computer, and obtained telephone numbers for Catholic churches in Yuma, Arizona. By playing the priest card, I wormed my way past secretaries and managed to speak with priests at several parishes. Most had never heard of Flood, Cruz, or Lundgren, but the pastor at Immaculate Conception surprised me by asking, "Who are you again?"

"Jacob Austin. I'm pastor at Sacred Heart in Oberlin, Ohio."

"What's your interest in these men?"

He was already defensive and I wasn't sure how to play this without scaring him off. I didn't want to mention the homicide investigations but decided to lay some of my cards on the table.

"There have been some … unusual occurrences at their church, and I've been asked by the local police to find out what I can."

"Are you at the rectory now?"

"No, but I will be in thirty minutes. The phone number is—"

"Don't bother. I'll find it. Call you there later. Goodbye."

Traffic was light, my foot was heavy on the accelerator, and I arrived at the rectory early. Colleen set up my budding Michelangelo with paper and a box of crayons at the kitchen table, then ushered me into the living room.

"Really, Father! Playboy? I found it when I took out the trash. Please tell me you buy it to read the articles!"

No explanation would satisfy her, but I gave it a try. "I didn't buy it, Colleen. I came across it while helping Sheriff Macon with a case."

"Uh huh. And our kitchen was the closest wastebasket you could locate? Where a five year old could find it?"

Unlike Colleen, RJ didn't snoop through the trash. Anything I told her would be public knowledge within hours, so all I said was, "It's a long story."

"And one I've no desire to hear." She shook her head. "Sometimes I swear, Father, you meet trouble more than halfway. I'll see you tomorrow." With that, she whirled around, left the rectory, and slammed the door.

Back in the kitchen, I watched RJ finish his latest masterpiece, a portrait of me complete with a Charlie Brown head and huge banana-shaped smile—definitely refrigerator-worthy. I was chuckling softly when the phone rang.

"I apologize for the cloak and dagger when you called earlier, Father Austin, but one never knows who a caller actually is or what he's up to. I wanted to look up the rectory phone number myself. You asked me about Jeremiah Flood's time in Yuma."

"I did. So you knew him and Rex Lundgren?"

"I knew Flood though an ecumenical group of clergy. Quite an orator by all accounts. The fire and brimstone type and a bit too zealous for my taste, but a nice man until his wife died. After that, he became … irritable and argumentative, downright nasty at times. The change was shocking. He once even mocked our reverence for the Virgin Mary, called the Immaculate Conception the *Spontaneous Combustion!* At first, I was confused by the change in his personality. Then rumors of his drug use swirled through the community. Next thing I knew, he left town. Let me emphasize, I have no first-hand knowledge. This was all *gossip* and quite possibly unfounded. That's why I hesitated to speak with you."

Gossip, indeed. With cocaine in his bloodstream, erosions of his nasal septum found at autopsy, and a bag of coke in his office desk drawer, his drug use was *more* than rumor. His frenetic speech pattern and erratic behavior certainly fit that of a user.

Rex Lundgren had told us that Flood decompensated after his wife died and couldn't stand to be in the Yuma church they had built together. He'd also said that he had moved into the vicarage with Flood to support him. So if Flood was using drugs in Arizona, most likely Lundgren knew about it. I began to wonder how involved he was in the whole operation.

"What's going on with Flood, Father Austin?"

"Wish I could tell you, but it's a police matter. Did you ever meet Mateo Cruz or Reverend Lundgren?"

"I did not. Never heard of Cruz, but Flood talked about Lundgren sometimes. Before he packed up and moved out of town, Flood and I were having cocktails and he'd had … one too many. He was bragging about the seminary he'd graduated from, a well-respected school, when out of the blue he started laughing. He said Lundgren's degree wasn't worth the paper it was printed on. Flood could be downright cruel and spiteful at times. I wasn't sorry to see him leave town."

"Do you have any idea what seminary Lundgren attended?"

"Sorry, no. The 'Universal' something, near San Francisco. Not a school I'd ever heard of. That's all I know. Listen Father, I have a meeting and must go. If I can help in any other way, give me a call. Bye."

After RJ went to sleep, I searched degree programs online and found the Universal Theological Seminary in Salinas, California. The school was not certified by any legitimate organization and was clearly a diploma mill. Pay the "tuition" and voilà, like magic you are an ordained minister!

Curiouser and curiouser.

I called Tree at home. "I, your personal confidential informant, have some new information for you, Sheriff."

"The department's money appears to be well-spent. Whatcha got?"

I told him what the pastor in Yuma had said, and what I'd found online about Lundgren's degree. "We've been assuming all along that Cruz worked for Flood. Now that we know Lundgren and Cruz grew up together, what if…"

"What if Lundgren got some bogus degree and enlisted his pal Cruz to help him fleece the congregation, using Flood's fiery sermons to draw a crowd? I was wondering the same thing. Hell, Cruz was in Grafton Prison for drug possession with intent to sell, so he already had connections to local suppliers. Getting his hands on coke or speed would be a snap." Tree paused. "I been busy too. Got a list of all the members of The Blessed and checked them out. Guess what? They're all prominent and wealthy."

"So The Blessed are also *The Well-To-Do.* That makes sense, Tree. Sounds like Lundgren may be selling tickets to Heaven at premium prices. Flood said Lundgren was the money man, the fund-raiser who handled that group. Tony was told he was too young to join The Blessed, but his father, a church deacon, is not a member either. Maybe that's because the Pagano family files in the wrong tax bracket."

"That all fits, Jake, but if The Blessed are *cash cows,* what's in it for them? The simple promise of Heaven? I doubt it. What hold could Lundgren possibly have over Flood and a bunch of rich people?"

"If Lundgren knew about Flood's cocaine habit, the threat of disclosure might have been enough to gain the upper hand. But that doesn't explain The Blessed. I don't think a second-string preacher like Lundgren could force powerful, wealthy congregants to do anything against their will."

"Where the money trail dead ends, a side road usually forks off to either dope or sex. After what happened to Tony, I'm betting on drugs."

"Since we're speculating here, let's take the logic one step further, Tree. After his wife died, Flood was depressed and volatile … and vulnerable. Lundgren moved into the vicarage in Yuma to support him, but maybe he didn't simply *know* about Flood's addiction. What if he *introduced* Flood to illicit mood elevating substances, then took control of the operation."

"Mood elevating, like coke and amphetamines? If Lundgren supplied drugs to keep Flood on a leash, maybe he's doing the same with The Blessed. Could be he's supplying just enough for a pleasant religious high for some, and providing more for those who enjoyed the buzz. Maybe even increasing their dosage over time, slow enough that folks wouldn't notice. Once he's got them hooked, it would be the fox guarding the henhouse."

"Remember when Flood went on a rant in his sermon about how the government outlawed peyote from Native American religious ceremonies and tried to ban sacramental wine from Christian churches during Prohibition? His tirade sounded fanatical and personal to me. Maybe Lundgren even provides *hallucinogens* to help The Blessed feel the presence of God."

"Easy buddy. Peyote? Acid? We gotta walk before we try to run. If it's true that Lundgren has chemical leashes on The Blessed, though, that's a kennel full of high-priced pooches—and potentially a lot of overflowing collection plates. Pretty damn clever. I think we're on to something, but I need evidence. I will, however, *unleash* my army of trained bloodhounds and see if they can pick up the scent. And you, Jake, should keep nosing around the kennel. Talk with you soon."

After Tree hung up, my focus shifted to worries about my appointment with Bishop Lucci and the Superior General of my Order in the morning. There would be questions about my friendship with Emily, and I had no answers. I slept poorly that night.

CHAPTER THIRTY SEVEN

Tuesday, April 8, 9:30 a.m.

Flood and Lundgren were a distant memory the next morning. After offering Mass, I drove to my meeting with Bishop Lucci and The Very Reverend Father Stefano Demarco, the head of my Camillian Order. They would challenge my relationship with Emily and my commitment to the priesthood—and if I couldn't deftly maneuver my way through their interrogation, there would be consequences.

On the wrong side of this Inquisition, I wore our traditional black Camillian cassock emblazoned with a red cross on the front, hoping that my Superior General would think of me as an ally rather than an adversary.

The bishop's secretary, who usually had more interest in fashion magazines and nail polish than lowly priests, jumped to her feet the second I entered Lucci's waiting room.

"Good, you're here," she said. "The Superior General just arrived. Follow me, Father."

She whisked me past an oil portrait of Demarco, which hung near the bishop's likeness in his antechamber, and we entered Lucci's office.

The aroma of freshly brewed coffee filled the air, mingling with the sweet scent of pipe tobacco and the rich, earthy smell of the leather-bound books that filled the floor-to-ceiling bookcases. The bishop was a Diocesan priest, not an Order priest like me, and he had taken no vow of poverty. His luxurious chambers were filled with lavish furnishings and artwork that added the fragrance of money and power to the mix.

The two major earthly deities in my religious life were standing by the window, engrossed in a spirited conversation. Lucci wore a violet zucchetto skull cap with a purple sash draped over his robes indicative of his rank.

A jewel-encrusted pectoral cross hung from a gold chain around his beefy neck. In contrast to my black cassock, Demarco wore a white one with our red cross on the front, a reminder that although we were on the same team, he was the captain, coach, and club owner.

Unlike the rotund bishop, Stefano Demarco was an imposing man, broad-shouldered and well over six feet tall. Although middle-aged, his slicked-back hair and meticulously-manicured beard were the color of printer's ink without a trace of gray. His complexion was sun-kissed, suggesting that he did not linger inside at meetings unnecessarily. I overheard them mention "The Greg," the Pontifical Gregorian University in Rome, where they had both received their religious education and doctorates. Lucci patted his political ally and benefactor gently on the arm and chuckled. Demarco nodded and took a sip of coffee, the Church pecking order on full display.

Lucci's secretary cleared her throat, announced my arrival, and scurried from the room so as to avoid shrapnel when my vocation detonated. The bishop introduced me, his eyes cold and hard as stones. My relationship with Emily had placed him in a compromised position with his friend and mentor, and he made no effort to hide his disdain.

In contrast, Demarco gave me a cryptic Buddha-like smile, his ash-gray eyes alive with curiosity. In a basso profundo voice with only a faint hint of an Italian accent, he said, "Ah, Father Austin, at last we meet in person." No handshake or offer of coffee. Apparently our meeting would not take long. "I've heard a great deal about you and your ... *exploits*." He pointed to a leather chair. "Please take a seat."

My *exploits?* Was he talking about saving Lucci's life and unmasking a fraudulent "miracle," or choosing to raise my nephew and clinging to my relationship with Emily? I sat and drew a slow, deep breath.

They took the two matching chairs across from me. Each waited for the other to begin, resulting in a painful silence.

Lucci glanced at Demarco and took command. "I won't beat around the bush, Father. Where do things stand with your lady friend?" He gazed at me as if he were dealing with a dullard who couldn't follow simple instructions. "I warned you to burn that bridge to your past. Have you broken off your relationship with her yet?"

Demarco's eyebrows knitted together and the corners of his mouth turned down. He glared at the bishop. For months, Lucci had kept him in the dark about Emily because I had saved his life in July, and Demarco was clearly displeased to be left out of the loop.

The bishop and I had assumed that my involvement with Emily was the reason the Superior General had called the meeting. We had both been mistaken, and Lucci's comment had inadvertently changed the agenda. Dread settled in the pit of my stomach.

The bishop had made it clear that he was no longer willing to protect me. He redirected Demarco's displeasure toward me.

"As your spiritual head, I've told you *repeatedly* that you needed to sort out this issue." He shook his head, his wattle and jowls swaying side to side. "I'd assumed you had. What steps have you taken?"

I hesitated, and Demarco leveled a stony, measured stare at me. "A woman? Yes, Father Austin, tell me about her and your ... *friendship*."

My first inclination was to lie, or at least to project a rosy, G-rated version of our relationship. I wanted to say that Emily and I had resolved our feelings for each other and we were now just pals. If Demarco suspected that I was lying, I would be drummed out of the priesthood in disgrace, and if he believed that the bishop had been complicit in the cover-up, Lucci's fast-track journey to Archbishop was at an end.

Lucci looked away and sipped his coffee—like a modern-day Pontius Pilate, washing his hands of any responsibility for my downfall. One thing was certain, if a career was to be sacrificed today, it was not going to be his.

Silence filled the room. Decision time.

I stared at the crucifix on the wall. There was no painless answer. I loved God and the priesthood—and I loved Emily—and I didn't want to give up *either*. It was as simple, and complex, as that. Denying my feelings for her was as absurd as asking the sun not to set in the west.

Over the past year, I had pondered our dilemma until my head throbbed and prayed until my knees ached. Unable to untie the Gordian knot that our relationship presented, I decided to place my faith and my destiny in the hands of a higher power—if not God, then my Superior General.

I came clean and told Demarco everything from the beginning, including my unwavering commitment to raise my nephew, and my passionate kiss with Emily. When I had completely bared my soul, I added, "But please understand, although I've struggled with my feelings for Emily, we've not been intimate. I've never violated my vow of chastity."

Silence filled the room as Demarco took it all in. He steepled his hands and tapped his fingertips together, inclining his head to one side as if listening to something faint and faraway.

Lucci squirmed in his chair, his eyes ping-ponging between Demarco and me until he finally said, "That's an exceedingly lax definition of chastity, Father. You're ignoring purity of conduct and intention. Kissing parishioners isn't the least bit *chaste* in my opinion. I'm done coddling you. You've had more than a fair chance. It's clear that—"

Demarco raised a hand to silence him, then turned to me with a *Lord-give-me-patience* expression.

"I've read your file, Father Austin, and know you came late to the priesthood. I entered the seminary when I was eighteen, so I've had many more years than you've had to contemplate the problem of love, as well as desire. Your feelings for this woman are … natural, nothing to be ashamed of. God will not judge you for that." He stroked his beard. "Anyone who *doesn't* desire marriage and family should rethink the priesthood, because a priest is married to the Church and is the spiritual father of his congregation. Contrary to what outsiders may think, it takes a *courageous* man to become a priest. You must be sure here," he tapped his chest, "who you are, and be unafraid to acknowledge that priests are called to be different. Not better. Simply different."

I was completely dumbfounded. Lucci's head swiveled in my Superior General's direction, a tinge of disapproval evident on his lips. He cocked one bushy eyebrow and his nostrils flared. His Excellency clearly had hoped for punishment and retribution, rather than understanding and forgiveness.

Demarco closed his eyes and pinched the bridge of his nose, then he rose to his full height, walked to the window, gazed out onto the city streets, and spoke softly. "It's hard to live with one foot in this world, and one in the next. We all hear the whispers, the derisive comments, the mocking. It can be painful. Although you may at times be shunned, know that the priesthood is a privilege and a grave responsibility that Jesus Christ himself has called us to. When the demands of the Church seem too much, remember that." He spun around and looked directly at me. "As you do the work of the Lord, Father, never forget the Lord of the work. It takes a man's man to be a priest today. Our calling is not for the faint of heart. It requires an inner strength to defy the insults and assaults of a cynical, secular world."

Demarco returned to his seat. "Let me be honest with you, Father. When you joined the Order of the Ministers of the Sick, you were a perfect fit for us. We have many Camillian members who are nurses, social workers, and therapists, but few physicians. I understand your need to care for your nephew, and I will support your effort. I also know that you must do what you must do with regard to this woman who has a hold on your heart—but we would hate to lose you if you choose her over the priesthood. Your loss would be particularly hard for me in light of the reason that I requested this meeting."

I was lost for words but managed, "Which was?"

"I've been impressed by the finesse with which you managed the bleeding statue case, your tenacity and courage when threatened by drug dealers and murderers, and your ability to work with law enforcement. I came here today to offer you a position as my personal consultant and investigator. You would be stationed with me in Milwaukee."

Lucci's mouth dropped open and his eyes widened.

My head was spinning. "Investigator? I don't understand."

"We Camillians are not without our problems. Reports of theft, violence, abuse, fraud, and even the occasional unexplained miracle land on my desk. And I've made it my personal crusade to root out pedophiles from our Order. I require someone willing to pursue the evidence wherever it goes. Someone I trust, who won't back down." He took a swallow of coffee. "Running our day-to-day operations and collaborating with Rome allows me little time to handle other problems. I need a right-hand-man. Since the day I first learned of your encounter with a serial killer, I've followed your exploits. From all the accounts I've heard and read, Jacob, you'd fit the bill nicely."

I was thrilled that the focus of the meeting had changed, but shocked at where the discussion had gone—and also by how intrigued I was by Demarco's offer. Truth be told, I had come to enjoy investigating mysteries and working with the sheriff. The investigator position would provide endless interesting opportunities and I desperately wanted to accept it, but it also presented obstacles.

"I must say, I'm honored and tempted by your offer, however I'm completely committed to raising my nephew."

"I understand and support your loyalty and compassion. Bring the boy with you to Milwaukee. But be honest with me. Is he the sole reason you're hesitating, or are you *unwilling* to leave your lady friend?"

"It's more complicated than that. My nephew's only five and has finally become comfortable here. And I have a support system in town to help me care for him. I'm not willing to uproot him by moving to Wisconsin." How much more to tell him? "You know how lonesome the religious life can be. Being assigned here restored my two closest friends to my life, so yes, I'm reluctant to move and give that up. But it's more than that. Emily is seriously ill and just had surgery for cancer. I want to see her through these dark times."

"That poses a problem. I can provide caregivers for your nephew in Milwaukee, and we need physicians to treat the poor at our hospitals too, but moving there is a requirement of the job." I hesitated and Demarco muttered, "You're a complicated man, Jacob, and you are not making this easy for me. But it may take a complex man to be my consultant and troubleshooter, and to do the work I require."

Bishop Lucci's expression drooped like soft tallow. He finally found his voice. "There's still the unresolved issue of your current relationship. It's unclear whether you'll even be a priest in a year from now."

I looked at Demarco. "With Emily fighting cancer, she needs all the support she can get. Please don't force me to desert her."

"Only you can decide what to do. Pray hard about it. The Lord will guide you."

"I *have been* praying, but God seems more prone to whispers and masquerades than straight answers."

Maybe He had already answered, and I hadn't wanted to hear His response. *Denial* can be deafening.

"Then pray harder, Father. He will respond. Maybe not with the answer you'd hope for, but He will guide you. Of this I am certain."

"And if Emily and I decide to pursue a relationship, and I leave the priesthood? What then?"

"I ... would be disappointed. You've done exemplary work with the sick, the poor, and the suffering at St Joseph's Hospital. It's clear you care deeply about Mother Church, and I trust your judgment in the face of adversity. I can't hire an outside private investigator for this work. It requires a *priest*, someone with knowledge of, and entree into, the religious world. No, leaving the priesthood would be a deal breaker. You must decide. Once and for all. And I'll need your answer in the near future. Here is my private phone number." He walked over, gave me his card, and offered a hand. I stood and we shook. "Go with God, Jacob. Ask for His guidance. And call me ... soon."

CHAPTER THIRTY EIGHT

Tuesday, April 8, 11:30 a.m.

I don't remember driving to the hospital. I'd gone into the meeting expecting Demarco and Lucci to force me into making a decision about my relationship with Emily. Now I also had to decide about accepting an assignment as my Superior General's consultant and investigator, a job I very much wanted, but one that would uproot little RJ and tear me away from Emily and Tree.

The Urgent Care waiting room was overflowing and rather than think about momentous decisions, I buried myself in my work. At lunchtime, I grabbed a sandwich and called to check on Emily's status. She was stable postoperatively and scheduled for discharge in the afternoon. I wanted to phone Dr. Glade and challenge her seemingly premature release from the hospital, but he was her physician and I understood that the decision was his.

It took most of the afternoon to clear the patient backlog in Urgent Care. I'd just poured a cup of coffee and parked my tired behind in a breakroom chair when Nurse Ochs entered, leveled a mischievous grin at me, and said that I had a visitor in room four.

Emily sat on the exam table wearing jeans and a loose-fitting, flowered blouse. She was drawn and pale but beaming.

"Hi, doctor."

"Em! What are you doing here?" I stepped toward her, intending to give her a hug, but stopped short. "I've been filling God's inbox with prayers for you since your surgery. It's wonderful to see you, but you should be in bed resting."

"Relax. I'm doing fine and wanted to share my good news. Do you have time to talk?"

"Of course."

"Dr. Glade is confident he removed the entire tumor. It wasn't as large or aggressive as it appeared on the mammogram. There was no definite evidence of spread, so he cancelled the mastectomy and closed my incision."

"That's wonderful, Em!" I couldn't stop myself and gave her a gentle hug, avoiding any contact with her surgical site. "I'm so happy for you."

"Easy, Jake. I'm not out of the woods yet. You know that. But if the pathologist confirms that all my lymph nodes are negative and my scans remain normal, I may not need radiation or chemotherapy. Fingers crossed."

"That's great news." I moved a negative pathology report to the top of my prayer list.

"If all goes well, I'll have over a ninety percent chance of a cure, but … maybe it's *you* who should go home to bed and rest. You sound completely exhausted."

"I am."

She chuckled.

"What's so funny?"

"I just thought of a joke. A Catholic priest, an exhausted parent, and a physician walk into a bar …."

"What's the punchline, Em?"

"He only needed one barstool."

"And three shots of Jim Beam."

The smile slipped from her lips. She paused and wound a strand of auburn hair around her finger. "I could use a favor, Jake."

"Sure. What is it?"

"Before the Diocesan Tribunal rules on my annulment request, would you ask Bishop Lucci to testify on my behalf? A good word from him might swing the vote."

A good word? Doubtful. The man lived by the rulebook, and had always taken a hard line against annulments. He was more about the letter of the law than the spirit, and not fond of exceptions of any kind. If our meeting with Demarco had gone better, maybe he would have considered the idea, but I was definitely in Lucci's doghouse, especially when it came to my relationship with Emily.

"He won't help. He and I have had another falling out. Besides, Cannon Law gives him no voice in the matter. The outcome rests solely with the three-judge panel." I watched her hope deflate. "Let's see what the Tribunal decides, and go from there, okay?"

I was about to tell her about Demarco's offer when there was a pounding on the examination room door and Nurse Ochs charged in. "Doctor, one of our patients is having chest pain. We're getting a stat EKG now. I'll grab a crash cart."

I gave Emily a peck on the cheek and followed Ochs down the hallway, glad for the diversion. The day had crashed over me like raging surf. I didn't know how to begin to make decisions about my future and needed time to think.

When my workday ended, I was still in a muddle. RJ was engrossed by a cartoon show on TV when I relieved Colleen. I set my black bag in my bedroom, removed my tie, and stared at the letter from the Episcopal Church, wondering if it was my Plan B. If I converted, I could remain a priest *and* have Emily fully in my life, but it meant leaving the faith I loved.

I picked up the envelope, hesitated, and threw it into the wastebasket. I had no plan B.

I closed the door, dropped to my knees, and made the sign of the cross. "Lord, Your servant's path has forked. I'm lost and confused. I can barely see the road ahead and don't know where it will lead. Please guide my heart and my head on the journey that pleases You. Thy will be done. This I ask in Jesus's name. Amen."

CHAPTER THIRTY NINE

Wednesday, April 9, 2:00 p.m.

Morning Mass went smoothly, and I was cruising through a quiet day in Urgent Care when Tree phoned.

"My attempt to get a search warrant for the Church of Eternal Release crashed and burned. Judge *Donna Even Thinkaboutit* said I didn't have enough hard evidence, so I'm gonna run a sting-operation at the seven o'clock worship service to get a closer look at the members of The Blessed. I could use your help, Jake. Can you attend tonight?"

My gut clenched into a knot. When Tree talked about "sting operations," it made me anxious. I had witnessed one in the past that had strayed beyond the letter of the law and verged on entrapment.

"I don't know, Tree. Tonight's not good for me. I want to spend more time with RJ, and I've been asking Colleen to put in too many hours caring for him as it is."

"Come on buddy, I need an operative inside the church to verify something for me. It can't be one of my troops because someone in that large crowd might recognize him, and I don't want to alert Lundgren that I'm eyeballing his operation. It's a memorial service tonight to honor Reverend Flood. You knew him and can go to pay your respects. No one will think twice. I wouldn't ask if it wasn't important."

"And by *operative*, do you mean *stooge*? You suckered me into that role once, and that's not going to happen again."

"Scouts honor. No shenanigans, I swear. I just need to find enough evidence to convince the judge to issue a warrant. I got two dead bodies now, and I want to shut that place down. You said it yourself, the church has stockpiled a mountain of cash to build a school. If Lundgren gets spooked, there's nothing to stop him from grabbing the money and disappearing. Please Jake."

"Okay, okay. I'll ask Colleen. But the last time I was involved in one of your schemes, you colored way outside the lines, and I darn-near had to perjure myself in court." After falsifying Mrs. Hudson's insurance form, however, I knew I was throwing stones in my own glass house. "Let me be clear. I won't lie to protect you, and I won't break the law, Tree." I thought I heard glass shatter.

"You won't have to. Promise. Try to get there early and weasel your way into the special prayer meeting Lundgren holds for The Blessed at six-thirty. See if you notice anything hinky."

"All right, fine, I'll go."

"Thanks. One more thing. Drink the Communion wine. That's important." Someone hollered Tree's name. "Sorry, gotta run. Later, buddy." And he was gone.

Was I to be back to my role as a human guinea pig? Here we go again.

Although I knew what was coming, I telephoned Colleen. "I hate to ask this, but can you stay late again tonight and care for RJ?"

"Think nothing of it. I'm always happy to sacrifice my own needs to suit your every whim, Father. And don't you fret about RJ. He had a splendid time with you at Christmas, and he's looking forward to seeing you again after Easter." She mumbled something in Gaelic which did not sound complimentary. "I must go now and cook and clean so that the manor house is ready when your Highness finally returns." Click.

We Catholics are masters at dispensing guilt, but Colleen had honed the skill into an art form.

I finished my shift, hurried to the rectory, ate dinner with RJ and Colleen, then threw on a sport coat. I was on my way out the door when a parishioner telephoned. Mrs. Burton's husband was once again donating much of his salary to the ponies at the racetrack. She was distraught and after I had settled her down, I set up a pastoral counseling appointment for the couple. In the meantime, I suggested that she contact Gam-Anon, which provides support to families of problem gamblers.

Our phone session took longer than I'd anticipated, and by the time I arrived at the Church of Eternal Release it was after six-thirty. Two dozen expensive, exotic automobiles were parked near the entrance, no doubt the carriages of The *Financially* Blessed attending the pre-service soiree.

As Tree and I had suspected, membership in this club obviously required a healthy bank account.

Only one car was parked next door at the vicarage. What surprised me was that it was the sleek red Lexus SC430, not the road-weary SUV I'd seen on prior visits. Tree and I had assumed that the Lexus was Flood's. We'd been mistaken. This hundred grand of steel and chrome belonged to the Right Reverend Lundgren. *Follow the Money.*

I was walking toward the church entrance when a motorcycle roared into the parking lot. Piotr, the church organist, hopped off, removed his helmet, and waved.

"Hey, Father. What a pleasant surprise. Didn't expect to see you here again."

"I'm paying my respects to Reverend Flood. His passing must be a huge blow to his congregation. By the way, thanks for helping the Sheriff to identify the man in the yellow sports car."

"No problem. I am here on a student visa and want to stay on good terms with the authorities." He stopped walking. "If I may ask, how are you involved in all this?"

A darn good question. "Sheriff Macon and I are friends. I passed your observation on to him. Has that man returned?"

"Not that I have seen."

"Reverend Lundgren has big shoes to fill now. Do you know him well?"

"I do not. I always dealt with Reverend Flood."

"Pity. I was hoping to join the prayer meeting that he holds before each church service but I arrived too late. Have you ever been?"

"The one for The Blessed? No, I am just the lowly organist. They are a select group, and one must be invited to that service. However, I am not sure I would care to join them. There is a … tension about them. They are, how do you say it, a bit tightly-wound? There seems to be … I don't know."

"Seems to be what, Piotr?"

"Friction in the group. Recently, I have seen bickering among the members. I come to church to worship God with my music, not for intrigue and politics." He eyed me warily, then began walking. "Sorry, I must go in, Father, and prepare my program."

I entered the church nave as the members of The Blessed were filing into the two front pews for the service. One elderly man with a mop of curly white hair intercepted Lundgren. They had a brief, heated exchange. When the man gestured angrily toward him, Lundgren stormed away.

As the rest of the congregation poured in, I slipped into the third row of pews. I sat near the old man but directly behind a huge bear of a fellow, hoping his bulk would shield me from Lundgren's line of sight. I wanted to overhear anything the elderly gentleman might say to the others, but he remained mute.

The service was much like those I had seen Flood perform, but lacked the same pizazz. No miraculous laying-on-of-hands healings or swooning worshipers at this service. Lundgren did, however, personally pass out the communion bread and wine to The Blessed as Flood had done.

The major difference in the service was Lundgren's impassioned appeal for donations to the school building fund in honor of Jeremiah Flood. Halfway through Lundgren's sales pitch, the old man in front of me grumbled softly and dropped his gaze to his hands.

When the service ended, Lundgren charged down the center aisle toward the exit, glad-handing worshipers along the way. After he'd passed by, an elegantly dressed woman turned to the old man and asked, "Well, what did he say?" The man just shook his head and walked away.

I slipped out a side door to avoid the adoring masses lined up at the church entrance waiting to congratulate the pastor on his sermon. I hurried to my car, and phoned Tree. "Okay Sheriff, I drank the communion wine. What now?"

"Stop by the station house on your way to the rectory and tell the desk sergeant you're there to have blood drawn. He'll understand. Did you notice any change in the behavior of The Blessed before and after the prayer meeting?"

"They were already coming out of the meeting room when I arrived, so I can't compare. The organist mentioned that he sensed friction among the group, and I witnessed a confrontation between Lundgren and an elderly gentleman before the service."

"Perfect. What'd the man look like?"

I described him.

"Where are you now, Jake?"

"In the parking lot."

"Good. I need you to find out what kind of car the old man drives and call me. Get the license plate number if you can. I'll explain later. Anything else?"

"Well, Lundgren served Communion to The Blessed, the same way Flood had. The rest of the congregation received less personal attention. Oh, one other thing. That expensive Lexus belongs to Lundgren, not Flood."

"Interesting. Call me as soon as you spot the old man's car."

I pulled onto the grass on the left side of the parking lot exit where I could see the drivers leaving the church. The elderly man must have bypassed Lundgren and gone directly to his car because he was one of the first to leave the lot. I called Tree.

"The man who confronted Lundgren is driving a silver Cadillac DeVille with a black vinyl top." I gave Tree the license plate number.

"Thanks, Jake. Your work is done. Get your blood drawn, and go home and play with your boy. I owe you big time. I'll stop by with a six-pack of gratitude. Later, buddy."

CHAPTER FORTY

Thursday, April 10, 1:00 p.m.

Part way through my Urgent Care shift the next day, Nurse Ochs informed me that a patient in the Emergency Room was asking to see me. When I arrived in the ER, I found Sister Angelica lying on a bed in cubical five wrapped in a hospital gown. Her once beautiful face was covered in bruises the color of rotting fruit, and there were deep gashes on her left cheek and forehead. X-rays of her abdomen and skull hung from the view box on the wall. Her right hand and wrist was grotesquely deformed and immobilized by an aluminum splint.

"Oh Father," she whimpered when she saw me. "I should have listened to you!"

"Angelica! What happened?"

"We got a call on the trafficking hotline about a nail salon on Harvard. The cops didn't seem to care, so yesterday I went to get my nails done and check the place out. When I walked back to my car in the parking lot behind the building, I noticed that my windshield wipers had been zip-tied together while I was inside. I assumed it was a prank by some kids." She began to sob, struggling to get the words out. "With no other cars in the lot, I should have driven away … but while I was taking the plastic cables off, two guys grabbed me. I couldn't get to the pepper spray in my purse. They … kept beating me, kicking me, stomping on my hands, warning me to mind my own business. They took my car keys and threw me in the back seat. One of them forced my mouth open and made me drink whiskey, kept pouring it in."

I dialed Tree Macon and told him what had happened. He said he was nearby and would come himself. I turned to Angelica. "Why didn't you bring your football jock friends to protect you?"

"Defensive linemen at a nail salon? I wanted to breeze in and out, and not be noticed. Guess I asked the wrong questions." She massaged her abdomen and moaned. "Next thing I knew, I came to on the floor in the back seat of my car smelling like a damn distillery, an empty booze bottle next to me. My front bumper was crushed against a bridge abutment." She forced herself to sit up and winced. Although a tear rolled down her cheek, I could see anger in her eyes. "I called 911 and told the police what happened. They didn't buy it. While we waited for an ambulance to arrive, they *ticketed me* for reckless driving and DUI!" A long moment passed as sorrow swept away her anger and she wept freely. "The doctor said my hand and wrist are going to need a lot of surgery and I might never …."

"Can you describe the guys, Angelica?"

"Big. Both Asian, like the girls in the salon. It's all pretty foggy, hard to remember details." She wiped tears onto the sleeve of the hospital gown, then the anger flared again in her eyes. "You know what this means, Father?"

"What?"

"I'm getting close. Close enough to rattle them. Maybe close to my sister." She blew her nose into a tissue, turning it blood red. "I can't prove it, Father, but that nail salon screams forced labor. It's got most of the warning signs."

The literature she had given me on human trafficking two weeks earlier lay unread on my desk, and I felt I'd let her down. Before I could ask my next question, Tree hurried in and took command.

"What warning signs, Sister?" He withdrew a spiral notebook from his uniform pocket and scribbled something. "Tell me about that nail joint."

"The three Asian girls working there, and I do mean 'girls,' looked like they should have been in junior high. They were all skin-and-bones and avoided eye contact with me. None of them spoke unless spoken to, and when they did, they all used the same few words in broken English, as if they were reading from a script. And anytime they opened their mouths, the old lady who runs the place glowered at them."

"Could it simply be a family run business, and the woman is their grandmother?" I asked.

"That's what I wondered. So after I paid the old woman, I gave my girl a nice tip. As I walked out the door, the old lady grabbed the cash and chewed her out. Not in English, but the message was clear. The windows, however, convinced me. The front windows of the shop had no metal bars or security shutters, but there *were* bars on the back ones. From the parking lot, it looked like a prison, like ....”

“Like the girls were locked up at night,” Tree said, finishing her thought. “Sounds like forced servitude to me. Any signs of violence?”

“The girl doing my nails was missing two teeth, and she had a bruise on one arm that could have been an imprint from fingers, as if she’d been manhandled or yanked to her feet.”

“I’m gonna need a formal statement, Sister, and I’ll have a sketch artist stop by,” he said, then focused on me. “Problem is, Jake, it’ll be hard to shut down the nail joint legally unless the girls are willing to testify, so you better touch base with Agent Novak. Fill her in and see if she’s willing to get her task force involved. Maybe they can do an extraction of those girls.”

CHAPTER FORTY ONE

Thursday, April 10, 2:00 p.m.

I found an unoccupied examination room and called Keri Novak, expecting to get her voicemail. Wrong again.

"Father, what a surprise. I'd say a *pleasant* surprise, but you only call when the crap is hitting the fan. What's up?"

I reminded her about Miriam's disappearance and filled her in on Angelica's attack at the nail salon. "Agent Gates told me about Save Our Kids, the team you're organizing that rescues victims of human trafficking. Could they help assist local law enforcement here?"

"S.O.K.'s not operational. Won't be for a couple years. It'll probably take me that long to fill out the damn bureaucratic paperwork. I'm still setting up training facilities, recruiting operatives, and interviewing prospects. That's why I'm at Wright-Patterson Air Force Base in Dayton today." She went quiet for a while. "Listen, Father, S.O.K. is hush-hush. Gates shouldn't have mentioned it. We don't want to show our hand too early. You can't breathe a word of this."

"I won't. Promise."

She sighed. "These clowns really beat up a nun to silence her? Makes me want to personally perp-walk the bastards into a cell. It's stories like this that led me to organize the strike force." A pause. "Let me think about it, and I'll call you when I'm done here. That's the best I can do."

"I understand. Thanks for your time. Bye."

I was disappointed, and after seeing what had happened to Angelica, I was also mad as hell. The ball was now in Tree's court, and I wanted to help in any way I could. I removed Agent Gates' card from my wallet and dialed his number. A woman answered.

"Philco Waste Management."

"Agent Gates, please."

"Never heard of any *Gates*. How'd you get this number?"

"He gave it to me."

"That right? Name?"

"Father Jake Austin. I'm calling on behalf of Sheriff Macon in Ohio."

"Hang on while I ask around."

Although I spend a lot of time on hold these day, this silence seemed to last forever.

"Gates here. I haven't forgotten about you, Father. How could I forget Keri Novak's personal confessor? Listen Padre, we have a backlog of cases, and these things take time. If we had come up with the name of a perp or a location, I'd have called. You gotta be patient." He sounded irritated, and I didn't want to alienate him. "All I can tell you so far is that your victim was being groomed by a predator of some kind."

"What does that mean?"

"He followed the standard script, befriending a vulnerable kid with no means of support. When Miriam couldn't pay the rent, he paid it, dropped off some food, and most likely threw in some free drugs because they were *pals*. The usual. That's where the online trail gets cold. They were scheduled to meet in person, and he probably offered her money for some minor transgression at that point, maybe stealing a bottle of wine—followed by gently guiding her to bigger and badder indiscretions, like cash for a hand-job or a blow-job. You get the picture. It's a process that leads to learned hopelessness, despair, and desperation. These scumbags are persistent and ruthless. But this one's trail is buried deep. We haven't been able to track him down yet."

"Sorry, I didn't mean to hassle you, but the violence associated with Miriam's disappearance is ratcheting up. Her sister was attacked yesterday and she's on her way into surgery. Any help would be appreciated."

Gates drew a deep breath. "Okay, hold on a sec." I heard computer keys clacking. "The only other thing we know, Father, is that the perp was messaging Miriam in Spanish. The girl is fluent in it. Traffickers love that. Once she's seduced into prostitution, they can sell her overseas, far away from prosecution by U.S law enforcement, perhaps in Venezuela where there's a high demand. Unfortunately, all Miriam's messages are routed through servers around the world, and tracing them to the sender is slow and tedious work. I'll call you when we have something solid. Gotta run. Later, Father."

CHAPTER FORTY TWO

Thursday, April 10, 4:00 p.m.

American girls being trafficked, both in this country and overseas? I couldn't wrap my head around it. When my shift ended, I stopped in to see Sister Angelica in the recovery room. Her hand and wrist were wrapped in a surgical dressing and she was groggy. I told her what Agent Gates had said.

"Spanish came easy to Miriam, Father, and she enjoyed it. She was failing everything else, but she always aced Spanish." Her words were slurred, and her eyelids were at half-mast. "After our dad died, she stayed in the apartment. I would stop by whenever the convent permitted. A couple times she had school chums over. Whenever they didn't want me to understand something, they'd switch to Spanish." She moistened her lips with a glycerin swab and sucked it like a lollypop. "With our Mom and Dad gone, I became … the party-pooper in her life, the enemy. They referred to me as *Sister Sister*, a member of the *God-Squad*—which made me even less cool than a parent."

"Did Miriam have a job?" She shook her head. "Then how'd she pay the rent?"

"She said her *friends* helped. The landlord told me Miriam was often late, but always paid, usually in cash. Two months ago, when he threatened to evict her, I gave her what little money I had. Next thing I knew, she was gone, vanished." Angelica fought her drooping eyelids back up. "But there's no way she'd leave her computer and game console behind. I took them for safe keeping, thinking she'd show up, but she stopped calling. I knew something bad must have happened. That's when I contacted the police and came to you for help."

"A seventeen year old living alone? Didn't Child Protective Services step in?"

"They tried, Father, but Miriam kept them in the dark. She convinced them that I was living there and taking care of her. Whenever they showed up to check, she said I was at work. She even gave them the number of a burner phone, and would speak with them as if she were me when they called."

I considered Gates' comment about predators befriending indigent teens. "You said her *friends* helped with rent and food. Do you know who they were?"

She yawned. "The two I met were from her school, but I don't remember their names."

"I'll pick up class yearbooks. Maybe you can ID them."

"Good idea. Thanks, Father."

She was asleep before I could leave the room.

I have a parishioner who works at the high school. I phoned and asked her to borrow recent yearbooks, then swung by her home after work and picked them up.

To my surprise, a county sheriff's cruiser was waiting for me when I returned to the rectory.

CHAPTER FORTY THREE

Thursday, April 10, 5:45 p.m.

Tree Macon stepped from the car and walked over. "What's with the shocked look, Jake? I promised adult beverages in payment for your help." He raised a six-pack of Guinness in the air and chuckled. "Heck man, you should get a sign that reads: 'Will work for beer.' "

He draped an arm around my shoulder and spun me toward the door. "My wife's out of town, and … when the warden's away, the inmates will play. I thought we could watch the Cavaliers beat the Celtics tonight. Besides, Colleen's a better cook than me, and I want to spend some time with my favorite five year old."

Tree, RJ, and I feasted on Colleen's tuna casserole, the one topped with Parmesan cheese, smoked paprika, and panko bread crumbs. I made a pitch to play Candy Land. Tree's presence would have made the board game particularly entertaining for me because it allowed me to watch his hard-ass image morph to candy-ass as he moved his playing piece from Candy Cane Forest to the Gumdrop Mountains.

RJ and Tree, however, went all macho and outvoted me, demanding to play soldier. As always, Tree and I fought valiantly against General RJ's plastic army but were soundly defeated moments before my nephew's bedtime.

After RJ was asleep, I popped the tops on two bottles of beer, handed one to Tree, and we settled in front of the television to watch basketball. We enjoyed an hour of hoops, light banter, and a sense of normality but at halftime, reality set in. I told Tree about my conversations with Agents Novak and Gates, and with Sister Angelica.

"Think you're in the wrong business, Father. You'd have made a super full-time confidential informant and professional snoop."

"Thanks, boss. That means a lot coming from you." I hit the mute button on the remote. "I'll take the yearbooks to Angelica tomorrow and see if she can identify Miriam's school friends."

"Good. But the 'sale of sex slaves overseas' is way above my pay grade. You'd better keep Agent Novak in the loop. We may need her. I'll have our undercover cops focus on the Hispanic community and get the word out to area cop-shops. Maybe we'll catch a break."

"Anything happen with the nail salon?"

"The deputies I sent got stonewalled by the old Asian lady who runs the place, and the young girls working there refused to say boo. We asked to see the rest of the building and the woman refused. Definitely looks like involuntary servitude, but without a warrant I'm dead in the water. This would be a perfect job for Keri Novak and her extraction team."

"Her teams not up and running yet, and may not be for a while. Anything come out of your sting operation at the church yesterday?"

"Not what I'd hoped. I had a couple of cruisers monitoring the cars as they left the church parking lot. They had the names and license plate numbers of all the members of The Blessed. I was hoping to catch someone driving erratically so I could demand a blood test. By the way, you were my control subject, and your bloodwork was negative, as expected. If Lundgren was doling out uppers, he didn't share them with the entire congregation."

"Wait. Back up the law-enforcement bus, Tree. I know cops can demand a breathalyzer test, but can they order someone to take a *blood* test?"

"Ohio's implied consent law is pretty tough, Jake. If the officer actually arrests you and suspects drugs, he can choose whatever type of test he wants—including urine or blood. And in some circumstances, he can use 'reasonable force' to take a sample."

"That sounds draconian."

"Harsh maybe, but you consent to the law when you get your driver's license."

"So tell me. Did you catch anyone?"

"Yeah, one speeder who was twice the legal limit for booze, but he had no amphetamines in his system. The guy's the church janitor, not a member of The Blessed. He boozes at the church 'cause his wife won't let him touch the stuff at home. It was his second DUI and when we pressed him, he let slip that he often sees members of The Blessed come to the church at all hours, day or night, for special one-on-one prayer meetings with Reverend Lundgren."

"Actually, that fits. I think Lundgren is using low doses to simply enhance the religious zeal of the service. His goal is probably to produce dependency on the church, not addiction. But the more habituated you are to a drug, the more often you want another hit. Sunday and Wednesday services might not be enough. Withdrawal symptoms start after a couple days, but if you weren't aware that you were being drugged, you might not think much about it. The symptoms are fairly nonspecific. Depression, fatigue, trouble sleeping, irritability, and anxiety. You might assume it was a mild flu or a cold and wait it out. Or you might even talk to your minister about feeling anxious and depressed, and Lundgren would give you some spiritual guidance and a hit of amphetamine-laced wine—and each time you'd come away feeling better. That kind of positive reinforcement in itself could be addicting."

"Makes sense. Most of the Blessed are ambitious, professionally successful people. A regular hit of medicinal energy in their lives would be welcomed. I haven't come across anyone who dropped out of the group or lodged a complaint." Tree's mobile chimed. He checked the number and silenced it. "But what if they complained to their physician instead of Lundgren?"

"For symptoms of anxiety, fatigue, and depression? Most doctors would do routine bloodwork and review the patient's current prescriptions, then look for psychological causes. No physician I know would initially run a tox screen for those common symptoms. Remember, most likely Lundgren dispenses frequent, *low* doses of the drug to keep them coming back. If the patient stopped going to church while sick, their blood levels would soon be undetectable. And if they returned to church, the next dose would make them feel better, and they'd probably credit their physician."

"Damn." Tree slapped his knee. "Lundgren's available 24/7 for a quick Bible reading and another hit. Nifty little scam. He's not selling, he's doling out drugs for free. And his grateful worshipers reward him with tax-deductible contributions."

"It's a hell of a setup. A tax deduction for getting stoned as well as laundering money in a tax-free church account? You're right, I am in the wrong business." I sipped my Guinness. "Do you think Flood was in on the scam? Could he have been an innocent dupe in all of this? The priest

I spoke with in Arizona said that Flood and Lundgren both left Yuma suddenly. Could be the heat was on, and Lundgren convinced him to move across the country. Flood was depressed after his wife's death and might not have resisted."

"More likely, Lundgren supplied cocaine to Flood when he was depressed and mourning his wife, Jake. Once he was addicted, good old Rex was not only Flood's dealer but also a potential blackmailer. If Flood resisted in any way, Lundgren could rat him out to the police." Tree dragged a big hand down his face. "If that's true, Rex *earned* his nickname, *T. Rex*, because he is the biggest, baddest predator in the swamp."

"And if Lundgren was recruiting thugs from Grafton for his operation by using Flood as the drug mule to sneak dope into the prison, he was never at risk of arrest himself. Smart." I took a long draw of my beer. "Besides the church janitor, did you stop any of The Blessed leaving the service?"

"We pulled over one member for a broken tail light, told him he was weaving, and tried to convince him to take a blood test, but the guy was a lawyer. He told us to go straight to Hell."

"What about the elderly man in the silver Cadillac who argued with Lundgren?"

"I stopped him myself. He rolled through a stop sign and was going five miles over the speed limit. It was obvious he was scared out of his mind, so I switched to my bad cop role."

Tree raised his voice, gesturing as he spoke. The more we reviewed the case, the more energized he became. "When the old man told me he was an accountant, I pressed him and he admitted to serving as the treasurer for the Church of Eternal Release. He was clearly a weak link in the chain, so I put the fear of God in him by making him drive to the station house, where I told him we had proof of financial malfeasance and fraud at the church. He nearly shit his pants. I also said Flood was murdered and he was a suspect since we'd found his fingerprints in the office."

"Is any of that true?"

"Heck no, but he didn't know that."

"What? Are you allowed to lie to suspects? Is that another Ohio loophole?"

"Not just Ohio, Jake, everywhere—within limits. We can't coerce a confession or use physical force, but we can play fast and loose with the truth. I'm a seasoned performer in the art of the bluff. That's why I always beat you in poker." Tree picked up a Lego from the floor and tossed it to me. "I also told the old guy we had an eyewitness who saw him arguing with Lundgren. That broke the dam and the truth came pouring out."

RJ cried out from his room, and I hurried to him. He'd had a bad dream, and it took some time to console him and get him to sleep. When I returned, Tree had the game on.

"Damn, this is hard to watch. You and I were better players than some of these guys, Jake. I don't think the Cavs will even get twenty wins this season. Let's hope they have a better player draft or they'll suck again next year. Is RJ okay?"

"He's fine, and back in dreamland." I grabbed a second bottle of beer for each of us and lowered the volume on the TV. "Don't leave me hanging, Tree. What happened at the interrogation of the church accountant?"

"He swore everything was fine with church finances. Income was exceeding expenses, debts were all paid, and money was pouring in for the school building fund."

"That's not exactly earth-shattering news."

"Hold your horses, I'm getting there." He took a slug of Guinness. "Then Flood died and guess what? Lundgren fired the old man as treasurer."

"Who'd Lundgren appoint?"

"Who do you think? Lundgren had training in accounting, so he *temporary* appointed himself. The argument you witnessed was about the lack of an independent auditor. You can bet that Lundgren will vanish with the money before a new treasurer is appointed and before construction of the school begins."

"So, the fox is guarding the hen house."

"Appears so. And there're a lot of eggs in the church's account. I'll ask the judge for a warrant to examine the church's finances, but I'm not getting my hopes up."

"With two dead bodies and you nosing around, if I was in Lundgren's shoes, I'd grab the money and run."

"I'm sure that's his plan, Jake, but you underestimate how greedy most scumbags are. Greed is like battery acid—it corrodes folks from the inside. Lundgren's got a good thing going but with Flood dead, he's lost his golden goose. Without the orator who drew the crowds to the church, his congregation will start to dwindle. This will likely be his last big score, so he's going to milk this scam as long as possible. I'm hoping he'll hang around one day too long."

We watched the Cavaliers amass a third quarter lead, then self-destruct in the fourth. Tree and I called it a night, both of us unsatisfied.

CHAPTER FORTY FOUR

Friday, April 11, 12:30 p.m.

My resident de jour in Urgent Care had attended an excellent medical school. He was nowhere near the top of his class but had somehow graduated sum cum laude in overconfidence. He was cocksure to the point of foolhardy and didn't have an ounce of common sense—a dangerous and potentially lethal combination. I didn't dare go to lunch and leave him unsupervised, so I sent him to the cafeteria and asked him to bring me a hamburger and a soda when he was finished. The longer he was gone, the safer my patients were. I should have sent him to Maine for lobster.

I was scrambling to keep up with the workload when the receptionist told me that Emily Beale was asking to speak with me.

My heart flipped a few premature beats as I mentally ran through a list of possible postoperative complications. Working in medicine can be a double-edged sword. We know *too much*, which can sometimes scare the hell out of us.

When the receptionist brought Emily back, I led her into an examination room, unable to mask the concern in my voice. "Em, are you okay? What's happened? What's wrong?"

"Nothing. I'm doing fine. I came to the hospital to lead my poetry therapy class."

My heartbeat returned to a normal rhythm. "You should be home resting. They could have survived one day without you."

Her face darkened. "A lot of doctors look down on what I do, but I didn't think that included you. My job is as important to me as yours is to you. And the psychiatry department thinks so too."

"No Em, I *do* value your contribution. I'm just worried about your recovery."

"Relax. I feel fine—physically." She left the last word hanging between us. "But I wanted to tell you that the Tribunal rejected my petition for an annulment. That door is closed, so any dream of a Catholic marriage is off the table."

The air in the room seemed to be sucked out, along with all the hope.

I saw the sadness in her eyes and gave her a gentle hug. "Well, I'm glad you tried. I know it's not what we wanted to hear, but we needed an answer."

I hesitated, but decided to tell her about Demarco's offer and my desire to accept.

She sighed. "Fate is working overtime to separate us." Her expression cratered, a naked plea etched on her face. "Does that mean you and RJ might be leaving town? That would leave a huge void in my world."

I made my move. "And a giant void in RJ's world and mine. So …why don't you come with us?"

The pink flush of surprise in her cheeks transformed to cold white rage. "Damn it, Jake, you know I can't do that! I have to care for my dad, and it took me *years* to build a comfortable life here after I lost my vision. I won't throw that away." She drew a deep breath. "So, you're going? You've decided?"

"No, I'm waffling. Any thoughts?"

She leveled a penetrating gaze at me that nearly drew blood. "It's not *my decision* to make." She turned and left for her poetry workshop.

My reckless resident came back with my lunch, and I resumed babysitting him through the afternoon. I had just guided him through the management of a woman with brittle diabetes when Emily returned from her class.

"I have a problem, Jake. A patient shared a poem with me today that might be important in the search for Angelica's missing sister. The girl who wrote it attempted suicide by slashing her wrists and was admitted to the drug rehabilitation floor after her surgery. She refused to talk with her psychiatrist, so he sent her to my poetry therapy class. The poor thing ran away from home when she was only fourteen and ended up in Hell." Emily paused. "The problem is that anything folks say in class is as protected as if they'd told it to their psychiatrist, and as sacrosanct as a parishioner's confession."

I understood the dilemma all too well—but if we didn't locate Miriam before she was shipped overseas, the chance of saving her was miniscule.

"I get it, Em. I won't compromise her in any way. Promise. You have my word." I placed a hand on her shoulder. "But Miriam's *life* is at risk. Please let me read it."

"If I asked you to tell me what someone said in the confessional, would you?"

I opened my mouth, and closed it again. It's not smart to argue with a woman who's more intelligent than you are.

"No Em, you're right, I wouldn't. I'd go to jail before I'd break the Seal of the Confessional."

Emily removed my hand from her shoulder and held it for a long time, then she opened her purse, set it on the exam table, and said, "I have to use the restroom. I'll be back in a few minutes."

No question about it. She was too smart for *my own good*. After she had walked out of the room, I removed the poem from her purse and read:

When the clouds were darkest, my savior
brought light to my world, gave me
food, respect, shelter, hope, dignity,
drugs, a reason to laugh again, more drugs,
introduced me to new friends, his friends,
to needles and highs I'd never imagined.
He promised a movie role, asked
only small favors at first, a hand-
job, blow-job, my caramel-colored body
for his toy, shared me with his friends   until
I refused—then he beat me, starved me,
locked the doors, offered me
to a different man every night, different men
inside me, inside my dreams, my nightmares,
sold my innocence to the highest bidder   until
I wondered if I would live to see sunrise,
wondered when I would eat again, sleep again,
wondered if I would ever be free
of the lost, broken, addicted wretch
cowering in my mirror.
—Sarah

Sarah's portrayal of despair and the bleakness of her words left me shaken. I slipped the poem back into Emily's purse. When she returned, I said, "This woman may be the key to finding Miriam. Thanks, Em."

"I have no idea what you're talking about." She picked up her purse, headed for the door, stopped and added, "She's been abused enough and is as fragile as spun sugar. Don't take advantage of her, treat her like exhibit one, a piece of evidence in a missing person case. She's terrified of that man, afraid he'll come after her." Emily snapped her collapsible red and white cane to full extension. "I mean it, Jake. No police."

Then she was gone.

I finished my shift without throttling my incompetent resident or allowing him to harm a patient, then met with the hospital administrator and reported his shortcomings. In the doctors' lounge, I booted up the computer and checked the hospital census. Two Sarahs had been admitted to the drug rehabilitation unit, one fifty-two years old and one sixteen. The latter listed her religious preference as "Catholic."

I placed my white coat in my locker, put on a clerical shirt and collar, and made my way to rehab. I'd spent too much time there when my father was kicking his drug habit, and a tsunami of ugly memories washed over me when I stepped from the elevator. I knocked softly at Sarah's door, entered her room, and introduced myself.

Her wrists were bandaged where she had slashed them, and the ravages of months of repeated needle sticks were visible on both arms. A recent bruise painted her left cheek blue-black, and an older one on her neck had turned yellow-green. She had the body of a young teenager but the haggard face of the homeless.

Sarah took one look at my Roman collar, threw her legs over the side of the bed, and sat up. She blushed when her gown rode up her thighs and quickly yanked the covers over her legs. Her hands trembled and her eyes drifted to the floor.

"I work for the hospital, Sarah, and I know you've been through a terrible ordeal." My heart ached for this woman-child. "Can I help in any way? I'd be happy to talk a while. Nothing you tell me will leave this room."

"I, ah, don't think I can like ... talk about what happened." She dropped her voice to a whisper. "I've done ... horrible things, unforgivable things. And now this." She pointed to the bandages. "I'm like *so ashamed*! Don't waste your time with me, Father. I've like completely lost my faith."

"That's the great thing about faith, Sarah. If you lose it, it's always there waiting for you to find it again. One thing I'm certain of is that God will forgive anything if you ask Him."

"I'm beyond help, Father."

"Not true. We all need help from time to time, my child. All you have to do is ask."

She began to speak, then stopped, her shame filling the room. The long painful silence that followed seemed endless.

How should I begin? Questioning her would feel like an interrogation. I had to invite her into the conversation with something open-ended, something nonthreatening.

"Well, Sarah, I hope you will help me. Someone I care about, a girl about your age, has gone missing. When her parents died, she felt lost and alone. I think someone befriended her, got her hooked on drugs, and took advantage of her. I don't know how to find her, or where to begin. Anything you tell me could help. Please, I'm very worried about her."

She hesitated, then slowly opened up, sharing her story. It started, as so many do, with a weak-willed mother and an abusive stepfather. Tears streamed down her cheeks as she recounted her early molestation. Exposing, touching, pornographic photos, and finally rape … and the decision to run away.

Unlike Angelica's sister, it was clear that Sarah had not been recruited online. I had hoped that she might provide insight into the cesspool of computer-based predators or a link to the person who recruited Miriam, but that was not going to happen. The dehumanization Sarah had endured, however, probably closely mirrored Miriam's ongoing agony.

My fists clenched. I had suffered at the hands of my drunken father before he'd abandoned our family, and there were times when I found the idea of a vengeful god appealing. But my sad tale paled in comparison to Sarah's.

I handed her a box of tissues and she recounted her terror as a fourteen year old, cold and hungry, trying to survive on the streets alone—and the overwhelming relief when a man took her in and fed her. Then came the molding of an innocent, slowly bending her to his will. Isolated from friends and family, she had no one in her life except for the three other women he "cared for." They grew completely dependent on his drugs and on him, and he led all of them down the slow slippery slope that her poem had so vividly described to the final shredding of their dignity.

"He made us call him *Daddy*, like he loved us, like he cared. How sick is that, Father?" She drew a deep breath and choked it back out. "When I tried to leave the first time, he beat me and locked me in a room for days. When he finally let me out, he showed me pictures he'd taken of me stoned, doing … things with strange men, horrible things. He said if I ran again, he'd send them to my mom and grandma, splash them across the front page of the town newspaper—and then he would *kill* my mother and little brother. I decided anything was better than that." She pointed to the bandages on her wrists. "Anything. Even this."

We cried together for a while. When Sarah finally gathered herself, I asked if I could contact anyone for her. She refused my offer, so I inquired about the three other women.

"It was so weird, Father. We had no one else. Daddy called us his *wives-in-law*, but we became more like sisters. Shared everything. Sometimes he would like take us to get our hair and nails done, as a reward for a big month or when we had dates with high-rolling johns."

"What was his name, and the names of the other girls?"

"No way, Father. The girl I was with when I slashed my wrists told him I died." A violent shiver enveloped her. "He thinks I'm dead. If I give up his girls or his name to you, he'll know I'm alive and come after me and my family."

Strike one. "Okay, I understand, but I have to ask about my friend. Was one of the other girls named Miriam?"

"No."

Strike two. I thought about what Sarah had told me. "You said this man sometimes took you to get your hair and nails done. Where?"

"Don't know where the place is. Some Asian joint. Whenever he drove us anywhere, he pulled down the window shades in the back of the van and locked our doors. *Child-proofing* us he called it."

"Do you recall the names of the workers or anything about the salon? Think. It might help me find the young girl I'm looking for."

"All I remember is that the old Chinese woman who ran the place was like almost as mean as Daddy."

Miriam had been missing for two months. I hoped she was still being groomed somewhere, the first stage of human trafficking. I prayed that we would find her before she reached the next two stages: transportation and exploitation—and her inevitable ruination. If she had already been shipped out of the country, all was lost.

"One last thing, Sarah." I removed two photographs and showed her one of Rex Lundgren that Tree had given me. "Do you recognize this man?" She shook her head. I offered her the CCTV image of Mateo Cruz. "How about this man?"

She tilted her head to one side and gazed at it a long time, then her eyes brightened. "I saw him once. When Daddy first took me in, there was also a young girl from Mexico living there. She was a *child* really, like not even in her teens. The poor kid couldn't speak a word of English and was scared to death. This guy in the photo came and took her away. We never saw Consuelo again."

I thanked Sarah for her help, gave her my card, and told her to call anytime. The instant I stepped from her hospital room, I called the sheriff's office.

CHAPTER FORTY FIVE

Friday, April 11, 5:30 p.m.

"Tree, I have some information, but you can't question my source, and I won't reveal the name."

"What are you, a frickin' reporter now? Don't play games with me. Been a bitch of a day."

"You want info on Mateo Cruz or not?"

"Cruz, huh? All right, all right. What you got?"

"My source was being groomed for prostitution with several others, and Cruz came and took a preteen Mexican girl away. We know Cruz and Rex Lundgren were buddies, and Lundgren may have coerced Reverend Flood into vouching for Cruz at his parole hearing."

"So maybe Lundgren's not merely fleecing his flock, but dabbling in prostitution too? Could be he's setting up a new sideline business for when he grabs the church funds and disappears. You think Cruz manages his Hispanic hookers and clients?"

"That's not an unreasonable assumption, given that Miriam was messaged on her PlayStation in Spanish and targeted for her fluency. If you can arrest Cruz for Tony Pagano's kidnapping and murder, he might give up the girls and rollover on Lundgren, and you can lock both scumbags up."

"Be happy to bust Cruz, if I can ever get my hands on the bastard! We've been scouring the area for nearly two weeks and he's still in the wind. That yellow sports car he drove to the church has mysteriously vanished from the roadways. Maybe he had it repainted or he has a second car. Our Automated License Plate Readers haven't ID'd him yet, so he's probably using stolen plates. I'm beginning to think the guy's a ghost."

"One other thing, Tree. My source's pimp occasionally took his girls to an Asian-run nail salon that sounded like that joint on Harvard. Maybe Cruz uses it too. Thought you should know. What can I do to help?"

"While I work on Rex Lundgren and Cruz, find out if Sister Angelica can identify Miriam's Spanish-speaking friends. And Jake, thanks. Good work."

When Tree hung up, I phoned Angelica.

"I was about to call you, Father. I recognized one of Miriam's classmates in a school yearbook. Marisol Suarez. I've been playing private detective and tracked her down."

"Darn it, Angelica! Are you *trying* to end up in the Emergency Room again?"

"I wasn't combing the streets. I let my fingers do the walking on social media. Everyone's life is an open book online, if you look hard enough. Marisol's working tonight at a tattoo parlor in Lorain, a place called TIT-4-TAT. How about you and I stop in for a little chat with her?"

"Come on, be reasonable. You just got out of the hospital. With your cheek sutured together and your face the color of a purple squash, your appearance wouldn't exactly encourage Marisol to relax and talk."

"You saying I'm no longer pretty? Good thing I gave up dating years ago, Father. Miriam's my sister and I want to help."

"Locating Marisol is a *huge* step forward. Besides, I'm in Lorain now, not far from her. I'll let you know what she says. Keep the faith and rest up. Sheriff Macon and I have a couple new leads, and we'll need your help soon enough."

"Okay, Father. Keep me posted."

I changed out of my clerical attire and found the address of the tattoo parlor, then called the rectory and asked Colleen to hold the fort with RJ until I got home. I expected a colorful rebuke in Gaelic, but when I explained that I had a lead on Angelica's missing sister, she didn't hesitate. The woman was God-sent. I couldn't make it through a week without her in my life.

On my way to the tattoo parlor, I called Agent Novak on her cell and filled her in.

"Shame my extraction team isn't active yet, Father. I'm driving to Cleveland tomorrow to recruit an ex-Navy SEAL and I think I'll stop in your neck of the woods on the way. Got a sudden urge to get my nails done at that salon."

"Thanks, Keri, you're the best."

"True, I am. And I only recruit the best, so if my unit ever needs a priest, Father, you're in."

Our previous collaboration involved a gun battle on a rooftop, the night air filled with blood and bullets and the smell of spent gunpowder.

"Thanks for the job offer, Keri, but I'll pass. See you tomorrow."

The TIT-4-TAT tattoo parlor was in a dicey part of town, five minutes from the hospital. The faded, green clapboard building hadn't seen a paintbrush since Jimmy Carter was president, and the porch was littered with cigarette butts. Raccoons had raided an old metal trash can next to the house, scenting the evening air with the fragrance of rotting garbage.

The small reception area was gloomy and filled with photographs of body art, many of a sexual or sadistic nature, conjuring up images of Hell's waiting room. The young woman manning the front desk was wearing a nametag that read MARISOL. One side of her head resembled a bristly pink porcupine, and the other was shaved clean. Dark eye shadow circled a vacant stare. The ring piercing her lip and the one through her eyebrow made me wince. Her spiked choker collar and black lipstick screamed Goth rebellion, and her tattoos suggested that this might not be a pleasant chat. The top buttons of her blouse were undone. A dagger inked on her neck pointed toward a skull with angry orange eyes peering from the cleavage between her breasts.

I wasn't sure whether she was a potential ally or worked for a pimp herself. I needed to tread carefully. I showed her the rebellious photo of Miriam at age seventeen, and said, "Your friend's missing, and her sister asked me to find her. I was hoping you could help."

"Sorry. Ain't seen Miriam in a couple months."

"Were you two close?"

A shrug. "Partied some. Hung out at her place after school sometimes and helped with her Spanish homework."

"Was she fluent?"

"Fluent?" A scoff. "Nah, but damn good for a gringa when I was done with her. Shit, I missed my calling. Shoulda been the head of the language department at some hoity-toity Ivy League college."

Things were not going as I had hoped. I paused a moment to consider my options but took too long.

"Come on, man, I got a job to do." She opened a spiral notebook to a page of images of scantily clad women entitled Bitches & Hos. You buying ink or not?"

I sat and flipped through the pages, feigning interest. There were rafts of photos of devils, skeletons, and zombies, but not a single image of Jesus. Then I hit the section on flag tattoos.

"You take credit cards?"

"This look like the Ritz to you? Cash only, mister." She eyeballed me. "You seem kinda old for skin-art."

I ignored her slur and made a point of thumbing through the money in my wallet—mostly singles, but she didn't know that.

Five pages of flags, but not one from Puerto Rico. I produced the CCTV image of the flag on Cruz's arm and showed it to her. "Got one like this?"

"Definitely not Bubba's work." She hooked a thumb toward the back room. "But I mighta seen that one before. Let me get a better look." She snatched the photo from me and studied it. "What the fuck is this? You a cop or somethin'?"

"Yeah, I'm *somethin*'—somethin' that can make your life easy ... or real hard." I tried for Tree's bad-cop voice, but came up with lame-ass priest. "So tell me. Where'd you see this tat?"

"Not sure. Honest."

I showed her the mugshot of Cruz that Tree had given me. "Ever seen this guy?

Her eyes grew large as quarters, but she remained silent.

"His name's Mateo Cruz. Goes by Duro." I decided to lay some cards on the table. "Don't BS me. This guy may have Miriam and if he does, she's in serious trouble. Time to choose which side you're on, Marisol. Either you're her friend and help us find this Duro clown or ...." I left the implication hanging in the air.

She squirmed in the chair, then focused on the mugshot again. "I think ... he dropped off some 'Molly' once at Miriam's place. I thought it was weird that he was giving us free party favors and didn't even ask for cash or a blowjob or nothin' in return. Never saw him again."

Free Molly. Ecstasy for school kids. Building trust. He was worming his way into their lives. I was certain of two things. Nothing in life is truly free—and Miriam had paid a high price.

I showed Marisol the photo of Rex Lundgren and she shook her head. I considered rousting Bubba from the back room for a few questions, but he was probably younger, meaner, and tougher than me. Having a strong aversion to pain, I had no desire to fight above my weight class. The sheriff's troops could question Bubba if necessary.

I filled Tree in on the drive home, relieved Colleen, and gladly traded human trafficking, prostitution, and illicit drugs for the warm embrace of the child I loved.

CHAPTER FORTY SIX

Saturday, April 12, 6:00 a.m.

Troubled by nightmares of children locked in cages, I awoke early. The cool night air had blanketed our backyard in a fog so thick that at first I thought it was smoke from a fire in the nearby woods.

I didn't have to work at the hospital, so Colleen had the day off. I had warned her that if Agent Novak arrived, I might need her help. Colleen and I had been reading children's Bible stories to my nephew, and I'd also begun taking him to Mass whenever I could and explaining the meaning of the service. His initial preschooler interest, however, had quickly worn off. So after making a pancake breakfast for him, I settled RJ in the glass-enclosed Quiet Room in the back of the church where I could keep an eye on him, handed him a box of Legos, and offered morning Mass. We had been through this routine before and he usually behaved well during the service, although I was always as nervous as a long-tailed cat in a room full of rocking chairs. The fog outside was so thick that the beautiful stained-glass windows in the church failed to bathe my parishioners in the usual rainbow of colors. I hoped this wasn't an omen.

The service went well and RJ behaved. After Mass, I tried to knock out some church paperwork in my study while he watched cartoons, but my mind kept wandering to drugs, murder, and human trafficking—and to Emily. I gazed out of the window and watched the sun battle the fog, slowly routing it as butterscotch light began to seep through the pane.

By the time my inbox was empty and my outbox full, I craved some fresh air and fresh insights into my volcanic life. RJ and I donned light jackets and began walking to the playground. A gentle warm breeze whispered through the trees like God exhaling His love into the vast, cold universe.

When the Almighty is in the mood, He can craft a spectacularly beautiful day and on that Saturday, He was hard at work. Everywhere I looked, crocuses, daffodils, and tulips were reawakening around us— new life, the next generation, young and vulnerable—like RJ, Tony, and Miriam.

After my nephew wore out the playground equipment, we stopped in town for lunch, then wandered through the MindFair Bookstore in the Ben Franklin. For the first time in a week, I was able to give RJ my full attention, which for me was a form of prayer. We thoroughly enjoyed ourselves, and on the way home he was babbling away about the two children's books I'd purchased for him. I couldn't help but chuckle.

My contentment didn't last long.

A black Crown Victoria was waiting for us at the rectory. Keri Novak hopped out. She was dressed in jeans and a sweater. It was the first time I had seen her wearing anything other than a pantsuit with an American flag lapel pin, or body armor. Even without her FBI outfit and howitzer-sized sidearm, she was an imposing woman. In her mid-forties with dark hair and dark eyes, she had the vigor and singular focus of a newly-minted Quantico agent. She was the job on two legs.

Keri came toward us with a formidable athletic stride, looked down at RJ, and the corners of her lips turned up. She extended a hand and her grip crushed mine. "Good to see you again, Father. I'm guessing this is your nephew." She bent down and her lips finally made it to a smile. "Nice to meet you, young man," she said, the words whistling softly through the small gap between her front teeth.

RJ slid close to me and examined his sneakers.

"No reason to be scared, RJ. Keri's a friend of mine. She won't hurt you." Although no criminal was safe in the county with her around. "A pink sweater and makeup, Agent? Flaunting your feminine side? I thought a model or pop star had arrived."

"Yeah, right. My girlish heart is all a twitter. When in Rome … or getting a manicure. Gotta look the part." She reached out to tousle RJ's hair, but he took a step backward. She scoffed. "That's the same reaction I get from most men." She stood again, the smile slipping from her lips. "Listen, Father, I need be in Cleveland tonight, so give me the address of the nail parlor and I'll be on my way."

"Undercover in a Crown Vic? You might as well paint FBI on the side of it. Let me get my nephew settled and I'll drive you. Besides, I want to fill you in on what's been happening here."

Colleen soon arrived and walked RJ into the rectory. Keri threw a gym bag in the backseat of my Ford Focus and got in. As we drove, I told her about Mateo Cruz, Tony's abduction and death, Cruz's connection with Reverend Lundgren, Flood's murder, Miriam's disappearance, and the attack on Angelica at the salon.

"Who the hell beats up a nun? Lowlifes just keep getting lower. And why are *you* playing cop again, Padre? Last time we met, I told you to stay away from scumbags and stick to preaching the Good Book."

"Not my choice, believe me." We rolled up to A Touch of Class Salon, located between a pawnshop and a half-demolished duplex. It would take a lot more than a *touch* to class up this neighborhood. "Should I come in, Keri?"

"Nah, park across the street and watch me through the front window. You'll know if I want company." She removed a credit card from her wallet and wiped it down with a handkerchief. "If you spot any Asian dudes who might be the bruisers who beat up Sister Angelica, flash your headlights twice."

Through the shop's window, I watched Keri laughing with the people inside. There was no sign of tension or duress. Except for the occasional stray dog, the street was as deserted as a gold rush ghost town. I half expected a tumbleweed to come rolling past the car. After thirty minutes, Keri left the salon. She got into the passenger seat and removed her pink sweater, revealing a white FBI sweatshirt underneath.

"There goes your feminine charm, Agent." She volleyed with a look that gave me frostbite. "So, what'd you think? Are those girls in danger?"

"Not at the moment, if they toe the line for the old lady who manages the joint. It's your run-of-the-mill sweatshop. Forced servitude is a serious problem in this country, especially among farm workers and domestic servants, but it doesn't get much press 'cause it's not as racy a topic as sex slavery." She removed her makeup and lipstick with a tissue. "Those girls traded their freedom for a ticket to the Land of Milk and Honey. They probably thought coming to the good old U. S. of A. would help pay off their family's debts in Asia. Funny thing about those kinds of debts—with added interest and charges for room and board, they never ever get fully paid off. Never."

I shifted my car into gear and she continued. "The girls are either illegals, or Cruella de Vil is holding their passports as leverage. They have no options. She'll feed them lots of hopes and dreams, but not much else. It's definitely slave labor, but the girls are in no imminent danger, so there's no need for S.O.K. or a SWAT team. I did get the nasty old biddy's fingerprints on my credit card, though. I'll run it through the system, call I.C.E., and let Immigration and Customs handle it." Keri snapped on her seatbelt and we headed back to the rectory. "If the girls are willing to testify against the old woman, they'll be allowed to stay in the country. Unfortunately, many victims refuse because they fear for their family's safety back home. Sorry to disappoint, Father. I know you were dying to rumble today."

"Not even a little. Thanks for checking the place out. With no direct link to the two recent murders or Angelica's sister's abduction, this nail parlor dropped to low priority with local law enforcement. When Angelica told me there were bars on the windows, I wanted to be certain the girls weren't being held prisoner."

"They may or may not be locked up at night but trust me, they're already economic and cultural prisoners."

I phoned Tree Macon and told him about the nail salon, adding that Keri had checked it out and was going to get I.C.E. involved."

"Good, 'cause I got my hands full. Agent Gates called. He tracked down the IP address of the online predator who recruited Miriam." I heard background shouting, and Tree raised his voice. "Got his name and an apartment number. Not sure if Miriam or other kids will be there. We're on our way to hit the joint with everything we got." He paused. "I'll do what I can to get her out in one piece, Jake."

"I know, Tree. Thanks, and be safe."

Early dusk had descended. A smattering of stars encircled a full moon, but my thoughts remained pitch-black. I turned on my headlights. Lost in her own concerns, Keri didn't break the silence.

As we drove down Russia Road toward town, a Lexus crossed the double yellow line and passed me, and all my alarm bells sounded—a bright red Lexus SC430, Reverend Lundgren's car. In a rural working-class county, there couldn't be more than one. I hit the gas and followed.

CHAPTER FORTY SEVEN

Saturday, April 12, 7:45 p.m.

The Lexus hung a hard left into the Lorain County Airport. A school bus parked near the entrance pulled out and followed Lundgren toward the airplane hangars.

"Heads up, Keri, we have a problem. That's Rex Lundgren's car. He's the preacher who's connected to Mateo Cruz, the guy who abducted a teenage boy. He's also a suspect in Reverend Flood's murder."

"Let's roll." She reached into the backseat and grabbed her gym bag. "Shit. Wish I'd brought my tactical vest. There's nothing nicer than the warm embrace of Kevlar." She removed a Glock from the bag and racked the slide, chambering a round. "Slow down, Father, and turn off your headlights. Surprise is our ally."

We went dark and I drove slowly into the airport complex, which was not much more than a single, concrete landing strip in the middle of what had once been a soybean field. We passed some small outbuildings and a fueling station before I saw the Lexus again, parked in front of one of the hangers near a single-prop Cessna. The school bus rolled to a stop next to it. I put my car into neutral, shut off the engine, and coasted as close to the hanger as I dared. In the moonlight I read "The Church of Eternal Release" painted on the side of the bus.

Rex Lundgren hopped from his car and unloaded two large suitcases. He set one down and pounded on the bus door. Mateo Cruz stepped out. Six young girls followed him. Although I'd only seen photographs of her, I recognized Miriam the moment she stepped from the bus.

"Sheriff Macon and I think Cruz and Lundgren plan to sell those kids as sex slaves overseas."

"Not on my watch!" Keri raised a finger to her lips and whispered, "I lost my son to predators. I'll be damned if I'll lose any more kids. Not tonight. Stay here and call for backup."

She clicked off the car's dome lights so they wouldn't come on, opened the passenger door, and crept into the shadows, using a dumpster as cover.

I dialed Tree, got voicemail, and left a message, then called 911 and told them that an FBI agent was confronting murder suspects at the county airport and needed assistance.

Keri slipped between the dumpster and the building, and cautiously approached the Lexus. Lundgren herded the girls toward the Cessna and began boarding them. The plane didn't look designed for eight passengers, then again Lundgren probably didn't care if the girls had seats or seatbelts. They were cargo to him.

Cruz unloaded multiple duffle bags from the car. I had no doubt they were filled with church funds. With Flood dead, Lundgren and Cruz had lost their breadwinner. They were cashing out, and taking the girls for one final score.

I cracked my window and listened. Silence. Not a hint of police sirens. I didn't like Keri's odds and rifled through her gym bag looking for a weapon, but found only clothing.

Unable to sit and do nothing, I eased out of my car into the cool night air and peeked over the roof, waiting for Keri to make her move.

Lundgren had five of the girls onboard when Miriam turned to run. Cruz grabbed her by the arm, threw her to the ground, kicked her in the ribs, kicked her again, and continued bringing duffle bags to the plane. Miriam lay writhing on the tarmac, weeping. Lundgren helped her to her feet, whispered something into her ear, then slapped her so hard it sounded like a gunshot. He shoved her toward the plane and pushed her inside. I fought the overwhelming urge to charge the bastard and beat him senseless.

I glimpsed motion to my right as Keri crept behind the Lexus, using it as a shield. She stood and shouted, "Freeze! FBI. Show me your hands!"

And they did: their hands held automatics. Shielded by the car, Keri assumed a shooter's crouch and got off a shot before they unleashed a hailstorm of lead and she ducked down.

I flashed back to my Army days, flattened against my car, leaned over the roof, and held out my cellphone in a two-handed grip as if I were holding a revolver. "FBI! Drop your weapons. You're outnumbered and surrounded!"

Cruz unloaded his magazine at me, ventilating the side of my Ford as I dropped to my knees. Keri stood and fired at him to take the heat off of me, but Lundgren sprinted to his right and got off a clean shot at her. She screamed, grabbed her thigh, and stumbled behind the Lexus.

Lundgren immediately climbed into the cockpit and revved up the plane's engine. Cruz directed another volley at Keri, then blew out my car windows, peppering me with glass shards. Two red stains seeped through my shirt. I plucked a piece of glass from my forehead and warm blood dripped into my left eye.

With Cruz focused on me, Keri fired again and I heard him cry out. A brief silence was followed by the wail of sirens in the distance. I peeked through a shattered car window. Cruz lay in a pool of blood behind two duffle bags slipping another clip into his automatic.

Keri limped toward him and waved her Glock. "Toss your weapon, asshole, or you're a dead man!"

Instead, he opened fire—directly at the Lexus's gas tank.

Keri tried to hobble toward the dumpster but was a step too late. The car exploded in a ball of flame, the roar echoing through the night. Shrapnel filled the air like a million Ninja throwing stars, piercing everything around it.

When the pinging sounds stopped, I peered over the hood of my car. The money that hadn't yet been unloaded from the car was tumbling from the sky like green snow. Cruz tried to sit, but collapsed into an expanding lake of blood. His weapon dropped from his hand. Keri lay face down, motionless, her FBI sweatshirt more crimson than white.

I was moving toward her when I saw the plane taxi down the access road toward the runway. Dear Lord, what to do? Help Keri or the girls?

But I knew exactly what Keri would do. She'd rain down hell on Lundgren, with or without her SWAT team. Having lost her own son, she would do anything to save another parent from that agony.

I wasn't Keri, but I was all those girls had now. I jumped into my bullet-riddled Ford, turned the key and prayed the engine would start. It rumbled to life and I took off after the Cessna. Smoke and steam poured from the engine compartment, and all the warning lights on the dashboard lit up like a Christmas tree.

The access road led me to the midpoint of the runway. The Cessna was at the far end taxiing toward me, picking up speed, heading into the wind for takeoff. I couldn't allow him to fly those girls to the Gates of Hell, but I was running out of options.

Even if I'd had a gun, I wouldn't have fired at a gasoline-filled airplane full of children. But if I drove down the center of the runway, maybe I could force him toward the fuel truck parked along the far side of the landing strip and make him come to a stop. Prison had to be better than a fiery death—right?

As the Cessna approached, I drove down the left side of the runway and began inching toward the centerline, hoping he'd veer away and brake before hitting the truck.

The bastard came directly at me. He never hesitated, never slowed, never moved an inch away. I shoved the accelerator to the floorboard and drove down the center of the runway directly at the plane in a desperate game of Chicken—a thug who didn't give a damn about anyone, verses a mad-as-hell priest who was good with God. I prayed he would blink.

What I couldn't afford to do was cause another fiery explosion. But if the plane got airborne and those girls were consigned to lives of prostitution and servitude, they would soon wish they were dead—or end up like Sarah, slashing their wrists.

I also couldn't allow the plane's wheels to leave the ground. It was decision time.

I blinked first, swerving left to let Lundgren think he had won the game of Chicken. As the Cessna approached, I swung a hard right into its forward landing gear.

The impact was deafening and mindboggling. The plane's front wheel tore loose and bounced away. My car ground to a stop as the propeller amputated my passenger-side mirror. The airbag plowed into me, and for a second I saw my dear-departed mother standing in a tunnel of light—then the tunnel rocketed away and was gone.

I don't know how long I was unconscious but when I came to, the plane's damaged fuselage rested on the concrete runway, its propeller bent and motionless. I was covered in blood spatter but so awash in adrenaline that I felt no pain. The inside of my car was filled with smoke, the engine dead. Although I didn't see fire or sense heat, I wanted to get those kids out of harm's way.

The driver's door refused to open and I crawled out of the passenger's side. The sirens were loud now, much closer. I staggered toward the plane as a police cruiser and ambulance rolled onto the runway from the access road, their flashing red and blue strobes lighting the night. The cavalry had arrived.

The cockpit door opened. Lundgren stumbled out, limping toward the school bus, a duffle bag in each hand. Images of Tony unconscious in his truck, Miriam smiling at her birthday party, and Reverend Flood's death-mask stare filled my mind. Somewhere inside me the angry young man I had once been, the headhunter on the gridiron, the soldier who'd shot a man at close range in the war, came to life and rose to his feet.

Vengeance is Mine saith the Lord, but in that moment it was *mine*!

Lundgren never saw me coming. I hit him from behind so hard I heard bones snap. His or mine, I didn't care. He tried to wriggle away, but I grabbed his leg and was on him like a lion on a gazelle. I pounded his face until it looked like ground beef, savoring the horror in his eyes, unable and unwilling to stop—until Tree Macon pulled me off him.

"Easy, Jake. Enough! We got this."

Tree pointed to Lundgren and a paramedic attended to him. Cruiser strobes bathed the night in rainbow colors, producing a bizarre version of the Northern Lights. The shriek of sirens was gone, replaced by a chorus of urgent whispers and shouted commands. The fire department was spraying the plane's engine compartment and what was left of my car with a purple foam, which gave off an acrid aroma mixed with the smell of smoke and gasoline.

Police and EMTs helped the six girls from the plane. They were wobbly and battered but moving under their own power. With my adrenaline levels fading fast, my injuries found their voice, the pain rose, and my last ounce of strength drained away. I slumped to the ground. Blood ran down my cheek and onto my lips, the sharp taste of iron and copper filling my mouth.

I spit a pink glob onto the concrete. Tree called an ambulance worker over to examine me, but she left when I said, "No, not me. Not now. Take care of the girls first."

I looked up at Tree. "How's Keri? Is she going to make it?"

"Don't know, it's touch-and-go. She's already on her way to the hospital. Still with us, but … it's not good."

Paramedics loaded Lundgren onto a stretcher, said something to Tree, and walked toward the ambulance.

"What'd they say?"

"Lundgren's knocking on the Pearly Gates. If I hadn't dragged you off him, he'd...."

I should have felt remorse or guilt, something—but I was cold and dead inside. If Lundgren met Saint Peter tonight, I hoped Peter would tell the SOB to go straight to Lucifer's fiery inferno.

"You scare the crap outta me sometimes, Jake." Tree reached down and helped me to my feet. "Let's get you to the hospital."

I glanced around for Miriam. "Let me check on the girls first."

"No, Doc, you're off duty. We're done here."

"Then *you* take me, so we don't tie up an ambulance."

He gazed at the wreckage of the plane and the remnants of my Ford, and led me by the arm to his car. I didn't have the energy or will to resist. We buckled in and he fired up his lights and siren. Fields and farms flew past my window. Neither of us spoke until we reached the hospital.

Tree screeched up to the Emergency Room entrance, threw the cruiser into park, and said, "No doubt about it, Jake. You're still one crazy mother. I worry about you, I really do. Don't know what to say. Only that tonight … you done good, buddy, real good."

CHAPTER FORTY EIGHT

Saturday, April 12, 9:00 p.m.

Before the Emergency Room physician arrived, Tree joined me in the small patient cubical, pulled the curtain shut, and took my statement. My adrenaline rush had faded and my entire body hurt. Fatigue draped me like a wet overcoat, the room swayed, and all I wanted was to fall into a deep peaceful sleep.

A nurse entered and took my vital signs. She asked Tree to leave, helped me into a patient gown, and drew several vials of blood. After she'd finished, the incompetent resident I had worked with on Friday came in to begin my workup. Most of his questions were unrelated to my current condition and symptoms, and I was in no mood to put up with his nonsense. On Friday I'd wanted to send him to Maine for lobster at lunchtime to protect my patients and get him out of my hair, but now that didn't seem far enough. Maybe Thailand for Pad Thai? I interrupted his irrelevant line of questioning and asked him to fetch the staff doctor.

Soon after he left, an ER physician threw back the curtain and sutured the laceration on my forehead, removed a shard of glass from my chest, and bandaged both of my hands, which appeared almost as battered as Lundgren's face had been.

While he was scribbling in my chart, I called Colleen. Although I felt the way I looked, I told her I'd had a minor accident and would be home soon. The nurse returned and handed my physician the results of my bloodwork. I realized I'd lied to Colleen when he ordered a stat CT scan of my abdomen, started an IV in my arm, and called Dr. Glade.

Emily's friend, Todd, was the technician on call. He began scanning my belly but frowned as he watched each picture come up. When the scan ended, he helped me into a wheelchair. I requested to see the images, and he rolled me to the monitor as Gavin Glade arrived.

We scrolled through a virtual tour of my internal organs. Glade summed up the findings with one word. "Shit!"

The scan showed free blood in my abdomen and a tear in my spleen. Not large enough to kill me immediately, but worrisome enough to make Glade scowl.

"Surgery?" I asked.

"Not if I can help it." Nothing made me happier than a surgeon who avoided opening patients up whenever possible. Glade checked my bloodwork, read through my chart, typed-and-crossed me for a possible transfusion, and helped me onto a gurney.

"If you spend a few days here on complete bedrest, Jake, you might be able to take your spleen home with you—and not in a jar. Think you can use a bedpan, do what the nurses tell you, and stay out of trouble for a while?"

"Heck yes, I'll behave. Anything to keep you from wandering around inside my belly."

He chuckled. "You'll love our luxury accommodations and the fine hospital cuisine, especially those mysterious, green gelatin desserts."

Before Glade left, I said, "EMS brought in an FBI agent earlier. How is she?"

"Novak? Bad. She's full of shrapnel and a bullet hit an artery in her thigh. A vascular surgeon has her in the O.R. trying to save her life and her leg." Glade scribbled something in my chart. "We'll worry about the shrapnel later, if she lives," he added and walked out of the room.

I called Colleen back and explained the situation. She volunteered to care for RJ at her apartment until I was released from the hospital.

Generous doses of pain medicines got me through a long, restless night filled with dreams of Lundgren holding a branding iron, searing children with the number 666, the mark of the Beast. When he strapped my nephew to the table, I awoke in a cold sweat.

CHAPTER FORTY NINE

Sunday, April 13, 9:00 a.m.

It was Palm Sunday, the first day of Holy Week, the most important week in the Christian calendar leading to Easter. Father Vargas was offering Mass at Sacred Heart Church in my stead, and here I was, confined to bed, completely useless. On the feast day commemorating the triumphant entry of Jesus into Jerusalem as the messiah and Prince of Peace, I stared at bandaged hands that had nearly beaten a man to death.

During this holiest of weeks, a time when I should have been looking forward to Easter and the celebration of Jesus's victory over death, instead my mind wandered back to murder. Visions of Tony Pagano before his young life was cut short morphed to images of Reverend Flood hanging from the rafters, then to the terror in Lundgren's eyes as I unleashed my wrath on him.

I should have been overwhelmed with guilt, but I felt no remorse for Lundgren or Cruz, the devils who had stirred a cauldron of chaos, conjuring up violence and death throughout the county. No, rather than celebrate Jesus as a peacemaker and the healer of a broken world, I felt many things—frustrated and angry—but definitely not righteous.

I was wallowing in dark thoughts when Emily stopped in to see me, snapping me from my melancholic reverie. She tapped her cane over to the bed, found my face, kissed my cheek, and pulled away, leaving me in the warm mist of her breath.

"Damn it, Jake. What were you thinking? You scared the hell out of me."

"Not my smartest move, that's for sure. But I'm doing fine and should be home in a couple days. How are you feeling since your surgery?"

"I'm okay." She shrugged. "Look at the two of us. What a fine pair of invalid bookends we are."

The conversation turned to everyday things, anything to avoid further mention of her breast cancer or my near demise, until her wristwatch alarm chimed and she hurried off to teach her weekend poetry therapy workshop.

The moment she walked out of the door, waves of conflicting emotions washed over me. I needed a break from those blue eyes, what they made me feel, what they made me want to do—and yet it hurt to be away from them.

I stared up from my hospital bed at the ceiling tiles. My Superior General had offered me a job I wanted to accept, but it required moving to Milwaukee—away from Emily and Tree and the life I had built here. He wanted an answer soon, and so did I. With little else to do but gaze at the ceiling, I had no distractions, no excuses. I needed to put on my thinking cap; no more procrastination. It was decision time.

CHAPTER FIFTY

Sunday, April 13, 2:00 p.m.

Sunday afternoon brightened considerably when Colleen brought RJ to my room, but my nephew screeched to a halt in the doorway, panic in his eyes.

It wasn't merely that the lacerations on my face had been sutured and I resembled Frankenstein. He had recently watched his mother die a slow, painful death in a hospital. His little hands were trembling.

"Are you okay, Daddy?"

"I'm fine sport. Just a bunch of bumps and bruises, like when you fell off your bike." He didn't appear convinced, so I slipped on a smile and changed the topic.

"I'm bored. Did you bring your toy soldiers?" He looked down and shook his head. "Well, bring them when you come to visit tomorrow, all right?"

He sat in a chair next to me. Normally, he and Colleen were both chatterboxes, but I had to drag conversation out of them. We spoke about RJ's school friends, the cartoons he enjoyed, and anything I could think of until Colleen said, "I might take the lad to a movie today for a bit of distraction, if that's okay with yourself, Father. He's been prattling on about somebody named Nemo for days. The show starts soon, so we best be off."

"A movie's an excellent idea, but come now, Colleen. Even I know that Nemo is a *fish*. What do you say, RJ? Nemo?" He lit up the room with a Cheshire-Cat grin. "Okay, but you have to promise to come visit me again tomorrow and tell me all about it."

He nodded, gave me a hug, and they left the room.

I was lost in thought when Sister Angelica knocked on the door frame. Her bruises and cuts were healing but her hand remained in a cast.

"May I come in, Father?" I nodded and she took a step toward me. "I brought a visitor."

Miriam walked in wearing a long-sleeved blouse and jeans, her head and eyes down. One arm was in a sling and an ugly purple bruise painted the left side of her neck.

"My sister wants to express her gratitude, Father, for what you did at the airport." She looked over but Miriam stayed mute. "She feels … ashamed of the things she was forced to do."

My being a priest undoubtedly made her embarrassment worse.

"Please come in. And you have nothing to be ashamed of, not one single thing. Those men were pure evil. *You* are not. You did what you had to do to survive." I raised the head of the bed with the electric controls. "I'm so happy to finally meet you, Miriam, and thrilled that you're okay."

"I doubt I'll ever really be *okay*, Father, but if it wasn't for you, I wouldn't be here. Same for the other girls." She raised her eyes to mine. "We were sure our lives were over. Thank you soooo much."

I knew how long it had taken me to heal my psychological wounds from the war and what a rough road she had ahead. I wiped moisture from my eyes and managed, "Your recovery would be the *best thanks* you could give me."

"We were contacted by a member of Project Healing," Angelica said. "After Miriam completes her drug rehab here, she's going to spend time at their shelter for exploited teenagers." Miriam's eyes wandered down to the floor again, and Angelica continued. "They're a faith-based organization that guides young women back to a normal life. They address all aspects of recovery—not only physical but also mental, emotional, and spiritual."

I had many questions about the treatment and the facility, but this was not the time. What I couldn't imagine was how a victimized woman could look at *any man* in the future with anything other than fear and loathing, let alone ever fall in love with one.

Then I remembered the preteen girl who could only speak Spanish—and Hope raised its head.

"A question, Miriam. Did you come across a Hispanic child named Consuela who couldn't speak English? Was she one of the girls on the plane?"

"No. Never met her. Sorry."

Probably gone to a life of forced sex and servitude in South America. Hope lay its head back down.

Angelica said, "And I may be starting a new life too, Father. I've been volunteering with the Human Trafficking Program as an advocate for abused girls. Bishop Lucci complained to my Mother Superior. They told me to quit … or else. I'm *not* going to do that."

"Damn it, that's ridiculous! You're exactly the kind of person we need in the religious life. I'll do whatever I can to help."

"Thanks, Father, I was hoping you'd say that. I could use an ally." Angelica wrapped her good arm around Miriam's shoulder. "Glad my sister got to meet you, but we have to go to rehab now."

They had entered the hallway when Miriam turned around, ran to me, and gave me a long warm, one-armed embrace. I didn't even try to fight the tears as they left the room. I was bawling like a baby when Father Vargas arrived to give me Communion.

CHAPTER FIFTY ONE

Monday, April 14, 1:00 p.m.

The airport debacle on Saturday and the bittersweet meeting with Miriam on Sunday were already in my rearview mirror. I had finished a hospital meal of mystery meat, papier mâché disguised as mashed potatoes, and a nondescript algae-green gelatin dessert when Tree dragged himself into the room, rumpled and unshaven.

"How you doing, buddy?" he asked.

"They ran me through the CT scanner again this morning. The bleeding's stopped. Dr. Glade says I can go home soon, if I take it easy."

"Glad to hear it. And Emily?"

"She says she's fine, but it's too soon to tell. She doesn't talk much about her cancer."

"I meant you and her—and the job that you told me about in Wisconsin. What are you going to tell the Camillians?"

"I know exactly what I'll tell them, but I don't have a clue what to say to Emily."

"Give you a little advice on how to approach both Emily and the Church? It's what I teach my deputies." Tree flopped onto the chair next to my bed. "Ask what A wants from B, and what B wants from A. Then find the compromise in between. Works for most disputes, and sometimes in my marriage."

I laughed. "And all this time you've been writing an advice column for the lovelorn when *I thought* you were a cop."

He returned my smile but it faded fast. "I have some bad news. Rex Lundgren joined his pal, Cruz, down in Hell. He died from bleeding in his brain and a ruptured liver. As far as I'm concerned, the Devil can keep him." Tree waited for my response, then his eyebrows drifted up. "You don't look too sad."

I didn't know how to respond. I was conflicted, but not saddened. And I doubted that Satan wanted that bastard's soul; even Lucifer has standards.

"Well, I'm not gonna lose a wink of sleep over that piece of shit, Jake. What you did was … wrong, but what Lundgren and Cruz did makes it *less wrong* in my mind. But I don't get a vote." He hesitated. "Gerta Braun is doing an autopsy to determine whether his death was due to the collision with your car … or with your fists."

He paused for a long time. "We have to perform an official investigation into his death, and I'm off the case because of our friendship. My initial report isn't enough to clear you of charges. That's up to the coroner and the District Attorney. An officer will come and take another statement. Tell him everything. Don't hold back. We're all rooting for you, buddy, but the law is the law."

Had I killed a man with my bare hands? He was an evil SOB to be sure, but another human being all the same. I'd never meant to kill him.

Or had I?

One more item to add to the steamer trunk of ugly memories that I've carried with me since I was a teenager. In the past, the consequences of my actions had fallen on me alone. Now, I had my nephew's welfare to consider. What would be the outcome of an investigation; prison? What would happen to RJ?

But I'd tell it true, and let the chips fall where they would.

Sweet Jesus, forgive this sinner and have mercy on my soul—and on my boy.

I changed the subject. "How's Keri Novak? She was in surgery when you brought me in. Dr. Glade said it's touch and go."

"Made it through surgery, but she's in ICU. Lundgren shot her in the thigh and nicked an artery, but the Lexus explosion was like an IED, peppering her with shrapnel. Prayers might be a good idea."

"That's all I've been doing since I was admitted. Do you have any good news?"

"Yeah, we caught the online predator who recruited Miriam and sold her to Cruz. When I demanded to know where Miriam was, he refused to answer and … accidentally tripped and fell down some steps—at least that's what my report says. I mighta bumped into him by mistake. He's been threatening a lawsuit, saying nasty things about me. Sticks and stones."

"Tell me Tree, what makes people like Lundgren and Cruz tick? How could they kill an innocent boy like Tony or sell another human being?"

"A giant scoop of greed stirred into a soulless broth. The whole damn world had no problem with selling my people for hundreds of years. Slavery, sexual and otherwise, is big business all around the globe." Tree heaved a sigh befitting his size. "North Korea supplies Russia with slaves. Belarus and China have state-sponsored forced labor camps, and there's a huge market for sex slaves in Venezuela, Iran, India, and Cuba. Not to mention 'baby trafficking' for adoption and mail-order 'bride trafficking.' "

"I still don't get it. Poisoning people with drugs isn't lucrative enough? Why take on the added hassles and risks of turning kids into prostitutes and transporting human cargo?"

"Hell, Jake, if you run out of cocaine, you're out of business. Not true for pimps. You can sell a drug once, but you can sell a girl a thousand times."

That thought withered me inside. "Was Flood duped or blackmailed by Lundgren? Or was he part of the operation?"

"We'll never know. Appears he was legit until his wife died and he got hooked on cocaine. My guess is Lundgren used Flood's drug habit to control him, but he knew at some point he'd have to kill his golden goose, so he and Cruz concocted their sex slave scheme. They targeted poor kids, especially girls fluent in Spanish. With his flight school training in the Air Force, Lundgren knew his way around a cockpit. He'd been renting that plane at the airport on and off, honing his skills and setting up an innocent pattern, waiting to make the final score when Flood's erratic behavior forced his hand."

"So Cruz groomed and managed the girls, and Rex was the getaway pilot on a human heist?"

"Yup. And as treasurer at the church, Lundgren filled a bunch of duffle bags with all the cash in the school building fund."

"And the money?"

"A lot of it was burned or blown all over the county by the explosion. What was left will be returned to the church. Lundgren had filed a bogus flight plan and once in the air, he and Cruz would have made a dash to South America and sold the kids. Hard for law enforcement to touch them outside of the country—another reason to pray hard for Keri's recovery. We need an organization like Save Our Kids to extract victims all over the world."

The enormity of the challenge wasn't lost on me. We had stopped Lundgren, but the world was full of other predators ready to step into the void.

Tree headed to his office, and I fell into a deep depression.

CHAPTER FIFTY TWO

Tuesday, April 15, 7:30 a.m.

Dr. Glade entered my room and stopped halfway to the bed. "Just heard the full story about the airport. Damn! Remind me not to piss you off, Father. I think God broke the mold after he made you." He chuckled. "You'll be happy to hear that Agent Novak is out of intensive care. Banged up, but she's gonna make it. That's one scary-tough woman! She's in a room down the hall and wants you to stop in."

He performed a physical exam and reviewed my chart. "Can't allow a slacker like you to tie up a hospital bed. Time to send you home. Take it easy for two weeks. I mean it, be a slug. Give your spleen a chance to heal." He handed me prescriptions for antibiotics and pain killers, a follow-up appointment, and a list of home-going instructions. "And Jake, I'm tired of patching you up, so no more crazy-ass hero shit. Okay?"

After he left, I was about to call Colleen for a ride home when my phone chimed. The screen showed area code 414. *Milwaukee.*

I'd had time to think the last few days, and had asked the questions Tree had suggested—What did Demarco want from me, and what did I want from him?—and I had my answer. I desperately wanted to accept the position as Church investigator and troubleshooter. Although I hated the violence, my time working with Tree Macon had taught me that I loved following the scent, loved the hunt, loved the challenge of putting clues together like a jigsaw puzzle. It excited and satisfied me in exactly the same way that making a difficult diagnosis in a critically ill patient did—and I wanted to continue doing it for the Church. Maybe *this* was the path I was destined to follow, the reason I had been called to the priesthood.

But I'd also decided that nothing was more important than my commitment to RJ, and to the close friends who allowed me to care for him: Colleen, Emily, and Tree. Nothing.

I thought I knew what Demarco ultimately desired, but I wasn't sure.

I picked up on the fifth ring.

"Father Austin, it's Stefano Demarco. I have a problem brewing that may require investigation. It's decision time. I need a man I can depend on, and I want it to be you. Are you in or out?"

He obviously hadn't heard about my recent injury, but that didn't matter.

"There's nothing more that I'd rather do, but I have to say *no* to your offer."

"This about your lady friend? That's a deal breaker."

"No, it's about my nephew. He's my first priority, and I won't uproot him and move to Wisconsin. He's doing well in school and has made friends, and I have a support system here to help me care for him." And I was also unwilling to give up the life I'd built in town with my friends and *chosen* family—Tree, Emily, and Colleen—just for a job. "I'm sorry. As much as I would love to accept the position, I won't put my nephew at risk."

"Not what I'd hoped to hear." I listened to a prolonged silence, then Demarco said, "And knowing that, what would you do if I simply transferred you here? As your Superior General, that's certainly my prerogative."

That caught me off guard. No question, Demarco had to be tough and at times cold-blooded to climb to the top of the Vatican pecking order, but he had thrown down the gauntlet. *My way or the highway.* He was strong-arming me. It was cruel—and it pissed me off.

He'd backed me into a corner. "Hardball is it? Really? You disappoint me. What would I do if you commanded me to uproot my nephew? I would submit my indult of laicization and leave the priesthood."

Demarco went silent for so long that I thought my phone had dropped the call or he had hung up.

"Damn! Excuse my French. You leave me no choice, Father." I waited for my Superior General to pronounce my sentence, but instead he said, "You're full of surprises, and full of determination and courage—which is *exactly* what I'm looking for." A deep sigh. "In my role as leader of our order, I sometimes have to be hardheaded, but I'm also a practical man. I fully understand and support your commitment to your nephew. That's not an issue." Another pause. "So if I promise to keep you stationed there in town, Jacob, would you accept my offer and be willing to fly where I need you, when I need you?"

"Absolutely, but there are two other problems."

On Colleen's last visit to the hospital, I'd told her about Demarco's offer and asked if she'd be willing to take on additional hours when I traveled. She jumped at the opportunity, saying she needed extra income to help support her brother in Ireland who'd had an accident on the job.

"With my work at both the church and the hospital, the burden of my nephew's care already falls heavily on my housekeeper, Colleen. She will need significant financial compensation if I'm also to intermittently leave town on assignment for you."

"You drive a hard bargain, Jacob. You should have been a telemarketer or a used car salesman. Fine, fine. I can live with that. And problem number two?"

"I already have too much on my plate. I can't just fly off to help you and leave Sacred Heart Church uncovered. Bishop Lucci has made it clear the parish is job one for me. He's not likely to help."

"Leave the bishop to me. If you become my investigator, then that job becomes your *first* priority. As for His Excellency," Demarco scoffed, "I can assure you that Lucci will assign an assistant pastor to help out at Sacred Heart if I … *request it* strongly enough. Consider it done. So, do we have a deal?"

"We do."

"I'll mail you the paperwork. When you complete and sign it, we can get down to business. Give my regards to Bishop Lucci, Jacob, and go with God."

I sat on the bed, stunned and ecstatic. Doing what I loved, both investigating and ministering as a priest, and staying where I wanted to be. We had struck the compromise I had hoped for, and my world had gotten a lot brighter and more interesting.

But there was still the problem that Demarco called *The Deal Breaker*: Emily.

I was pondering that conundrum when Tree knocked and entered. He was wearing his uniform and a serious expression.

"I just met with the coroner and the District Attorney, Jake."

My heart skipped a couple beats. "What did Dr. Braun find on Lundgren's autopsy?"

"Broken ribs, internal injuries, and a broken arm from the crash, but he died from a brain bleed, from …," Tree pulled out his spiral notebook and read, "brain stem herniation secondary to an epidural hematoma." He put the notepad away. "She decided that the cause of the bleed was *inconclusive*, due either to the crash … or the beating you gave him, or both."

All the air left my lungs and the room. "And?"

"And … it was an *interesting* morning. While we were discussing your case with the District Attorney, he received a phone call from Quantico, and the FBI Director weighed in with his opinion. Didn't hear exactly what he said, but there was some shouting and he wasn't shy about expressing his feelings concerning your case. Shortly after the call, the D.A. decided he didn't have enough evidence to prosecute you, given that you were aiding a federal agent in the arrest of a dangerous fugitive. You're off the hook, Jake." Tree grinned. "You have lived to 'fight another day'—but don't, okay! No more scrapes, or they might be used to indicate a pattern of violence and bite you on the ass."

He patted me on the shoulder and headed to his office, leaving me to ponder the difference between insufficient evidence and not guilty—particularly in light of the long-arm-of-the-law's heavy thumb on the scales of justice.

CHAPTER FIFTY THREE

Tuesday, April 15, 2:30 p.m.

After my discharge orders were completed, I called Colleen and asked her to pick me up and drive me to the rectory. I shed my hospital gown, slipped on my Cavaliers sweatshirt and a pair of khakis, and walked to Keri Novak's room.

The car explosion had left her wrapped in more gauze and bandages than an Egyptian mummy. It was a stupid question but I asked, "How are you feeling, Agent?"

"Like I've been put through a blender. And I'll be setting off metal detectors from now on." She waved me over. "Heard what you did. That bastard, Lundgren, got what he deserved. Don't you dare feel a lick of guilt, Father!"

Easy for her to say. "I'm on my way home now, Keri, but I wanted to thank you." She nodded. "Get well soon. We need you and your S.O.K. team rescuing kids and making the world a safer place."

She saluted and I returned to my room. No sooner had I sat on the bed than I heard the tapping of a cane coming down the hallway—it was Emily.

While confined to bed for days, I had given considerable thought to our relationship and its ramifications, and finally knew what I wanted.

I wanted to remain a Catholic priest, marry Emily, and raise RJ with her—which, of course, was *never* going to happen. But you can't live by *what ifs* … only what is. Sometimes the hardest thing is to accept the inevitable.

Now that the Tribunal had denied the annulment of her marriage, even if I left the priesthood, we couldn't marry in the Catholic Church— and neither of us wanted to abandon our religion. We were trapped in our own personal Catch-22. And ever since her cancer diagnosis, Emily had made it clear that any talk of marriage was out of the question.

What I feared most was the loss of her friendship and her involvement in RJ's life. I didn't want to risk the *wonderful* relationship we'd built in an attempt to attain a *perfect*, but impossible, fantasy. If we had to forgo marriage and a physical relationship, then I still wanted the rest of the dream—a family in every other sense of the word.

At least that left Emily free to marry someone else in the future if she chose. The idea rankled me, yet I loved her enough to wish her that happiness. That's the funny thing about love. It blurs the distinction between giving and receiving, you and me, yours and mine.

But until some hypothetical day in the future when she might actually marry, I wanted to keep her in RJ's life and mine. Demarco would understand and accept that Emily was important to RJ's welfare, and that I needed to support her through her illness. Lucci would bitch and moan and make my life hell, but he wouldn't dare openly oppose Demarco.

Emily and I had circled the question long enough. Time to give up the foolish fantasy and answer it.

The tapping in the hall ceased and she appeared in the doorway.

"I heard you're going home, Jake. That's great."

"Thanks. Join me for a few minutes. There's a chair five feet to your right." She tapped over and took a seat. "How are you feeling, Em? Any news from Dr. Glade."

"That's one reason I stopped by. Things aren't as rosy as they first seemed. The pathologist found evidence that cancer spread to one of my lymph nodes. The odds are still in my favor, but that probably means chemotherapy and radiation. As if surgery wasn't bad enough, now poisoning and scorching? Heck," she said with a self-deprecating expression, "I've been on *blind dates* that were more fun than that! But … I'll get by."

Emily was amazing. Somehow she always managed to keep her sense of humor no matter what challenges she faced.

"I'm so sorry, Em." I walked over and gave her a hug. "Know that I'm here for you. I mean it. Anything you need."

She leaned away from my embrace and hesitated. "I meant what I said about us, our relationship. I refuse to put you and RJ through the same nightmare that your sister's leukemia caused you both. No way. Not again.

That alone takes any possibility of marriage off the table. The cancer's *my* problem."

I wilted a bit as I walked back to the bed and sat. She meant well but married or not, RJ's world and mine were already irreversibly tied to her well-being. It was *our* problem too. Any hell she was subjected to would be an inferno for us as well.

"I've come to doubt much of what I once believed, Em. The only two truths that I'm sure of are my love for God, the Church, and the priesthood … and for you. I hate to admit it, but I see no way out of our predicament. If we can't marry and remain in the Church, then I want the next best thing—you and RJ and Tree in my life as an unconventional family." I fumbled for the right words. "God chose to put me on the path to Him, and *I choose* to walk it together with you. We're never going to have a classic love story, but we can write our own story, right here in town."

"So you told Demarco you wouldn't take the investigator position? You're staying?"

"I'm staying, but not giving up the job. Demarco folded his cards and made me his jet-setting consultant. I can fly out on assignments when he needs me."

"I can do unconventional. After all, I live at a hospital. Being childless, however, has almost been as hard on me as being sightless, so it's important to me to keep RJ in my life." She grinned. "It's *him* I've been after all along, you know." She stood and tapped her way over. "So this is our life now? Our new normal? You, me, RJ, Colleen, and Tree?"

"It is." That was good enough for me—it would have to be. Seeing the unattainable woman that I loved every day at the hospital, however, would be the invisible cross I would have to bear. "This may not be easy."

"Nothing worthwhile ever is, Jake."

"So it's us against the world?"

"Count me in. Look out world!"

From the doorway, Colleen cleared her throat. "There'll be no more shilly-shallying, you two."

RJ dashed into the room and, to my surprise, didn't object when I gave him a kiss.

"Get a move on, Father. I've a homecoming dinner in the oven, and I'll not allow you to dawdle and turn a beautiful prime rib into shoe leather."

CHAPTER FIFTY FOUR

Easter Sunday, April 20, 11:45 a.m.

Maundy Thursday, the day Jesus held the Last Supper with his disciples and washed their feet as an example of humility, had come and gone. As an act of remembrance on that day, Catholic popes have washed the feet of priests for years and most recently the feet of prisoners. Jesus is my role model and the Pope is his representative on earth, but I had drawn the line. There was no way I would be washing the feet of my pedophile snitch at Grafton Prison under any circumstances.

The sorrow and somber reflection of Good Friday led to the Holy Saturday vigil, the miraculous resurrection of our Lord, and then the joy of Easter Sunday.

Dressed in white vestments of celebration that matched the Easter lilies lining the altar, I smiled when I saw Emily, her father, and Colleen sitting together with RJ in the glass-enclosed Quiet Room in the back of the church. Colleen had an Easter feast of baked ham with a brown-sugar glaze and all the fixings cooking at the rectory, and I'd invited Emily and her dad to join us for what I hoped would be our *First Supper*, one of many that our strange blended family would enjoy in the future.

Spills of rich multicolored light tumbled from the many beautiful stained-glass windows into the church. Their designs seemed to retell the events of the last two months. The window labeled "Wicked Fruit" showed a cluster of purple grapes next to a bloody dagger, which to me represented Lundgren and his corrupted church. Nearby, a window was titled "Nets and Fishes"—with me a willing fish in the Almighty's net. But the window labeled "The Sower," which cascaded rainbow colors onto the crucifix, seemed to symbolize hope—a hand sowing seeds, as I hoped to nurture a crop of good friends and a fine young boy in the town I loved.

I stepped to the altar, inhaled the intoxicating aroma of fresh flowers and incense, and celebrated my time with the Lord, savoring the amazing serenity it always brought me. As I raised the body and blood of Christ in my hands, I felt His arm around my shoulders. I had been truly blessed. As painful as it had been, Emily and I had made the right decision, and my life was as it was supposed to be. Without a doubt, the Almighty worked in mysterious ways.

When the Mass ended, I stood for a moment at the altar watching my parishioners file out, and for the first time in a long while I was completely at peace. I entered the sacristy and was changing clothes when my cellphone chimed and the 414 area code appeared. *Demarco.*

"I'm sorry to bother you on Easter, Jacob, but I have a serious problem and may need you to look into it. How soon could you be on a plane?"

Let the fun begin.

AUTHOR'S NOTE

In addition to being entertaining, I hope this novel provides readers with a new perspective and useful information about human trafficking.

The "Save Our Kids" (S.O.K.) extraction team described in the story is fictional but was modeled after the numerous raid-and-rescue groups currently in existence, including the **International Justice Mission (IJM)**, **Operation Underground Railroad (OUR)**, as well as their FBI counterparts. Working in conjunction with law enforcement, these groups rescue victims worldwide and aid in the arrest of traffickers. Although their tactics may be controversial, the anti-trafficking industry has learned a great deal over the past decade about what does and doesn't work.

"Project Healing" is also fictional, but there are many groups that provide safe, secure homes in undisclosed locations for trafficking victims, along with physical, emotional, and spiritual support during their rehabilitation and recovery. A few such organizations include: **Selah Freedom**, the **Salvation Army**, **International Justice Mission**, **Children of the Night**, **Free the Slaves**, and **Shared Hope International**. I support one group financially, and I hope you will consider helping in any way that you can.

The **Human Trafficking Resource Center** described in the novel is real, and its contact information [1-888-373-7888, Text 233733, and www.humantraffickinghotline.org] is accurate and can be lifesaving.

ABOUT THE AUTHOR

Born and raised in the Cleveland, Ohio, area, John Vanek received his bachelor's degree from Case Western Reserve University, where his passion for creative writing took root. He received his medical degree from the University of Rochester, did his internship at University Hospitals of Cleveland, and completed his residency at the Cleveland Clinic. During the quarter century he practiced medicine, his interest in writing never waned. Medicine was his wife, but writing became his  mistress and mysteries his drug of choice. He began honing his craft by attending creative writing workshops and college courses. At first pursuing his passion solely for himself and his family, he was surprised and gratified when his work won contests and was published in a variety of literary journals, anthologies, and magazines. John lives happily as an ink-stained-wretch in Florida, where he teaches a poetry workshop for seniors and enjoys swimming, hiking, sunshine, good friends, and red wine. For more information, go to www.JohnVanekAuthor.com.

CPSIA information can be obtained
at www.ICGtesting.com
Printed in the USA
LVHW052357100921
697540LV00005B/359